**No one was aware of the storm**
**Not the Hurricane Hunter crew t**
**Not the family marooned on a resort island while**
**searching for their missing teen.**
**A deadly Category Five hurricane has never hit**
**the Georgia coast in modern times. Until now.**

"Buzz Bernard bursts on the scene with EYEWALL, a compelling and suspenseful tale told with the insight and authenticity of one who has walked in the world of the famed Hurricane Hunters and endured the harsh realities of a major, devastating storm. Great characters combine with razor-sharp suspense and leave you breathless. A one-sitting, white-knuckle read."
—Vicki Hinze, award-winning author of *Deadly Ties*

"A well-crafted tale you can't put down; characters you care about; a spot-on insiders look at hurricane forecasting and flying."
—Jack Williams, author and founding USA TODAY Weather Editor

"A dramatic and frenzied story of how an angry hurricane collides with the frailty and heroism of human nature. After reading the exciting and emotional EYEWALL, I admire even more those who work to protect us from the next category five."
—Michael Buchanan, co-author and screenwriter, *The Fat Boy Chronicles* and *Micah's Child.*

"Riveting . . . Intrigue, power struggles . . . Frightening reality from several perspectives . . . EYEWALL will keep you more than interested. Having been on location interviewing survivors of a Cat 4/5 hurricane that hit Charleston SC in 1989 (Hugo) and witnessing the destruction left in its wake I fully understand how a Cat 5 might impact a barrier island along the southeast coast of the United States. The author takes us there and describes in frightening detail the impact of this scary scenario."
—Marshall Seese, retired anchorman and meteorologist, The Weather Channel

ii

# EYEWALL

### A Novel

## H.W. "Buzz" Bernard

**Bell Bridge Books**

Bell Bridge Books
PO BOX 300921
Memphis, TN 38130
ISBN: 978-1-61194-001-5

Bell Bridge Books is an Imprint of BelleBooks, Inc.

We at BelleBooks enjoy hearing from readers. You can contact us at the address above or at BelleBooks@BelleBooks.com

Visit our websites – www.BelleBooks.com and www.BellBridgeBooks.com.

10 9 8 7 6 5 4 3 2

Cover design: Debra Dixon
Interior design: Hank Smith

:Lwe:01:

To Evelyn M. Bernard

aka "Mom"

A belated 95th birthday present

**Eyewall: the ring of violent squalls and towering thunderstorms surrounding the eye of a mature hurricane.**

## The Saffir-Simpson Scale of Hurricane Intensity

| Category | Winds (mph) | Damage | Example |
|---|---|---|---|
| 1 | 74-95 | Minimal | Diane* (Northeast, 1955) |
| | | | Agnes* (Northeast, 1972) |
| 2 | 96-110 | Moderate | Floyd (Eastern Seaboard, 1999) |
| | | | Frances (Florida, 2004) |
| 3 | 111-130 | Extensive | Katrina Louisiana/Mississippi, 2005) |
| | | | Wilma (Florida, 2005) |
| 4 | 131-155 | Extreme | Hugo (South Carolina, 1989) |
| | | | Charley (Florida, 2005) |
| 5 | >155 | Catastrophic | Camille (Mississippi, 1969) |
| | | | Andrew (Florida, 1992) |

*Both Diane and Agnes produced extreme flooding leading to extensive damage

# Chapter One

**AIRBORNE, 175 MILES SOUTHEAST OF THE
GEORGIA COAST
LABOR DAY SUNDAY, 0800 HOURS**

Dead ahead of the aircraft, a massive redoubt of roiling clouds, the eyewall of Hurricane Janet, billowed toward the heavens and poked into the underbelly of the stratosphere. Between the aircraft, an Air Force Hurricane Hunter, and the towering wall, layers of white and gray clouds, innocuous outliers of the storm, cluttered the skyscape. But the eyewall itself was obsidian, foreboding.

Major Arlen Walker leaned forward in the pilot's seat, scanning the sky through the cockpit windshield. Beads of cold sweat spotted his forehead. His muscles were tense, strangely alert to some undefined threat. It was as if he'd been awakened in the dark to the heavy creak of a floorboard, or the rustle of bushes outside a window when there is no wind.

He understood—or thought he did—that the probable source of his apprehension was not Janet but the strange events of the previous day. Thus, there should be no rational, no logical reason for his unease. Or was there? He stared at the barrier of clouds, trying to take their measure, guess at what lay within them. Janet was a mere category one, the lowest intensity on the rating scale, yet if you could judge a storm by its looks . . . He spoke into the intercom, addressing the on-board weather officer, Captain Karlyn Hill. "Karlyn, this thing might have teeth. Is it still looking like penetration at 5000 feet?"

Her voice came back. "Yes, sir. The Hurricane Center said she'd still be a cat one on our first pass. If she isn't, we'll do the next fly through at 10,000. And kick the asses of those guys next time we see 'em."

**Walker considered her** words, her tone of voice. Whistling past the graveyard? Colonel Bernie Harlow, the copilot, didn't think so.

"Attaboy, girl," he said. Walker gripped the aircraft's controls and stared at his looming adversary. "Give me a heading, nav," he said.

"Zero-four-five," Major John Best called out.

Walker turned the aircraft to the new track, then glanced at the cockpit radar. They were minutes from the edge of the eyewall. On the radar, solid red and magenta returns indicated torrential precipitation. They were approaching a palisade of rain. "No way this thing is a one," he said.

"Yeah," Karlyn responded. She usually added a commentary or light-hearted one-liner before penetrating the eye of a hurricane. This time she didn't.

The plane was doing a little dance now, a constant jiggle as it barreled toward the bulwark of bruise-colored clouds.

"Winds are going up fast," Karlyn said.

"Is there a better way in?" Walker asked.

"Don't see one."

"Break it off, Major?" Colonel Harlow asked.

"Negative. Let's do the mission. It's not a cat five." Harlow was testing him.

"Let's hope," Best chimed in.

"'Half a league, half a league, half a league onward. All in the Valley of Death rode the six hundred,'" Harlow recited, holding his gaze on the eyewall.

"What's that?" Walker asked. "Tennyson. 'The Charge of the Light Brigade.' The Brits. Crimean War."

"If I recall my history, that didn't end well."

The plane rattled more sharply now, the jiggle lapsing into a hard shake.

"No. It didn't." Harlow looked at him. And in his eyes, Walker caught a flicker of doubt, something he'd never seen before.

## KEESLER AFB, MISSISSIPPI
## THREE AND A HALF HOURS EARLIER

Major Walker trudged toward a WC-130, a bulky four-engined Air Force Reserve Hurricane Hunter, squatting on the ramp at Keesler Air Force Base, Mississippi. The plane bore no resemblance to a sleek commercial airliner. With its landing gear almost flush against its plump fuselage, the high-tailed craft looked like an overweight duck floating on a sea of concrete.

As Walker neared the plane, he could see the ground crew making its final preflight checks. Overhead, a Milky Way of insects swarmed around the stanchioned lights that lit the tarmac in glaring brightness. A power cart tethered to the airplane coughed noisily, sputtered, then resumed a steady purr.

A rotund sergeant from the crew approached. "Morning, sir," he said. "She's lookin' good. Double your money back if she craps out on you."

"You guys didn't do the preflight on the previous bird, did you?"

The sergeant laughed. "The one that aborted because of hydraulic problems? No, sir. They must've had the second string on that one."

"Take off's in forty-five minutes. If we bust two recon flights in a row, the Hurricane Center will really get its knickers in a twist."

"This ain't Delta, sir. We'll have you rollin' down the runway right on time."

"Thanks, Sergeant. Give your guys a high-five for me."

"I will, Major. By the way, what's the scoop on Janet? Still no big deal?" He swatted at a bug orbiting his head.

"Looks that way. At last report, 75 mph; a minimal hurricane. So I guess we'll just slap the plane on autopilot, put our feet on the yoke and snooze through the trip."

"Yeah, but it's still a hell of a way to spend Labor Day Sunday."

"You're out here, too, Sarge."

"Me? Not to worry, sir. I'll be home shortly. Got a pig on a spit, an apple in its mouth."

*Pig on a spit. Kind of the way I feel, too, but I don't know why.* The sergeant snapped off a crisp salute which Walker returned. *No, I do know why.* Yesterday, of course.

**He and his wife Donna** had been visiting a traveling carnival, something neither of them had done in years. It had been designed as a fun trip, one he hoped might ameliorate some of the tension that had been festering between them for over a year now.

She spotted the palm reader's tent first. "Go ahead," she said, nudging him in the ribs with her elbow. "For kicks. And who knows, maybe what you hear will validate your decision."

*Don't start*, he pleaded silently, and ducked into the tent, not only to cater to Donna's whim but to escape the harangue he knew would follow.

The interior of the tent was shadowy, dimly lit. Dust motes, caught in shafts of sunlight that streamed through gaps in the canvas, swirled like fish in an aquarium. A faint odor of something cooking, meaty and greasy, permeated the air. He stood for a moment, allowing his eyes to grow accustomed to the duskiness.

In front of him, a rickety chair stood next to a small table covered in black cloth. At least there wasn't a crystal ball on it. "Anybody here?" he asked.

"Yes," a voice said from somewhere outside the tent, the words raspy and broken. "Sit."

He sat. A flap in the wall of the tent behind the table opened, and a bent, wizened lady entered. She limped to a chair on the opposite side of the table and lowered herself onto it, slowly, carefully. She smiled at Walker, revealing yellowed, broken teeth. Her skin was crenulated and age spotted, her eyes, inky, riddled with cataracts.

"You are right handed?" she croaked.

"Yes."

"Let me see your right hand. Put it on the table. Palm up."

She bent her head close to his palm.

Walker leaned back slightly, catching the stench of her breath: decay, alcohol, onions. "You're a palm reader?" he said, trying to be polite, though he knew it was pseudoscience, trickery, cheap theater.

"Chiromancer," she corrected, tracing a skeletal finger over his palm. "You are an athlete?" She looked up.

"No." He decided not to tender any personal information, much less to tell her he was a pilot and, in civilian life, a banker. She was the fortuneteller. Let her figure it out.

"Maybe you are going to a sporting event soon, like baseball or football?"

He shook his head.

She lowered her gaze and continued moving her finger across his palm. "So. It is odd, I sense you in a coliseum. A large stadium." She stopped, then retraced an area. "No," she whispered, *"trapped"* in a stadium. No way out. No stairs. No exits. No gates. And . . . I don't like this." She snapped her head up and stared at him through her maculated eyes.

*Theater. Pure theater.* He leaned back, away from the foulness of her exhalations that had become uneven and labored. From outside the tent, he could hear the laughter of children, the shout of a carnival barker, the trill of carousel music.

"It makes no sense," she said, gripping his hand now, hard. "There is an aura about the stadium. Something suggesting great danger. And there are others with you. All of you are being stalked. I sense evil." She released his hand but continued to fix him in an unwavering gaze. "I do not understand," she continued. "I can only tell you, do not go."

"Go where?"

"To the stadium."

"What stadium?"

"You will know."

"How will I know?"

She shrugged. "Maybe you won't until it is too late." She stood and turned to go.

"Here," he said. He reached into his wallet for money.

"No," she responded. "I fear it does not end well. I do not take money for that." She shuffled out.

Walker remained seated, staring at the now-closed flap through which the harridan had exited. He hadn't been aware of it earlier, but his temples were throbbing, blood pulsing through his brain almost audibly. As if it would clear his mind, reorient his thoughts, he shook his head vigorously, as a horse might warding off a bothersome fly. Finally he stood and went back outside, squinting against the late-summer sunshine.

"Well," Donna said, "do you feel better about what you decided now? After a little help from your friendly local soothsayer?" She snickered and took a swallow of beer from a plastic cup.

He looked at her, momentarily puzzled, forgetting why he'd scuttled into the tent so quickly in the first place. But now he remembered, and could see she was winding up to throw a beanball. *What the hell.* "You mean, what *you* decided."

"Don't be such a dick head. At least admit it was *our* decision. I thought we agreed your career in the Reserve was shot to hell. No more promotions. Stuck in-grade."

"It doesn't matter, I love to fly."

"The point is, not only is your Reserve job in the toilet, so is your bank job," she snapped. "Your real job."

"I'm an assistant vice president."

"Dime-a-dozen. You should be an executive vice president by now, climbing the corporate ladder, investing your extra time at the bank instead of tootling around in cloud formations with your tin-soldier flyboy buds."

A calliope started up somewhere on the carnival grounds, filling the afternoon air with loud, discordant sounds; a small boy, swirls of blue cotton candy held aloft in each hand, darted past them, pursued by a smaller child, a sibling or playmate.

"I resent that remark, Donna."

"Resent it then. You think I fucking care? I'm the one stuck at home, living in middle-class poverty because you can't get ahead."

"Middle-class poverty?" It sounded laughable. "What the hell is middle-class poverty?"

She faced him—a pit bull now, not the soft, cuddly puppy he'd married. "Not being able to afford the country club," she barked. "Driving a ten-year-old car. Having the same furniture now as when we got married."

"We're hardly destitute."

"You can do better. I want something more for you, not just me." She took another swill of beer.

No, you want it for you, he wanted to shout. But he held his return fire. He'd never heard his father raise his voice to his mother in forty years and wasn't about to alter that tradition now. He'd been raised to respect the sanctity of marriage, though he wondered how much sanctity—how much life—was left in his. He now thought of the waterbed he and Donna shared as the Dead Sea.

Corny as it seemed to some, he'd made a commitment on his wedding day and intended to honor it. But of late he'd begun to wonder if a commitment wasn't just an abstraction to hide behind to avoid doing something more difficult.

Donna waited for him to respond, but when he didn't, she apparently took his silence as tacit agreement with her position and continued her rant. "You were close, buddy, real close. If you hadn't decided to tender your resignation to the Reserve, I was damn near ready to bail out. Someday after one of your little military gallivants you would've walked in the door to an empty house. You don't think I wouldn't have taken you to the cleaners?" She paused, then added derisively, "Not that that would've produced a big load."

"Enough, Donna. Drop it. My last flight is tomorrow."

"Make sure," she said. She tossed her beer cup, only half empty, onto the ground, pivoted and strode away.

Walker went back to where she had stood, picked up the cup, and jammed it into a trash bin. As he did so, he caught a glimpse of the tiny, gnarled soothsayer peering out at him from her darkened tent. Then, like Donna, she was gone. But the old lady's warning lingered: *Do not go.*

# Chapter Two

## ST. SIMONS ISLAND, THE GEORGIA COAST
## LABOR DAY SUNDAY, 0500 HOURS

Alan Grant opened the slider of his rented condo on St. Simons Island and stepped out onto a deck that overlooked the beach. A gust of wind barged through the door into the family room, scattering paper plates and cups. An empty pizza box, bearer of last night's dinner, thudded onto the tiled floor.

"Damn it," Alan said, and pushed the slider shut as quickly and quietly as he could. It was well before dawn and Trish and the kids were still sleeping. He didn't want to wake them. He took a sip from a cup of coffee, and watched the sea oats below him whip back and forth in the stiff breeze. Lit by spotlights, they seemed to be performing a frantic ballet. The oats topped a sand berm that separated the condo from the beach, and he could hear the surf washing against the far side of the berm. The water had come up during the night, responding to a steady northeast wind that had been blowing for the last two days. The kids would be disappointed today: no building sand castles or wading in the swells. The beach and ocean would be off-limits. Well, a little sightseeing wouldn't hurt them. God knows, there were enough historic forts, plantations and churches on St. Simons to keep visitors occupied for days.

That, in part, was why he loved the island. It retained, despite a steady population growth, a keen sense of its heritage and laid-back charm. Even on holidays, it wasn't overrun with tourists. He could come here and unwind, reconnect with his family, enjoy good restaurants, flail at golf balls and whack them, though not by design, into the multitude of marshes that guarded the island's courses.

He'd had his fill of Florida's Panama City Beach with its sweaty throngs of drunken kids, keg parties and wet T-shirt contests. At times, it seemed more like an overcrowded, third-world vacation spot than anyplace fit for families. And South Carolina's Myrtle Beach had lost its appeal, too, surrendering to an explosion of high-rise condos, crowded roads and cheesy gift shops.

Even though a hurricane watch had been posted for St. Simons, the storm was expected to swirl by offshore and hit South Carolina. As was usually the case. Tropical systems had an aversion to the Georgia coast, indented as it was from the Atlantic Ocean.

Over the wash of the surf, the rustle of sea grass filled the predawn air. And accompanying the whisper of the swaying grass came an amalgam of odors: salt, decay; life, death. He set his cup on the railing of the deck, gripped the barrier with both hands and leaned forward into the wind. Its rush on his face, mingled with a mist of ocean spray, invigorated him.

Yes, he needed this time off, away from the demands of being CEO of his own development company, to rest both his mind and his body. To escape the morons with whom he had to deal daily. To pump new life into his spirit. To spend uninterrupted time with his family— reconnect with his wife, son, and daughter.

He turned as he heard the slider open. Trish, her nightgown whipping around her bare legs, her eyes bleary and unfocused, managed a smile as she walked toward him. They traded a hug and kiss. He could taste wintergreen and pepperoni on her lips.

"Go back to bed, honey," he said, "it'll be another couple of hours 'til it's light."

She rubbed her eyes. "I was worried about the hurricane."

"It's okay," he said, "it's going to miss us."

"I hear cars on Ocean Boulevard. I think some folks are leaving."

He clapped his hands together. "That's great, hon', you know what that means?"

A gust of wind caught her nightie and lifted it above her hips. She screamed, mock terror, and brushed it back into place with her hands.

He laughed. "You could have just called to me, you know, instead of coming out here and titillating the entire neighborhood."

"Be serious," she said, turning a weak shade of crimson.

Even after two kids she still looked great. Tennis and workouts at Curves had done their job. He was tempted to ask for something beyond coffee and bagels for breakfast, but Trish was concerned and had not arisen before sunup merely seeking a little predawn delight while the kids slept.

"It means," he said, reverting to his earlier train of thought, "with people leaving, there'll be less traffic, we won't have to wait in line at restaurants, and it'll be easier to get tee times."

"You don't think we should leave?"

He reached out and drew her to him, her brown hair wrapping around her forehead as another puff of wind cartwheeled across the deck. "I didn't build Grant Development Enterprises into a multimillion-dollar business," he whispered in her ear, "by making bad decisions. And I'm not going to make one now regarding my own family."

"I know," she said.

"Look," he continued, "we'll get some wind and rain today, but nothing worse than a winter gale. We can go visit an old fort or plantation someplace, we can play video games or maybe just go to a movie. Tomorrow, the weather will be great again. Everybody will be back on the beach and out on the golf courses."

"You're sure?"

"We'll be fine. Let's get out of the wind now."

She turned and walked toward the slider.

He patted her on the rump. "Harlot," he jested.

Over her shoulder she said, "How'd you like something other than coffee and a bagel for breakfast, sailor?"

"I've been at sea a long time, m'lady. Something other than food would be most welcome." Predawn delight after all.

She pointed toward the bedroom. "I'll tend to your needs, swabbie. But first, some coffee." She disappeared into the kitchen.

He went to the master bedroom where he sat on the edge of the bed and removed his shoes. Then his shirt and pants. *Perhaps there is a God after all.*

A throwaway line. He was certain there wasn't. He was sure his successes and blessings were self-generated, not the arbitrary gifts of some disinterested and imagined deity. He controlled his own direction and destiny, and thus had little sympathy for the minions who didn't or wouldn't, drones who wasted their lives in the hives of large corporations and the nests of mega churches. He soared above them, seeing things and imagining concepts they couldn't.

He'd been one of the first to envision the huge profits to be realized in developing upscale communities for the coming surge of Baby Boomer retirees. In the northern exurbs of Atlanta, he'd designed and built Sunrise Estates, a sprawling complex of small luxury homes, condos and continuing care facilities integrated with shops, restaurants and clinics, all accessible by foot, bicycle or golf cart. Automobiles were optional. Community bus service linked Sunrise Estates to

Atlanta's rapid transit system. And a thrice-daily limo service made it easy to reach Hartsfield-Jackson Airport.

Shortly, Trish padded into the bedroom, stopping at the foot of the bed. She stood in silhouette, steam spiraling from a mug of coffee in each hand. "I bear you good tidings of great joy," she said.

"I'm sure you do, wench." He could feel himself growing hard. "Reconnect" took on a new meaning. He patted the rumpled sheets. "Put the coffee down and come into my bed."

She placed the mugs on a nightstand, stripped off her nightie, knelt beside him and whispered in his ear: "I'd rather you come in me, sailor."

They made love to the thunder of the wind and rain, their own breathless cries briefly challenging the clamor of the storm as they soared to a climax. Afterward, they lay on their backs, holding hands and listening to the gale-swept downpour rattle against the windows.

Eventually, Alan rolled onto his stomach and ran his hand gently over Trish's perspiration-drenched breasts. "It feels as though m'lady has seen some heavy duty action," he said.

She stifled a snicker. "Like they say about horses, 'rode hard, and put away wet.'"

"You ain't no horse, wench."

"No, but sometimes I feel like the Lone Ranger. Thanks for this time together . . . Tonto." She raised herself onto her elbows and kissed him. "Now, let me get dressed before the kids wake up."

"Remember what we used to do on rainy days? All day?"

"Of course I do. That's how we got Sandy and Lee."

Alan sighed. "So, times lost and gone forever, I guess. I'll shower while you get dressed."

"Then roust the kids out. I'll spring for breakfast in town."

After showering, Alan walked down the hallway to the children's bedroom. He opened the door and flipped the light switch on and off several times. "Lee. Sandy. Up and at 'em. Pancakes and eggs beckon."

Lee, eight, poked his head out from under his covers. "I thought this was a vacation, Dad. Why do we have to get up?"

"Because it's morning and it's time for breakfast and I know it'll take me two hours to drag you two out of your cocoons. Rise and shine."

Lee pulled the covers back over his head. There was no movement in the bed where Sandy, his fifteen-year-old sister, slept.

"Looks like somebody wants cold water poured on her," Alan said loudly. He stomped over to Sandy's bed and yanked back the comforter. Except for a pillow and half-a-dozen stuffed animals, the bed was empty. "What the hell is this?" Alan snapped. He wheeled toward Lee's bed. "Where's your sister?"

"Dunno," came Lee's muffled voice from underneath his covers.

Alan stepped into the hallway. "Trish," he called, "you haven't seen Sandy this morning, have you?"

"No. Why?"

"She's not in her room."

"What!" Trish came down the hallway at a trot. "Did you check the bathroom? The sunroom?"

"No. You can look, but I don't think you'll find her. It appears like she—someone—put stuffed animals in her bed as a deception." His heart hammered against his chest cavity. He heard Trish dashing around the house, screaming Sandy's name, opening and slamming doors, flinging the slider open to check the deck.

He couldn't quite believe it.

His daughter was missing.

# Chapter Three

## ATLANTA, GEORGIA—THE NATURAL ENVIRONMENT TELEVISION NETWORK LABOR DAY SUNDAY, 0500 HOURS

In the stillness of the predawn hours in Atlanta, Georgia, Dr. Nicholas Obermeyer, a seasoned hurricane expert, leaned back from his computer monitor and closed his eyes. He'd long harbored a gnawing apprehension that a meteorological disaster far worse than those unleashed by Katrina or Andrew loomed in the future. But until now, his concern had been low-grade, hypothetical.

He opened his eyes and looked again at his monitor, at a satellite image of Hurricane Janet. What he saw was no longer hypothetical. It was reality. He was watching a wolf in sheep's clothing, teeth bared, hackles raised, malevolence in its eyes, stalking toward the coast of the Southeast U.S.

The broadcast operations area of The Natural Environment Television Network, former home of the venerable Weather Channel, was nearly empty this Labor Day Sunday. The air in the quiet facility was chilly and stale; part of the HVAC system had been shut down as a cost-saving measure over the holiday. Yet despite the coolness, Obermeyer perspired freely. In earlier images on his monitor, he'd recognized something that others had obviously missed: a subtle change in the river of air flowing over North America; a slight shift in the jet stream dictating the future of Janet. Neither the numerical models nor the forecasters at the National Hurricane Center in Miami had yet diagnosed it.

Janet, a weak hurricane, at least on the relative scale of such storms, was swirling just a little over two hundred miles east of northern Florida. The storm's proximity to the coast left no margin for forecast error. Until now, that hadn't been a concern. The prediction had seemed simple and straightforward. Janet was expected to strengthen only slightly and punch into South Carolina near Hilton Head.

Warnings had been issued and evacuations ordered from Charleston to Savannah, but the public's response so far had been slow and lacking urgency. It was, after all, a holiday weekend, and Janet was, after all, a minimal hurricane. The problem was, official forecasts to the contrary, she was about to become something entirely different. Something more. Something dangerous. Something—dare he think it—catastrophic.

A door slammed. Obermeyer looked up. Sally Ainsworth, the producer in charge of weekend programming, gave him a quick wave then scurried off down a hallway. He went back to studying the hurricane's satellite imagery. Filaments of moisture, computer-colored a deep red, streamed away from the top of Janet, arcing out in different directions. Near the center of the storm, lighter colors suggested an absence of clouds and the birth of a well-defined eye. It was like seeing the flash of distant artillery fire and awaiting the thunderous explosions that would follow.

For thirty years, he'd studied rapidly intensifying hurricanes, and over the last ten had forged a theory, the essence of which he'd scribbled onto an old-fashioned paper checklist. Inflow, outflow. Stability, instability. An upper-air low pressure center here. A high pressure ridge there. On and on. Twenty-two factors. Until this morning, he'd never seen them all positive, all favorable. Now he was looking at a monster-in-the-making.

He stood, paced the room and considered his next move. He couldn't sound the alarm alone, a Paul Revere riding on television signals into people's homes crying, "Janet is coming. Janet is coming." He needed an ally. Preferably, one in the government. He'd done the solo Paul Revere act before and, despite being right, nearly been burned at the stake for his efforts.

He decided on a phone call to an old friend, Richard Keys, a meteorologist at the National Hurricane Center. And despite the preponderance of evidence that Janet was about to become a beast, Obermeyer understood his usual point-blank proselytizing might not serve him well with his colleague. Their long-standing, amiable relationship notwithstanding, Keys still represented government officialdom, something you didn't want to toss bombs at. Obermeyer elected a subtler approach.

"Hey, Rick, it's Obie," he said when Keys answered the phone.

"So you got the midnight shift, too, buddy?" Keys responded. "Who'd you piss off?"

"Everybody."

"That's not hard to believe."

"Thanks for your vote of confidence," Obermeyer said. He fumbled around his cluttered desk searching for his checklist.

"I know you too well. In fact, I know you well enough to realize you're not calling to talk about the Braves or your love life."

"I don't have a love life."

"I know that, too. So it must be about Janet."

"She's intensifying."

"Agreed, but we're going to wait until the next recon flight gets into her to see how much stronger she really is."

"Wasn't there a flight due in overnight?"

"Yeah. It got halfway there and aborted; hydraulic problems or something. Anyhow, we're not that concerned about major strengthening. We think what we're seeing right now is just the typical early-morning growth spurt."

Obermeyer grimaced. *No, it's not.* "I'm not so sure," he said. He found his checklist under a stack of technical journals, pulled it out, ripping a corner off it in the process, and studied it once more. "I think it's more than that. I suspect that little kink in the jet stream over Alabama we thought would keep Janet kinda flabby might not be up to the job."

He heard his friend tapping on a keyboard, probably calling up the latest upper-air analysis on his computer monitor. Obermeyer waited, giving Keys a chance to study whatever it was he'd requested.

Finally Keys said, "Yeah, I agree. But we've got the right area warned, so it shouldn't make much difference whether Janet steams in as a category one or minimal two."

Obermeyer leaned back in his chair and closed his eyes. "I was thinking a bigger bang than that."

Rick sighed softly. "Okay, lay it on me."

"Sometimes, a little shift in the upper-level winds makes a big difference. In this case, the difference between a hurricane being held in check or getting supercharged. I'm seeing things that really concern me. Signs that Janet is about to explode."

"Look, the computer models have been doing a good job on her. I don't think it's time yet to start gnashing our teeth and rending our garments. Let's wait until the recon bird reports back to see where we stand."

Obermeyer sensed his friend circling the wagons. Rick had

worked for the government too long. He was a good soldier, a competent forecaster, but had become infected with the virus of bureaucratic inertia. One last try, Obermeyer decided. He held to his circuitous approach. "Remember the Butterfly Effect?" he asked. He rocked forward in his chair and squinted at the satellite image on his computer.

"Yeah, something about a butterfly flapping its wings in Brazil and causing a tornado in Texas."

"Meteorologists having fun with chaos. Meaning small changes in the atmosphere over there—" Obermeyer gestured with his hand, forgetting his friend couldn't see him. "—can cascade into huge changes, changes that wouldn't have otherwise occurred, over there." He gestured in a different direction.

He stood up and began pacing again, almost yanking the phone set off his desk. "My point is, a little alteration in the winds over Alabama and we've got Janet on steroids. And if we've got Janet on steroids, we've got a hurricane that's going someplace other than where we think it is, because its steering winds have been shot to hell. Bottom line: no time left to warn people. Janet's too close to the coast. Everybody's thinking a Hilton Head landfall. Everybody's thinking a cat one, maybe a two; not so bad."

Rick expelled a long breath before speaking. "Jesus, you're starting to sound like that Senator McCarthy guy back in the 1950s who saw a Commie behind every tree. You're seeing a Katrina behind every cloud. Maybe it's time to put you out to stud. Aren't there some cute on-camera meteorologists—what did you call them? OCMs?—you could chase around the network up there?"

"The cretins who run the network fired most of them when they bought the operation from the previous owners."

"Then maybe you'll just have to hang around an assisted-living facility someplace. Listen to me, partner. Take a deep breath. Relax. Wait until the Hurricane Hunter reports in. We'll take it from there."

Obermeyer wasn't surprised at Rick's recalcitrance, but if nothing else, he'd had to make the call to him as a professional courtesy. "What time is the bird due in?" he asked, a pro forma question. He'd already made up his mind what he was going to do. He wasn't waiting.

"About three hours." Rick paused. "Hey, Obie?"

"Yeah?"

"Don't do anything stupid. Something unofficial. They'll string you up by your balls off the Washington Monument. One word, old friend . . . ”

Obermeyer waited, but knew what was coming.

“ . . . Rita,” Keys said.

Rita. Hurricane Rita, the storm that had followed Katrina in an assault on the Gulf Coast in 2005. The storm that had triggered a reverse land rush out of Houston. Only it hadn't ended up as a rush, but more of a slow-motion ooze of cars, trucks and buses jammed bumper to bumper leaving the city. A needless mass exodus.

At least Obermeyer had thought it was needless and said so on the air, refusing to toe the official line. His meteorological hubris was almost his undoing. Despite the fact he turned out to be right—Rita spun inland east of Houston and weakened—federal and local governments wanted his head on a platter.

He was pilloried by the feds and even his own network, the corporate powers-that-be refusing to stand up for him, likely under pressure from the FCC.

In the end, his popularity in the media as a maverick who took on the establishment saved him. Appearances on the cover of *Newsweek* and front page of *USA Today* cemented his fame or, depending on your viewpoint, infamy.

“Obie? Obie? You still there?” Keys' voice snapped Obermeyer from his reverie.

“Yeah.”

“Did you hear me?”

“I heard you.”

“But . . .?”

“But I think we've got something really dangerous on our hands. Janet's not going to be a cat one, or even a two, and she's not going into South Carolina.”

“Oh, my God. You're going to do it again, aren't you? Hey, I wasn't kidding about getting strung up by your balls. You pull another Rita-like stunt and that'll be the stake-in-the-heart for your career.”

“Good-bye, Rick.”

Obermeyer, before he hung up, heard his friend shout, “Don't do it. Listen to me, Obie. Don't do it.”

# Chapter Four

**KEESLER AFB, MISSISSIPPI**
**LABOR DAY SUNDAY, 0500 HOURS**

In an attempt to ease the discomfort and doubt that had settled around him, squeezing him in a vise grip of foreboding, Major Walker drew a deep breath. It didn't help. All it produced was a lungful of diesel fumes from the power cart, their aftertaste as acrid as the realization that this would be his final flight with the Hurricane Hunters. The papers requesting his release from the Reserve sat on his desk in squadron headquarters, awaiting his signature. A task he'd attend to after the mission.

He didn't look forward to resigning. He loved flying, but if there were a chance to rescue his marriage, at least whatever was left of it, he needed to abdicate that love. Yes, he was old fashioned. More than a few friends had pointed that out. "Why not bail out of the marriage?" they'd asked. "Find a woman who will love you unconditionally, support your career in the Air Force?"

"No," he'd answered, "my vows were for better or for worse. I still believe in them."

And even though recently there'd been more worse than better, there once had been something of value between him and Donna. Something worth trying to salvage. Yet, to be honest, he wasn't sure his heart was in it any longer.

He'd left active duty after six years, surrendering to Donna's complaints about him being constantly absent from home, flying missions all over the world with the 314th Airlift Wing out of Little Rock. After that, he latched onto a Reserve job with the 302nd in Colorado Springs, piloting C-130s equipped to drop retardant on wildfires. A super job. How many guys get to fly low-level bombing runs with cargo planes? And he flew them lower than anyone else, and dumped his loads of red-colored slurry with greater accuracy than anyone else. Every time he nailed a run, which was frequently, his crew would paint a flame-icon on the nose of his Hercules, as C-130s are called.

But Donna again. She wanted to be closer to home, the Deep South. When the job with the Hurricane Hunters, the 53rd Weather Reconnaissance Squadron, opened up, he was lucky to get it. And Donna was happy. At least for a while.

Then her dissatisfaction grew again, disguised initially as concern over his future. "All I want," she said, her voice syrupy-sweet with a Southern lilt, "is for you to better your life, expand your opportunities, receive the recognition you deserve."

By "expand your opportunities," she meant, "forget the Reserve." By "receive the recognition you deserve," she meant "more money." What she really desired was for him to plow his energy and passion into his civilian job at the Raintree National Bank in Biloxi. Scale the corporate peaks, then move to a bigger bank. Eventually there would be a corner office with a view at Wells Fargo, SunTrust or Bank of America.

But he was content with his life, save for his marriage, and happy to navigate within the shallower waters a career with the Hurricane Hunters demanded. Without question the Reserve gobbled up time and effort that might otherwise have been invested with Raintree. But what Donna couldn't grasp, or was unwilling to grasp, was the immense fulfillment and excitement his military job delivered: flying into—attacking even—the most powerful storms on earth. An oak desk in a corporate prison offered no such drama.

Eventually, after a lukewarm performance report from his Air Force superior, Donna no longer hid her disdain for his Reserve career. Her brickbats no longer dripped honey, they became venom-tipped, and their marriage degenerated into the tension-riddled, vitriolic relationship that existed today.

"A penny for them?"

He turned. Captain Hill, Karlyn, the aerial reconnaissance weather officer, moved alongside of him. He knew a little bit more about her than he probably should have. Long-legged, athletic and attractive, he suspected she'd been a Lorelei for more than a few men. When not putting in time with the Reserve, she was a popular TV meteorologist in Charlotte.

"Just thinkin' about this old bird," he said.

"It's not old. It's a brand new J-model."

"I was speaking generically. About the family tree. My dad flew into Vietnam on one of these back in '65. Probably an E-model."

"Bullshit." She elbowed him softly in the ribs. "You've told me that story before. No penny for you."

Sometimes she was a little too insightful for her age.

"Look, you show me yours, I'll show you mine," she said, then clapped her hand over her mouth. "Oops. We already did that, didn't we?"

"Not quite."

"My, aren't we touchy. Bad hair day?"

"Sort of."

"Me, too."

He looked at her, into her dark brown eyes. In truth, he wasn't good at reading women, but thought he saw a certain pleading in Karlyn's gaze. "Okay," he said, "we'll grab a cup of coffee when we get back. Talk about it—your bad hair day."

"I'll hold you to it," she said, and headed toward the short, drop-down steps in the forward portion of the aircraft.

She was a good officer, it seemed to him, albeit a bit reckless at times. She'd once told him her passions in life were meteorology, motorcycles and mountains. She loved flying into hurricanes, she said, because it was "in-your-face meteorology." Motorcycles? She owned a Honda Gold Wing and a 1940 Indian Scout, a classic. And she'd scaled most of the major peaks in the Far West: Rainier, Adams, Hood, Whitney, and Shasta. Next, she said, McKinley in Alaska. He guessed—well, he knew—her recklessness washed over into her sexual behavior.

A yellow fuel truck roared to life, pulling back from the Hurricane Hunter.

"Sir, sir."

Walker looked behind him. First Lieutenant Van Smithers, the squadron's public affairs officer, was striding toward him, a civilian in tow. The civilian carried a canvas duffle bag and wore a loose-fitting windbreaker with the letters AJC embroidered on the front.

"This is Don Hemphill," Smithers said as he reached Walker. "He's a columnist with the *Atlanta-Journal Constitution*. He's going to be tagging along with us today."

"Sorry, I'm a little late," Hemphill said. He set the duffle bag on the ground, then extended his hand to Walker. "I had trouble getting to sleep last night, and after I finally did, I almost slept through my alarm."

He and Walker shook hands. The newspaperman appeared a bit

rumpled; his eyes, red and baggy. Walker judged him to be in his fifties, but his thinning, graying hair coupled with large bifocals that perched crookedly on his nose probably made him look older than he really was.

"Little apprehensive about flying into a hurricane?" Walker asked.

"Well, I guess. A bit. I've heard it's pretty safe though. That you've never lost one of these things." He gestured at the airplane.

"True, at least in the Atlantic Basin."

"What do you mean by 'at least in the Atlantic Basin?'"

Walker registered that the nuance hadn't slipped by Hemphill. "The only One-thirty that ever went down in a storm," Walker said, "was in the western Pacific. 1974. A Hurricane Hunter from Guam flew into Typhoon Bess. Radio contact with the bird was lost on its second penetration of the eye."

"A typhoon's the same thing as a hurricane, right?"

"Same thing. Just a different name in a different part of the world."

Hemphill made some notes on a small pad of paper, then looked up. "How long has the military been flying into hurricanes?"

"Quite awhile, actually. Joe Duckworth, a major in the Army Air Corps, flew into the first hurricane in 1943. Crazy bastard used a single-engine trainer. The first sanctioned mission, though, was in 1945. A B-17 out of Miami flew into a hurricane over the Bahamas. We've come a long way since then." Walker checked his watch. "Grab your bag there, Mr. Hemphill. The bird flying the previous mission had some mechanical problems and had to turn back. So the Hurricane Center wants us to be on-station on time, if not sooner."

Hemphill stooped to retrieve his bag. "Mechanical problems?" The words seemed to wobble out of him, fettered by uncertainty.

"You'll be fine, Mr. Hemphill," Walker said, patting him on the back. "The plane's in great shape, and Janet's not a particularly strong hurricane, so this should be pretty much of a milk run."

Walker didn't say anything, but there had been a Navy reconnaissance aircraft lost in the Atlantic Basin. In 1955, a two-engine P2V carrying a crew of nine and two newspapermen went down in the Caribbean during a low-level penetration of a strengthening hurricane. Its name, ironically: Janet. *No need to mention that to Hemphill. Maybe after the flight.*

"Good morning, Arly." Walker's copilot, Lt. Col. Bernie Harlow, the squadron commander, fell into step beside him. Harlow had informed him at the preflight briefing that he, Harlow, would be flying as copilot today. "Hope you don't mind," he'd said, "I decided to give the scheduled copilot a break. You know, holiday off, time with the family. You've still got the left-hand seat. I'll just be along for the ride."

Walker doubted that. Harlow, as the squadron commander, was also his rater, and the two hadn't seen eye to eye on Walker's last performance report. The colonel certainly wasn't a hard-ass, in fact, he was well respected by his peers, but the report had injured Walker's career: he'd been passed over for promotion. More fuel for Donna's fire, her campaign against "middle-class poverty."

"Good morning, sir," Walker responded. He couldn't bring himself to call the colonel Bernie, as most of the other officers did. He didn't feel a casual kinship with him. The performance report was at the root of it.

Harlow, black and ruggedly handsome, greeted Lt. Smithers, then introduced himself to Hemphill. He turned back to Walker. "If you're all set," he said, "I'll have 'em pull the plug on the power cart."

Walker nodded. "And Colonel?"

Harlow waited.

"If you want the stick today, that's fine with me." Harlow, in addition to being Walker's boss, was also the more experienced pilot. He was an Air Force Academy grad who'd won a Distinguished Flying Cross during Just Cause in Panama. The story was he'd held an AC-130H "Spectre" gunship in a tight pattern over Panamanian Defense Forces HQ while taking heavy ground fire. His skill and bravery had allowed his gunners to level the building while at the same time leaving structures just a few yards away unscathed. But despite his success in the Air Force, Harlow had left active duty after ten years and now flew 767s for Delta.

"Arly," Harlow said, stepping close to Walker so he could be heard over the roar of the power cart, "your flying skills are unquestioned. You're one of the best damn pilots in the squadron. I'd fly second seat with you anywhere, anytime. You're drivin'. Now let's go throw a rope around Janet."

Left unsaid was the real point of contention between the two men: the fact that Harlow viewed Walker as sometimes unable to make quick decisions, "indecisive" was the term he'd used. Walker disagreed, viewing himself as assiduously analytical and thoughtful, but certainly not indecisive.

Their polarized viewpoints were typified by an incident that had occurred the previous year. Walker had been returning to Keesler from a recon mission when he was asked if he could divert to perform a low-level search for a yacht damaged and adrift in the Gulf of Mexico. He'd asked for a few minutes to consider the request, but by the time he responded—in the affirmative—the mission had been handed off to a Coast Guard C-130. Harlow, Walker was sure, saw the delay in terms of a scorecard: Coast Guard 1, Air Force 0.

Walker countered that his navigator had needed time to calculate if they had enough fuel on board to perform an effective search. Low-level flying burns more fuel, and if they hadn't had enough to make more than a cursory sweep, it wouldn't have been worth it.

But Walker lost his counterargument and chance for promotion. In the military, all it takes is one black mark, one pass-over, and your career is effectively comatose. His was on life support, though with his resignation pending, that made no difference now. And although Harlow said he was just along for the ride, it was more than that. Still, at this point, it was academic.

The colonel and the rest of the flight crew, passenger in tow, mounted the stairs into the aircraft. Walker loitered on the tarmac, strolling to the front of the plane to complete his personal, preflight good luck routine. He reached up and patted the Hurricane Hunter's bulging black snout, the radome. "One last time," he whispered, "get me safely through the eyewall one last time."

He climbed into the aircraft, leaving behind the humid clutch of the morning, and was met by the familiar arid staleness of the plane's interior. With its exposed cables, ducts and wiring harnesses, and its awkward webbed canvas seating for passengers, the C-130 was the antithesis of a passenger jet. To him, however, it was like settling into an old armchair—comfortable, functional, reliable. And yet he remained oddly ill at ease. *It's just the final-mission yips,* he tried to reassure himself, the gnawing fear soldiers get that something will go wrong on their final patrol. But he knew it wasn't that. It was something else. He didn't want to admit it, but he'd fallen prey to the sleazy carnival act, the campy vision of the wizened soothsayer the previous day.

To convince himself the disquiet that gripped him was imagined, he ran through a mental checklist. The plane was in top mechanical shape. The hurricane they were reconing was only a cat one. And his crew was experienced and competent. *Palm readers be damned.*

He strapped himself into the pilot's seat and turned to Harlow.

"Let's wind 'em up, Colonel."

The first of the plane's four powerful turboprop engines whined slowly to life. But the disquieting malaise of uncertainty continued to close in on Walker, swirling around him like a thick, scudding overcast.

# Chapter Five

## ST. SIMONS ISLAND, GEORGIA
## LABOR DAY SUNDAY, 0540 HOURS

Alan Grant knelt by his son's bed and drew the covers back as gently as he could.

"Lee," he said, "tell me what happened in here. Where's your sister?" Lee lay on his side, his head facing the wall.

"Dunno."

"Roll over and look at me."

"No."

"Lee," Alan snapped, "Roll over and look at me. Now." He placed his hand on his son's shoulder but didn't force him.

Lee turned, but kept his eyes shut.

"Open your eyes, Son. Tell me what's going on."

Lee opened his eyes. "I dunno, Dad. Nuthin'."

"Lee."

Lee looked at the floor.

Alan heard Trish enter the room, felt her presence behind him, sniffed the vague aroma of Azurée. "She's not in the condo," she said, a quiver in her voice. "Where is she, Alan? What happened? What—"

Alan held up his hand, signaling for silence. "Lee," he said, "remember what we've always said, 'no secrets in this family.' I'm here to help, Son. Whatever it is, you know Dad can deal with it. Ya trust me?"

"Yeah."

"Talk to me."

Lee squirmed, covering his crotch with his hand. "I gotta go to the bathroom, Dad."

"Soon as you tell me where your sister is."

"She said she'd bust my iPod and cell phone if I snitched." His wriggling became more vigorous.

"You don't wanna wet your bed, do you, Son?"

"She snuck out to meet some guy." Lee leapt from his bed and

25

dashed for the bathroom.

Alan turned toward Trish. "Some guy?"

Trish shrugged.

"We've been here one day and she runs off with a guy?" Alan said.

"Probably someone from Atlanta she knew was going to be here at the same time we were."

"Who?"

"I don't know all of her friends."

The toilet flushed, but the door to the bathroom remained shut.

"Lee," Alan said, "get back out here."

Lee stuck his head out the door, his eyes wide with apprehension.

"It's okay, buddy, just finish your story. Who's the guy? When did your sister leave?"

"I don't know the guy, Dad. Some dude from Atlanta she knew before. She left about a half-hour ago."

Alan and Trish looked at one another. The unspoken message: She snuck out while we were making love.

"To go where?" Alan said.

"Dunno."

"Lee."

"They were going to meet on the beach someplace, go for a walk, get some breakfast, spend the day together."

"Why couldn't she have just asked us? Been above board about this?"

Rain, in rising and falling crescendos, beat a staccato rhythm against the bedroom's window.

"Cuz she said you wouldn't approve."

"Why?"

"The guy's a punk. I seen him once—"

"Saw him."

"Yeah. Anyway, he's got pins and rings and stuff sticking out of his nose and lips. Purple hair that sticks up like a wheat field. He's a jerk."

"Why do you say that?"

"He told me to f-off."

"He's older than your sister?

"Yeah, I think."

"But you don't know his name, where he's staying, who his folks are?"

Lee shook his head.

"Okay. Get dressed." He turned to Trish. "Fifteen years old and she runs off with somebody from the Addams Family?"

"It'll come as a shock to *her* she's only fifteen."

"She is what she is, whether she wants to believe it or not."

"What do we do now?" Trish's voice was edged in panic. "With the hurricane coming and everything?"

"Don't worry about the damn hurricane. Worry about Sandy." He draped his arm over Trish's shoulders. "First, we'll try her cell phone. Which will be turned off. Then we'll get in the car and go on patrol. Hit some breakfast places. Lee said they were going to breakfast. There aren't that many restaurants open Sunday morning around here."

"And once we find her," Trish said, "goddamn, is she gonna be grounded."

"She can kiss her cell phone goodbye, too," Alan added.

"Good. Can I have it?" Lee piped in.

"Get dressed," Alan said, "we're going to search for your sister."

Outside, the rain had ceased, at least temporarily. The first rays of daylight streaked a leaden overcast. Gray low-hanging stratus, like herds of pewter-colored buffalo on an inverted prairie, raced overhead. Tendrils of Spanish moss, drooping from massive live oaks, danced and twisted in the restive wind.

Alan herded Trish and Lee into the family Range Rover, then drove to a small area on the south side of the island known as The Village. There they checked a couple of breakfast spots, but there was no Sandy, no kid with purple hair that stood up like a wheat field.

From The Village, Alan made his way to Frederica Road, the main north-south avenue on St. Simons. He headed north. In the opposite lane, a steady stream of traffic moved south.

"Lots of people leaving," Trish said.

"The hurricane has them spooked," Alan responded. "Let 'em go. The causeway back to the mainland will be jammed."

They pulled into several strip malls along their route, checked out a handful of restaurants— most of them closed for breakfast—but didn't spot Sandy or the boy. Alan continued north onto Lawrence Road then Couper Road to Butler Point and the Hampton Club, the northern-most part of the island. He came back south, stopping at the tourist attractions of Christ Church, almost two centuries old, and Fort Frederica, an 18th century Colonial bastion.

"Try her cell again," he said.

Trish dialed, listened, then placed the phone in her lap. "Only her voice mail," she said. She drew her fist to her mouth and closed her eyes.

On Frederica Road once more, this time going south, Alan slowed to a crawl, caught in the exodus of residents and tourists. They'd been searching for the better part of an hour, and though neither he nor Trish wanted to suspend their effort, they decided to give in to Lee's increasingly strident complaints of hunger. They pulled into a new eatery, Wake Up, in Redfern Village just north of the island's airport.

They ordered breakfast, then poked desultorily at their scrambled eggs and stared out at the dull morning light while Lee attacked a second helping of blueberry waffles. The odor of slightly burnt coffee and greasy sausage wafted from the kitchen and drifted through the restaurant. Soft rock music tumbled from tinny overhead speakers.

"Damn Sandy," Alan muttered to Trish. "I'm with you. She's gonna be grounded; grounded until she gets married."

"It's going to be hard for her to get married if she's grounded until then."

"Well, TS. That's her problem."

Lee, syrup dripping off his chin, looked up. "What's TS, Dad?"

"Use your napkin, Son." Alan tapped his chin.

"What's it mean? TS?"

"Tough—"

"Situation," Trish interrupted before Alan could finish.

"Oh." Lee jammed another forkful of waffles into his mouth.

A waitress—bleary eyes, tangled hair—sauntered over to them. "More folks, coffee?" She exuded the faint essence of stale beer.

Alan shoved his cup toward her. "Rough night, huh?" He wondered if she were capable of uttering a coherent sentence.

"Gonna get rougher. That storm's coming. What's his name?"

"Janet?"

The waitress's eyes swam in a strange Brownian motion. She snickered and said, "That's not a his's name." Her hand shook as she refilled his cup. She slopped coffee into his saucer. "Oops. Sorry. My bad." She pulled a rag from her apron, dropped it on the floor, picked it up, dropped it again, retrieved it a second time, then reached toward the saucer with it.

"Never mind," Alan said. "I'll take care of it." He grabbed a handful of paper napkins and dabbed at the saucer. The waitress weaved her way off toward the kitchen.

"It's not coming, is it?" Trish asked.

"What?"

"The hurricane. You said it would miss us."

"Look at me," he said. "Look me in the eye."

She tilted her head up.

"We'll be fine," he said, fixing her in his gaze. "You know you can trust me. Right?"

She nodded.

"This thing will blow by and we'll have a good laugh tomorrow. Don't be listening to some hungover teenager with the IQ of a Pop-Tart. And don't go watching any television, either. Nothing but sensationalists. They love to get people running in circles, waving their arms and screaming 'Disaster's coming, disaster's coming.'"

"And yet they were right about Katrina, weren't they? Look what happened to New Orleans."

Alan worked to hold his frustration in check. If was enough that his daughter had run off. He didn't need to deal with the imaginary threat of a hurricane, too. "We aren't in New Orleans," he said. "Besides, that was a man-made disaster, an engineering failure. It wasn't storm surge or wind that wrecked the city. It was piss poor construction of the levees. Even if a hurricane hit St. Simons head on, it wouldn't do the same thing here because there's nothing to break. There aren't any levees or seawalls. There don't need to be." He paused and waited for a response, but none came, so he continued. "You don't really think the ocean, even in the worst of circumstances, would ever overtop this island do you?"

She lowered her eyes.

"Do you?"

"No," she whispered. But there was a lack of conviction in her voice that disturbed him. And it disturbed him not so much because of her obvious apprehension, but because of her lack of trust in his judgment.

She looked up at him again. "Where's Sandy?" she said. Her face had tightened into a mask of anxiety. Her lips were pressed together as if stitched to one another. Outside, the sky had become blacker, the clouds lower, the wind stronger. Fronds on a row of palms across the street whipped frantically back and forth as if trying to ward off some impending doom.

Alan tossed a twenty onto the table. "Come on," he said, "we'll find her." He stood and extended his hand to Trish. "I haven't let you down yet, have I?"

She smiled wanly.

"Can I have another glass of juice, Dad?" Lee asked.

"Not now, Son. Maybe later. We've got to find your sister."

"Sandy's a jerk."

"Out of the mouths of babes," Alan said softly.

"I'm scared," Trish whispered. Her eyes were red and misted, on the verge of tears.

As they stepped out of the restaurant, the wind attacked, yanking at their clothes, ripping at their hair, spitting mist and grit into their eyes. Small branches tumbled through the parking lot in advance of a wall of rain sweeping in from the northeast. The family dashed for their Range Rover, Alan tugging Lee with one hand, encircling Trish's waist with the other. As they clambered in, the downpour hit, pelting the vehicle in a thunderous barrage.

Alan started the engine and turned on the wipers, but the blades, even on high speed, were unable to clear the windshield.

"We'll wait a few minutes," he said, "this shouldn't last long."

"Is this the hurricane, Dad?" Lee asked.

"No. I think it's what's called an outer rainband. You know how when you play your video war games they sometimes have Special Forces, small groups of soldiers that sneak into enemy territory ahead of the main force?"

"Yeah."

"That's kind of what these rainbands are. They race out ahead of the storm center, hit hard and quick, and don't stick around very long."

"Will there be more?"

"Probably. It'll get stormy at times, but I don't think it'll be real bad. The eyewall of the hurricane, the worst of the wind and rain, is forecast to miss us."

Lee nodded, then said, "But you know, Dad, sometimes those weather guys are wrong." He suddenly looked way too serious for an eight-year-old.

The wipers continued to beat a rapid tattoo, but remained no match for the cloudburst. Trish leaned her head against the passenger door window and peered into the rain-washed morning.

Alan stared at his son, the boy's innocent statement hovering in the vehicle like the Sword of Damocles.

# Chapter Six

## ATLANTA, GEORGIA—THE NATURAL ENVIRONMENT TELEVISION NETWORK LABOR DAY SUNDAY, 0545 HOURS

Nicholas Obermeyer drew a deep breath. The discussion with his friend Richard Keys at the National Hurricane Center hadn't ended well. But his next conversation would likely end up even worse: something akin to two Bullet Trains colliding.

He knew he didn't have time to struggle through the network's chain of command, so he bypassed the producer on duty, Sally Ainsworth, and dialed the home phone of Robbie McSwanson, the executive vice president of production. McSwanson, a spare, red-haired Scot, had been hired from Fox several years ago immediately after Asian-Pacific Communications had purchased the venerable Weather Channel from its corporate owners and renamed it The Natural Environment Network. Now all that was left of the old channel was nothing more than a handful of mostly pseudo meteorologists. And even those had been relegated to bottom feeders in an operation more interested in airing documentaries and infotainment programs than weathercasts.

Under The Weather Channel, Obermeyer would never have had to plead to go on the air live. Janet, a mere category one or not, would have been headline news from the get-go and he would have been in front of the cameras immediately.

McSwanson, however, was more interested in programming that brought steady, predictable income than with any notion of public service or the occasional soaring peaks in viewership that came with the high drama of dangerous weather.

Not only that, but Obermeyer and McSwanson had locked horns in a previous life. The Scotsman had been news director at the Houston station where Obermeyer worked when the "Rita Incident" occurred. Only the intervention of a producer built like an NFL offensive tackle had kept McSwanson and Obermeyer from throwing haymakers at each other in the newsroom. The episode served to enhance McSwanson's inherent low regard for Obermeyer specifically and meteorologists in general. "Wee boring people," he called them. But wee and boring or not, Obermeyer needed an executive blessing for what he was about to do. At least he *wanted* such a blessing.

Getting it, especially from McSwanson, would be extremely problematical.

Obermeyer's temples pulsed in painless throbs and his grip on the handset tightened with each successive ring of McSwanson's phone. On the seventh ring, someone picked up. "What?" The tone of voice suggested a person more asleep than awake.

"Robbie, it's Obie." Something on the other end of the line crashed.

"Shit."

"You okay, Robbie?"

"No, I'm not okay. I knocked the damn clock off my bed stand. And I'm guessin' it's five-forty in the friggin' mornin', not five-forty in the afternoon."

"I'm sorry to wake you—"

"Spare me. Ya never been sorry for anything ya done."

"And a joyous good morning to you, too, sir."

"Cut the shit. Just tell me what ya want." McSwanson's voice was thick and watery, as though something phlegmy was lodged in his throat.

"We need to start wall-to-wall coverage of Hurricane Janet. Now. I'm not talking thirty-second cut-ins or our usual three-minute weather spots at the top of every hour. I mean at least five minutes out of every fifteen. I want to recommend, unofficially, of course, that south coastal Georgia be evacuated."

McSwanson breathed heavily into the phone, not saying anything.

"Robbie?"

"Yeah?"

"Did you hear me?"

"Not very well. I coulda sworn ya said ya want to recommend south coastal Georgia be evacuated."

"I did."

"So what the hell am I missin' here? Last I heard we had a category one on our hands headin' for South Carolina, not Georgia. Did the Hurricane Center change its forecast?"

"No."

Again McSwanson fell silent. When he finally spoke, his words came out wrapped in a growl. "Although I know it's a stretch, just give it to me straight. What are ya seein' that nobody else is?"

Obermeyer started to speak, but to his surprise, no words came out. He cleared his throat and tried again. "A cat four or five landfalling somewhere along the south Georgia coast by early evening."

A hammering sound erupted in Obermeyer's ear: McSwanson, he guessed, beating his phone against a desk or table. The hammering stopped.

"Piece a crap," McSwanson shouted, "I knew this thing was a piece a crap. It sounded like ya said somethin' about a cat five hurricane."

"I did."

"On the Georgia coast?"

"Yeah."

"I don't suffer fools, Obie."

*My god, Robbie, how do you stand yourself?* Obermeyer held the phone away from his mouth in case he accidentally verbalized his thoughts. Under The Weather Channel, his judgment, experience, and integrity would never have been challenged.

"Obie, you there?"

"Unfortunately."

"What?"

"In case you missed my point, not that I had a chance to make it, I think Janet is about to become a monster. And when that happens, it'll change course. South Georgia will be its target, probably somewhere around St. Simons Island."

"And the Hurricane Center hasn't figured out that St. Simons, not . . . what was that other place?"

"Hilton Head." *Nice to see you're keeping up with the news, Robbie.*

" . . .that St. Simons, not Hilton Head, will be ground zero? How come you're so much smarter, Obie?"

"I'm not. The Hurricane Center will come around. Look, the overnight recon flight into Janet had to abort. If it had made it, I think we'd know for sure Janet already is a hell of a lot stronger than a cat one. The next flight in will confirm it, I'm positive, but every minute counts."

"Why?"

"Because there are thirty thousand, maybe thirty-five thousand people on St. Simons this weekend. They've got twelve hours to get off. And there's only one way out, over a causeway across the Atlantic Intracoastal Waterway."

"Let 'em hunker down. It's not like the island is gonna become Atlantis or something."

"Damn it, if I'm right, that's exactly what it'll be like. Humor me. Pretend I actually know what the hell I'm talking about." Obermeyer massaged his temples with his thumb and forefinger and wished that he'd cold-cocked McSwanson when he'd had the chance in Houston.

McSwanson paused, seeming to consider his response, then said, "When's the next recon plane due in?"

Obermeyer checked his watch. "A little over two hours."

"And if it confirms what you're thinkin', how much longer for the Hurricane Center to update its warnings?"

"Maybe half an hour or so."

"Wait 'til they do it."

"Almost three hours? You don't get it, do you? That could be the difference between life and death for a lot of people."

"Hypothetical life and death. Ya aren't sure yet."

"Hypothetical? You wanna tell that to the friends and family of the folks who don't make it? That dead bodies floating in the surf are just hypothetical?" Obermeyer's words came out clipped and firm, honed by restrained anger.

"And if you're wrong, ya wanna explain to the emergency managers, FEMA, the National Hurricane Center and the board of directors of this company why ya started a panic, a stampede, to evacuate the island? This is that Rita thing in reverse. Ya got your résumé up to date, Dr. Nick?"

"How in the hell can you measure thirty thousand lives against getting a handful of government agencies pissed off?"

"Government agencies?" McSwanson shouted. "This thing could go all the way to the White House if you pull one of your dumb ass, arrogant stunts again."

"It's not a stunt. Listen to me—"

"A few stinkin' hours, that's all I'm askin' for," McSwanson interrupted.

Obermeyer imagined McSwanson sitting on the edge of his bed, his eyes bloodshot and pinched; his narrow, freckled face sleep-creased and folded; his uncombed hair looking like windswept prairie grass.

"Ya hear me, Obie?"

"Yeah, I hear you." *Three hours. No frigging way.* He hung up. He imagined something else now. McSwanson slamming the receiver down, launching himself from the bed and muttering muted curses as he stumbled toward the bathroom. He'd be at the network in less than an hour. "Insufferable asshole," Obermeyer said to no one. He brushed a patina of moisture from his forehead. Suddenly unsure of the course he'd chosen, he bent forward to cradle his head in his hands, his forearms resting on his thighs. He walked his thoughts into a quiet forest and out onto the shores of a still lake. There he managed to reach a state of vague composure. After a moment, he sat up, reached for the phone and dialed an internal extension.

"Sally," he said, "McSwanson wants me on the air immediately."

# Chapter Seven

## AIRBORNE, EN ROUTE TO HURRICANE JANET
## LABOR DAY SUNDAY, 0550 HOURS

The WC-130 completed its climb-out from Keesler. Karlyn unfastened her safety harness and walked back to where their guest sat. He looked vaguely uncomfortable and slightly apprehensive. "Mr. Hemphill," she said, "I'm Captain Karlyn Hill, the weather officer on this mission." She raised her voice to be heard over the reverberating thrum of the huge turboprops. The Air Force didn't waste money soundproofing its aircraft. "It's going to be a couple of hours before we reach Janet, so if you'd like to follow me to my position, I'll give you a brief overview of what goes on in a Hurricane Hunter." She looked at Lieutenant Smithers and added, "Okay?"

Smithers nodded. Karlyn led Hemphill to the weather officer's console, a sprawling array of computer monitors, digital readouts, switches, dials and cables.

"So, a milk run, the major said?" Hemphill asked, not paying much attention to the console.

"Well, you never know, sir. But yes, this should be pretty much a routine mission. It might get a bit bumpy; that's probably the only excitement we'll have. Janet's not a particularly powerful hurricane."

He smiled at her, a thin, forced expression. "Still, I suppose things aren't always what they seem."

"You're a philosopher, Mr. Hemphill?"

"No, ma'am, just a newspaperman who's been around the block a few too many times."

The airplane shimmied, a good solid shake, and both Hemphill and Karlyn reached for the back of her seat to steady themselves.

"A preview of coming attractions?" Hemphill asked.

"Just making sure you've got your sea legs."

"More likely making sure I've got my Dramamine." He winked at her. "I do." He patted his shirt pocket.

She shrugged. "Honestly, you probably won't need it."

"Let's hope." He looked at a notepad in his left hand and clicked a ballpoint pen to life with his right. "Well, before you brief me about the aircraft, could you tell me about the squadron? I understand it's composed of reservists, not active duty personnel."

"The 53rd became a Reserve unit in 1993. Prior to that it was active duty. Its lineage actually goes back to 1944 when it was the 30th Weather Reconnaissance Squadron flying missions out of Gander, Newfoundland, over the north Atlantic."

"But now you're all part-time Air Force folks?"

"Not all. A lot of us are. I'm a TV meteorologist in Charlotte. Our pilot's a banker in Mississippi. Our copilot flies for Delta. A couple of other crew members are Air Reserve Technicians—ARTs—civil servants who work full time at the squadron but wear uniforms and hold Air Force ranks."

Hemphill scratched a few notes on his pad, then said, "Okay. So let me play devil's advocate for moment."

Karlyn waited, having a pretty good idea what the next question would be.

"Why do we need Hurricane Hunters? With all the radar and satellite technology we have, wouldn't that be a much more cost-effective and safer way to monitor these storms?"

"To be blunt, yes. It would be more cost-effective and safer, but not nearly as informative. Radar, for instance, can't tell us anything about a hurricane until it's almost to the coast. Too late for warning purposes. And determining the strength of a hurricane using satellite imagery is still an estimate, not a definitive measurement."

"Effective rebuttal," he said.

"My daddy used to tell me, 'If you really want to find out what the cannibals are up to, you have to walk naked through their village.'"

"Your dad was an explorer?" Hemphill smiled.

"Nope. A commercial fisherman in Astoria, Oregon. But he was always telling cannibal stories and jokes. You know, stuff like 'If a cannibal ate a clown would it taste funny?'"

Hemphill laughed. "But you guys aren't really walking naked through the village, so to speak, are you?"

"No, sir. We go in cloaked in technology. On our way out to a storm, we take continuous measurements of wind, temperature, humidity and air pressure, and transmit them to the National Hurricane Center in Miami. It's all automated, done by a system that's tied into the aircraft's navigation computers." She pointed out some of the features on the console and gave Hemphill a simplified overview of how everything worked.

A shudder abruptly ran through the WC-130 and Karlyn grabbed the edge of the console. "Hang on, Mr. Hemphill, we're gonna get a bump." The shudder turned into a jolt and the aircraft suddenly sank. Hemphill dropped his notepad and, like Karlyn, latched onto the console to steady himself. The turbulence passed and the Hurricane Hunter's flight smoothed out.

"Okay to let go now?" Hemphill asked, a bit of a quiver in his voice.

Karlyn nodded. *Why the hell are we getting bounced around like this so far from the storm?*

Hemphill bent to retrieve his pad. "So, where were we?" he asked.

"About finished, I think. Oh, there is one more thing. Within the last few years we've started using something called 'Smurf.'"

"Smurf?"

"The stepped-frequency microwave radiometer. The sensor's mounted on the underside of a wing. Just don't stand underneath it or you'll never have babies."

Hemphill closed one eye and cocked his head at her.

"Kidding," she said.

"So, Smurf. What does it do?"

"In simplest terms, it looks at the microwave radiation emitted naturally from wind-whipped sea foam and calculates wind speeds."

"Really?"

"Really. Satellites, with a lot of limitations, have been doing it for years."

"But before Smurf, how did the Hurricane Hunters measure wind speeds?"

"Same way we still do, to augment the Smurf data." She inclined her head toward a seat and console across from hers on the right side of the aircraft, but facing in the opposite direction, forward. A sergeant sitting in the seat looked up.

"That's where the dropsonde operator sits," she said. "Technically, the weather reconnaissance loadmaster. That's Master Sergeant Louie McKenzie." She leaned toward the sergeant and raised her voice. "Louie," she said, "this is Mr. Hemphill from the AJC."

The sergeant smiled and raised a hand in greeting.

"When we get into the hurricane," Karlyn continued, speaking to Hemphill, "Sergeant McKenzie will periodically launch dropsondes."

She patted a vertical tube immediately behind and to the left of the sergeant. "This is the launch tube. The sergeant stuffs a sonde, a little cylinder, in here, releases it and it floats toward the ocean while radioing all sorts of weather data, including wind speed, back to the plane."

"It *floats* down?"

"Yes. After a sonde is dropped, it deploys a little stabilizer, a sort of drogue parachute to slow its descent."

Hemphill bent over the tube for a closer look. "Pardon my French," he said, "but this looks more like something you'd piss in."

"Wouldn't work for me," Karlyn said.

Hemphill blushed. "My bad."

"That's okay, sir, I'm used to working around guys."

"Which brings to mind a question. How did you get into this business? Flying into hurricanes?"

"You mean because I'm a female?"

"Well, I gather you represent a minority."

She rested one hand on her console, just in case they encountered more turbulence, while she spoke to Hemphill. "There aren't that many of us, that's true. But hurricane hunting isn't exclusively testosterone-dominated anymore."

"But how did you get started, I mean in weather?"

"Big storms have fascinated me ever since I was a kid. I went out with my dad a few times on his fishing trawler. We got caught in a Pacific gale once and he was terrified for me. But I was having a ball. It ignited a genuine passion within me." She smiled at that memory.

Hemphill wrote quickly.

"After that, I was hooked. I went to the University of Washington—"

"Seattle, right?" Hemphill interrupted.

"Right. Majored in atmospheric science, went through Air Force ROTC and came out as a second lieutenant. Then four years on active duty. I was stationed at Langley AFB in Virginia when my commitment was up. At the time, I was dating a guy from Norfolk who was a television news reporter." *Dating? Yes, for public consumption. It was a bit more than that.* "He thought I'd make a good TV weathercaster and worked with me to cut some demo tapes. That's how I got the job in Charlotte. And then when a slot opened up with the Hurricane Hunters, I jumped on it. I guess flying through eyewalls is as close as you can come to combat without getting shot at."

"Eyewalls," Hemphill said, "tell me about them."

"Nature's nightmare," she answered. "An eyewall is the engine room of a hurricane—a circular wall of massive clouds and brutal squalls."

"Oh, I love that. Nature's nightmare." Hemphill wrote the words, then circled them twice. "So, what's it like, flying through eyewalls?" There seemed a certain hesitancy in his question.

Karlyn liked that, liked that first-timers were a bit apprehensive. It made her job sound more romantic, more adventuresome than it really was. But she had a canned answer she used to rattle rookies' cages: "Think of that crazy, big-ass roller coaster at Six Flags in Atlanta. Goliath."

Hemphill stopped writing and snapped his head up. "Goliath? That mega-coaster monster?"

"Yeah. That one, only wilder. Goliath out of control."

"Out of control?" His eyes widened slightly.

Karlyn laughed lightly and patted his arm. "Pulling your leg," she said. "Sorry. I shouldn't do that. Truth be told, the trip through an eyewall is often uneventful. A bump or two here and there and that's it. Once in a while it can get pretty rough. But let me put it this way: I've never been scared."

"That's comforting. I guess."

"In a mature storm, say a major hurricane, one with winds over 130 mph, we'll fly in at a higher altitude. It'll still be bouncy, but it gives us a big margin for error. C-130s don't make good seaplanes. It's low-altitude penetrations into unexpectedly strong storms that get hairy."

Hemphill furrowed his brow. "Does that happen often?"

"Not often, but a NOAA Hurricane Hunter got a big surprise back in 1989 when it flew into Hugo too low. The storm was strengthening rapidly and the crew wasn't aware of it. The plane got whacked around, lost an engine and ended up stuck in the eye until an Air Force One-thirty came in and led it out."

"Great," Hemphill muttered. He looked around the interior of the plane, shifting his gaze quickly from one side of the aircraft to the other.

"A question?" Karlyn said.

"I was briefed on the PFD, the personal floatation device," he said. "But how about life rafts?"

"We've got a couple. They'd be kind of academic, though, if we had to ditch in thirty-foot seas. We wouldn't survive more than a matter of seconds with or without life rafts."

Hemphill exhaled a long breath and stared at the floor.

"Relax, sir. It's not like you're riding in the *Titanic*." Using the Goliath analogy, she decided, had been a bad idea.

Hemphill lifted his head and looked at Karlyn. "So what altitude will we penetrate Janet at?" he asked, the professional journalist again.

"Since she hasn't buffed up yet, probably 5000 feet. If she were weaker, we might go in even lower. Stronger, we'd make our penetration at ten."

The plane bounced again, this time hard, rocking left and right, then wallowing up and down. Karlyn sailed into the side of the aircraft, Hemphill landing heavily against her. The interior of the plane was padded, but she knew she'd come away with a bruised shoulder.

"I'm sorry," Hemphill said. "You think Janet's trying to tell us something?" He steadied himself and pulled Karlyn upright.

"We're a long way from Janet yet," she said. "But maybe we'd better get strapped in."

"Okay. No argument from me." He hurried back to where he'd been seated next to Lieutenant Smithers, flopped down and cinched up his lap belt. Karlyn watched as he dug into his shirt pocket and fished out the Dramamine tablets.

She slumped into her own seat and tightened her harness. From somewhere deep within her brain, a synapse fired, and a yellow caution light snapped on. It was unusual this far from a hurricane to encounter turbulence of the magnitude they had this morning. *Some sort of warning shot over our bow?* She drew a long, slow, deep breath. *No, it's probably just me. My circuits are fried. I've got 220 volts of personal shit running through a 110-line.* The caution light flickered out. Still, the rough ride continued to nag at her. It was like a low-grade fever that refused to relent.

# Chapter Eight

## ST. SIMONS ISLAND, GEORGIA
## LABOR DAY SUNDAY, 0655 HOURS

The squall abated and Alan pulled the Range Rover away from the restaurant. "We'll go back to the condo," he said. "Maybe Sandy will call there. And it'll give us a chance to regroup. Refocus. Settle our emotions. Maybe we're going about this all wrong. Maybe we need a new approach."

"Maybe we need help," Trish said.

"No. It's our daughter. Our problem. Ours to solve."

He sensed Trish's gaze boring into him. "You mean *yours* to solve," she snapped.

"Ours," he repeated. "*We'll* find her. Don't bail out on me now." He glanced at his wife. She turned away from him and stared out through the windshield.

Alan steered the SUV onto East Beach Causeway, a stretch of road over the marshes that permeated the eastern side of St. Simons. A stately Great Egret, in search of breakfast, stalked slowly and deliberately through the brackish waters of one of the bogs. A small deer, seeking shelter from the wind, darted across the road in front of the vehicle, racing toward a copse of live oaks. On the eastern horizon, the sky darkened to obsidian once more as another arc of squalls churned toward the island.

Alan reached Ocean Boulevard and turned south, creeping along in a solid line of cars and trucks, evacuees from the low-rise condos, beach homes and bungalows that jammed the area. Alan wheeled the Range Rover into the parking lot of the King and Prince Resort. "I'm gonna run in here," he said. "Maybe our two delinquents showed up at a classy joint for breakfast. If they did, somebody might remember them."

He came out shaking his head and slumped into the driver's seat of the vehicle. The next squall hit, rocking the SUV in powerful gusts. Rain sheeted across the parking lot, hiding what few vehicles were left in waves of liquid grayness. Alan leaned his forehead against the steering wheel. "I don't know," he said. "I just don't know. Why do kids do stuff like this?"

"Cuz she's a jerk," Lee said from the rear seat, reinforcing a point he'd made earlier.

Trish rested her hand on the back of Alan's neck. Rain peppered the Range Rover, pinging against its metal and glass like volleys of buckshot. Alan raised his head from the steering wheel.

"No, that's not it, Son. She's not, not really. That's what's so mystifying. She can be pouty, stubborn and rebellious, but she's never pulled a stunt like this, just boogying off without telling us."

"You're still thinking of her as your little girl," Trish lectured. "She's growing up, asserting herself, flaunting her perceived independence. You haven't been around her as much as I have the last few years. You're still seeing her in black and white TV reruns, like old Ozzie and Harriet shows, and I'm catching her in high-definition color: flaws, blemishes and all."

Alan conceded Trish was right. He still pictured a pre-kindergarten Sandy sitting on his lap, laughing when he tickled her, hugging him goodnight when it was time for bed. He still saw her, seven years old, in her soccer uniform, eyes filled with tears, running to "daddy" for comfort after she let an opponent's winning goal past her.

Ten years old: blushing, deep crimson, then giggling when asked about a boyfriend. *"You seem to be spending an inordinate amount of time in front of mirrors lately,"* he pointed out.

*"I'm still your little girl, Daddy,"* she'd responded after she quit giggling.

He realized now that might have been her first foray into manipulative behavior. At the time, though, neither one of them would have recognized it as that. It certainly wasn't deliberate on Sandy's part.

"Should we call the police?" Trish asked.

"They've probably got their hands full with all these idiots trying to get off the island," Alan answered. "I'm afraid we're on our own."

"No. You just want us to be on our own. I'm going to try." She dialed 9-1-1. Alan listened as she gave Sandy's description to a dispatcher. She answered several questions, gave the dispatcher their cell phone numbers, and hung up. "You were right," she said to Alan.

"What?"

"The dispatcher said the police would keep their eyes open for Sandy, but that they had other priorities at the moment." A look of nascent desperation clouded her face.

**Back in the condo,** Alan stood behind the rain-flecked slider and watched the gray ocean roll over the beach. Breakers washed onto the sandy berm below him, flattening the sea grass on its crest, then retreated, carrying a portion of the protective dune back out to sea. To his right, foam torn from the tops of the breakers slid across the concrete pad surrounding the swimming pool and blew across the surface of the pool's green water.

Trish joined him, grasping his hand. "So what now?" she asked, her voice broken and unsteady. He realized he had no other plan, no other approach. They could mount a search again, but with the increasing rain and wind and snarled traffic, that likely would prove just as futile as before.

"Let's stick it out here awhile," he said, camouflaging his lack of an alternative course of action. "Sandy just might come back."

"Surely she would have phoned or come back by now . . . if she were able," Trish said.

"Don't go jumping to conclusions. Like you told me, she's probably just asserting her independence." But he, like Trish, was beginning to sense there was something wrong.

He turned toward his son. "Lee," he said, "do you know where Sandy met this guy?"

Lee was seated on the floor in front of the couch listening to his iPod. He removed his earphones. "What, Dad?"

"Where did Sandy meet this kid she ran off with? At school? Around the neighborhood? At a party? Where? Do you have any idea?"

"I think on the Internet."

"What?"

"You know. On one of those Internet chat rooms. All the kids use them."

"She was in a chat room?" He looked at Trish.

Her gaze moved from him to Lee then back to him.

"Chat room?" Alan repeated, directing his question toward Trish.

She shrugged.

"You didn't know?" he asked, a bit more sharply than he knew he had reason to.

"Did you?" she said softly.

He ignored her retort. "So this guy might have no other connection on St. Simons outside of trying to hook up with Sandy? He could be anybody. A criminal. A pervert. Shit." He felt like slamming his fist through the slider. His daughter could be in a much worse situation than he'd initially imagined. Not just in trouble. In danger.

Trish moved to the couch, sat and buried her face in her hands. Her shoulders heaved as she sobbed quietly, the same fears that gnawed at Alan undoubtedly running wild in her mind. Lee, wide-eyed, glanced at her, then slipped the earphones back on his head and turned away.

The slider shook and bowed as a powerful wind gust hurled a phalanx of rain against it. Alan stared through the glass, focusing on nothing. His daughter was out there someplace, in the storm; in the hands of someone she shouldn't be.

He felt in his pants pockets for the keys to the Range Rover.

# Chapter Nine

## ATLANTA, GEORGIA—THE NATURAL
## ENVIRONMENT TELEVISION NETWORK
## LABOR DAY SUNDAY, 0655 HOURS

One of Dr. Obermeyer's professors at Florida State University, a short, dark-haired Brooklynite who wore Coke bottle-bottom glasses and had a propensity for patting coeds on inappropriate parts of their anatomy, used to say, "People, when you're forecasting, remember: common things happen frequently, uncommon things happen rarely. So, when you hear hoofbeats, think horses, not unicorns."

Obermeyer stared at the whirling infrared image of Janet on his computer monitor. "Unicorns," he said softly. "Dammit, I hear unicorns."

"You think they escaped from a folklore zoo and snuck in here overnight?"

*A folklore zoo?* He swiveled in his chair to see who had spoken. It was Sherrie Willis, one of the network's new On-Camera Meteorologists. He didn't know Sherrie personally, and although she seemed like a pleasant enough young lady, he suspected her title of meteorologist was gratuitous, like most of the recent hires. She was, for all practical purposes, merely emblematic of a trend now underway at the network. That trend being to replace the few remaining Weather Channel holdovers with "blonde bimbos whose chest sizes are larger than their IQs and who don't know a cumulus from a condom."

That observation had been vocalized by Obermeyer once after an on-air segment. But he'd forgotten to switch off his mike and the remark was overheard by a producer. Obermeyer's indiscretion earned him a visit to the CEO's office, a tongue lashing worse than he'd ever gotten in army boot camp, and a stern warning to keep his opinions to himself.

"Think you can do that?" the CEO had demanded.

"I think what I can do," Obermeyer had responded, "is make sure my mike isn't live before I express them."

He looked up at Sherrie. "You're here early, Blondie."

"Sherrie."

"Sorry, it's like the clone factory exploded."

She smiled vacantly, the remark seeming to race past her, ungrasped—like a fart in a full gale.

"What about unicorns?" she asked.

"They're mythical. And in this case, metaphorical."

"You're sure about that?"

"I'm sure."

"Did you know they're mentioned in the Bible? Old Testament. King James version." She smiled again, same smile as before, and brushed a tumble of blond hair from her forehead. She locked Obermeyer in an unblinking gaze with flat, gray eyes. "In case you're wondering," she said, "and I know you're not, I have a Master's Degree in meteorology from Cornell." Her smile abruptly disappeared, subsumed by a subtly clinched jaw.

He was being challenged, though her manner seemed to suggest an intellectually considered summons rather than an emotional one. Had he miscast her, misjudged what she represented? He studied her for a moment, then said, "King James version?"

"In subsequent translations they became wild oxen. Maybe that's what you're hearing. Wild oxen."

"Probably a stampede." He paused, then asked, "So how'd you slip past the palace guards?"

"I wore falsies and told them I thought convection was a rock group."

"Welcome to the insurgency, Sherrie."

Her gaze softened and her jaw relaxed. "So what's with the unicorns—the oxen?"

He pointed at his monitor. "Janet. About two-hundred miles east of Jacksonville, top winds 80 mph, or so the Hurricane Center says, and moving northwest at fifteen. Officially forecast to make landfall this evening somewhere around Hilton Head as a strong cat one or weak two."

"But you see—hear?—something different?" Sherrie leaned in closer to the monitor, looking intently at the image he'd been examining. She smelled vaguely of roses and honeysuckle. Vibrant, classy. The result of a concerted effort, he judged, to overcome a three a.m. rise-and-shine. She'd obviously drawn the short straw for the holiday weekend. Not that she'd be overworked. Live weather segments were few and far between.

"See these?" He pointed to streamers of moisture feathering out from the top of the storm.

"Janet's exhaust system."

"You probably got straight A's at Cornell."

She shrugged. "I know what supercharges hurricanes. The more air you blow out the top, the faster it swirls in at the surface."

He took a can of Dr Pepper wedged between two books on his desk and tipped it to his lips. Some of its contents dribbled onto his dress shirt. "Shit," he said, "fresh from the laundry . . . oh, sorry."

A strange glimmer, the visual equivalent of a secret handshake, crept into Sherrie's eyes. "I usually just say 'fuck it'," she said, "and get a fresh blouse."

He suppressed a grin, wiped his mouth and dabbed at the brown spots on his shirt with a paper towel. He nodded at the monitor. "The supercharger is kicking in. Look how well defined the eye has become." A dark pinhole had appeared in the center of Janet's cloud shield.

"So, stronger than 80 mph now?"

"A lot."

"Didn't they recon it last night?"

"No. A flight was scheduled, but aborted. The Hurricane Center wants to wait until the next bird gets into the storm before they jack up the winds on the advisory." He stopped. Should he continue? Did Sherrie really care?

She cocked her head, apparently waiting for him to proceed.

*So, an ally?* He reached for the checklist on his desk and held it up for Sherrie to see. He explained his reasoning to her, pleased to have someone who listened, who understood. "Plus," he added as he finished, "Janet's about to cross the Gulf Stream."

"Higher octane fuel."

Obermeyer nodded.

"So how strong?"

"Remember Wilma?"

"Yeah, it went from a tropical storm to a cat five in twenty-four hours or something like that?"

"And from a cat one to the most intense hurricane known in just eighteen hours, an historic rate of strengthening. After Katrina and Rita in 2005, Wilma and her 185-mph winds kind of ran under the public's radar since it happened in the northwest Caribbean and the storm weakened a lot before whacking Florida."

"So you're seeing a Wilma, except next door to the U.S. and not in the Caribbean?"

A soft background hum, the white noise of the air conditioning system, filled the operations area while Obermeyer considered his response. After a brief pause he said, "That's part of it."

"Only part?" Sherrie squatted down, bringing her eyes level with his. "What's the rest of it?"

"The rest of it," Obermeyer said, "is that when a hurricane strengthens dramatically, it builds an upper-level high pressure area over itself. And that changes the steering of the storm."

"Almost like it develops a mind of its own?"

He shook his head. "Probably more like a design of its own. Everything is predictable about hurricanes. We just aren't clever enough to have figured out all the nuances yet."

"So, not Hilton Head?"

He shook his head. "South Georgia. Probably around St. Simons Island."

"Jesus." She stood up. "That area isn't even warned."

"And the computer models will never see it coming."

"But you do?"

He shrugged. "I'm not infallible. Nobody is in this business. Look, people want yes or no forecasts. Is it going to rain or isn't it? Are we going to get a foot of snow or not? Is the hurricane going to hit here or there? The fact is, we're never certain, which is why we think in terms of probabilities. That's the only honest way to forecast. But the public won't stand for it. They see it as a cop out." He felt to see if the spot on his shirt had dried. It hadn't.

He continued. "So I have to make the call. I have to balance my confidence, the chance that I might be wrong, against the downside of not sticking my neck out. In this case, the downside is enormous: an awful lot of people could die. I'm willing to fall on my sword to prevent that." He glanced at a wall clock.

"What?" she said.

"I have a show to stack. I'm going on the air in fifteen minutes."

"Doesn't McSwanson usually make that call?"

"I talked to him already."

"And he agreed?"

He looked at the ceiling, stalling for time, mulling over candidate answers. In the end, he decided to ignore the question. "I'm going on the air," he said.

She gazed at him intently, her eyes narrowing. "Well, your word 'insurgency' was carefully chosen, wasn't it? Come on, I'll help you stack. You can finish your story. And grab some more paper towels. We gotta do something about that shirt."

They walked to the other end of the first floor, to a set, Storm View, where Obermeyer would do his show. As they selected—stacked—the images he would use on-air, he continued to talk. "The Georgia and South Carolina coastlines are more vulnerable than most to storm surges. A lot of people aren't aware of that."

"I wasn't," Sherrie interjected.

He nodded. "It's because the coasts there are so shallow so far out into the ocean. The shallowness allows more water to build up for a given wind speed. For instance, a cat four hurricane would generate a surge of around fifteen feet above normal tide levels along most shorelines."

"And in Georgia?"

"Maybe twenty-five feet."

"And a cat five?"

"As much as thirty feet. All of St. Simons, under water. The highest point on the island isn't much more than twenty feet above sea level."

Sherrie let out a long, low whistle, like a guy might, and released the computer mouse she'd been using to move graphics into a queue for Obermeyer. "Maybe you'd better give the emergency management folks down there a call," she said.

His heart rate began to ramp up. He was wading into a swamp so deep and tenebrous he might never come out. In fact, he probably didn't need to worry about having to fall on his sword, the alligators he was soon going to be up to his ass in would take care of that.

"There's no need to call them," he said. "Thirty seconds after I finish my on-air segment, the phones here are gonna light up like a 9-1-1 switchboard after a terrorist attack. The Hurricane Center, Georgia EM, the state police, Glynn County EM, FEMA—"

"And Robbie. Don't forget Robbie."

"He's probably the least of my worries. This is going to be a pissing contest between me and the rest of the world until the Hurricane Hunters get into that storm. And even then, things might not get resolved."

"Wait a minute," she said. "Before you stumble off down Harakiri Lane, let me try to disarm you."

He checked the time again. "Okay, you've got seven minutes to save me from myself."

"When was the last time the Georgia coast took a direct hit from a hurricane?"

"I know where you're going with this," he responded. "You're right. The Georgia coast is not a good target for hurricanes, it's concave." He cupped his left hand and held it sideways in front of him. "Down here," he said, tracing with his right index finger from the base of his cupped hand to his wrist, "is Florida, a hurricane favorite. An elongated target." He wiggled the fingers of his left hand. "Up here. North Carolina. Sticks out into the Atlantic Ocean with a 'kick me' sign on it." He tapped the center of his palm. "In here, Georgia. Nestled safely away from the line of fire." He paused. "Unless, of course, a storm barrels in directly from the east or southeast. Like Hugo did in South Carolina."

Sherrie laughed softly. "Way to dodge the question. You should've been a politician."

"Okay," he said, "1979. David, a cat one made landfall near Savannah."

"And the last major?"

"Whose side are you on, anyway?"

"Yours. I'm just trying to make sure your bullshit meter doesn't peg."

He shook his head. "Thanks, but it's still in the green zone. And to answer your question, in the 1890s, two major hurricanes, believe it or not, whacked Georgia. So it's not immune."

"Two?" Sherrie said.

"In 1893, a storm with 120-mph winds and a surge of just under twenty feet made landfall near Savannah. Nobody knows how many people in the Low Country near Savannah and in South Carolina died, but it was several thousand. An even stronger hurricane hit farther south in 1898, on Cumberland Island. The surge and waves pushed twenty feet of water over the island."

"But a cat five?"

"A five is a rare animal anywhere. But just because something hasn't happened, no matter how improbable, doesn't mean it can't. God knows, we've learned that lesson in spades recently. Terrorists flying airliners into the Twin Towers. Katrina flooding New Orleans. The Boston Red Sox winning the World Series."

"That's disgusting," she said.

"What?"

"I'm a Yankees fan." She pointed at the set. "Better get up there, Cassandra. Three minutes. Check your mike and your ear fob." She patted her ear. "And try to keep your jacket buttoned. Covers up the Dr Pepper disaster."

"Cassandra?"

"Greek mythology. Her prophecies, like warning of the fall of Troy, were never believed. She ended up murdered."

"Because of her prophecies?"

"Because she was fooling around, I think."

"And the lesson for me is . . .?"

"I don't think the fooling around part applies, so it must be that even being right doesn't necessarily assure your survival."

"Thanks for the morale boost."

"Neither does poking your finger in the bloodshot eye of a foul-tempered Scotsman."

Obermeyer drew a deep breath and listened in his ear fob to a booth announcer who said: "And now, from Storm View, The Natural Environment Network brings you a special report on Hurricane Janet. Here's our hurricane expert, Dr. Nicholas Obermeyer."

As he began speaking, he heard a phone ring somewhere in the operations area. He knew without seeing a caller ID it was Robbie.

# Chapter Ten

## ST. SIMONS ISLAND, GEORGIA
## LABOR DAY SUNDAY, 0715 HOURS

"I'm going to look for Sandy again," Alan said, "I can't sit here and do nothing."

Trish stood, brushing the tears from her eyes. "I'm coming, too."

Alan stepped toward her and wrapped his arms around her shoulders. "No," he said softly. "You and Lee stay here, in case she calls or comes back. I'll stay in touch with you on my cell."

"Okay, okay. Please find her, Alan. Please." The word came out in a sob.

He kissed her cheek. "I'll—" An image on the TV screen caught his eye. "Where's the remote?" he asked. Trish pointed to it. Alan grabbed it and turned up the sound.

A voice was saying: "Although no official evacuation orders have been issued, given the proximity of the hurricane to land along with its expected rapid intensification and change of course, I urge people on Georgia coastal islands and in low-lying areas to leave now."

A banner at the bottom of the screen identified the speaker as Dr. Nicholas Obermeyer, Hurricane Expert. On-screen, a satellite image of Janet was being displayed. The hurricane's eye was tiny, smooth and perfectly circular—much different from the image Alan had seen the previous evening. Then there had been no eye. Janet had been nothing more than a benign blob of clouds.

Obermeyer continued talking. "The water-rise with Janet could be phenomenal. I hope to have more details on just how much very soon. But I can tell you this, many low-level escape routes will be flooded well before the eye of the hurricane nears the coast. That means by early afternoon."

The image of Janet was replaced by that of Obermeyer. He stepped close to the camera. Although he appeared harried and a bit tired, his liquescent eyes projected both authority and concern. "An Air Force Hurricane Hunter," he said, "will be in the storm shortly and will be able to give us more details. But given the potential urgency of the situation, I can't emphasize enough how quickly things could turn deadly. I'll be back with an update in thirty minutes."

Trish gripped Alan's arm. He turned to look at her. For the first time he read more than concern in her eyes; he saw genuine fear. "Don't worry about it, hon'," he said. "Remember what the guy said, 'no *official* evacuation orders have been issued.' And even if they are, it'll just be the county covering its ass. The EM guys are terrified of getting their tit caught in the ringer. Remember Hurricane Floyd? What was that, eight, ten years ago? Two million people in the southeastern U.S. trying to escape the boogeyman. What happened? World's largest traffic jam. Floyd fizzled and flooded someplace in the Carolinas."

"I don't like the sound of this," Trish said.

"Look, we're on the safest coast in the Southeast. I'll bet there hasn't been a hurricane here in a hundred years. And what did I tell you about watching television? It's all about ratings, all about the bottom line. Hype and fear-mongering work every time. Viewers flock to their sets." What he refused to voice, refused to admit, was that he, too, had been shaken by what he'd heard and seen—a warning of flooded escape routes and an image of an angry, one-eyed leviathan prowling toward the coast. *That's okay. A little fear gets the adrenalin pulsing. It's not like we're about to be blasted by a cat five.* He jingled the Range Rover's keys in front of Trish. "I'm off," he said. "I'll find our daughter."

"No, wait. I don't think we should separate. Not with that hurricane coming. If you find Sandy, then you'd have to come back here to pick up Lee and me before we could get off the island. That would waste time. Let's stay together."

"What if Sandy comes back here and finds the place empty?"

"She has a phone. She'd call us. Besides, where are you going to search that we haven't looked already?"

"I was thinking of Epworth."

"Epworth? What's—"

"Epworth By the Sea. It's that Methodist retreat and conference center on the west side of the island near the causeway. Remember? We drove through it last time we were here. Acres and acres of land along the Frederica River. Lots of palm trees and live oaks. Youth groups from all over the Southeast come there in the summer. I was thinking . . ." He stopped, not sure he wanted to articulate his thoughts.

Trish steepled her forefingers in front of her lips. Wrinkles creased her forehead. "Go ahead," she said.

He hesitated, then said, "If a kid had something, well, unpleasant in mind, what better place to sneak off to with all its dorms, motels and cabins?"

"Alan!"

"Time to stop thinking nice," he countered.

"Then let's look together. Let's not get the family spread out all over the island."

"No," he said firmly, "you and Lee remain here. This won't take long. It's not that far away."

Trish sat on the couch, arms folded across her chest and looked out the slider at the slanting rain. "As always," she said, "you're in charge. Go on."

"I'll be right back."

But as soon as he was on his way, he realized he wouldn't be right back. The number of vehicles on the road had increased substantially. The evacuation advice from Dr. Ober-whatever had obviously been taken to heart. Now Alan was caught in a traffic jam that rivaled Atlanta's worst on any given Friday afternoon. Muttering profanities, he crept forward a few feet per minute, through barrages of rain sheeting through the grayness and armies of palm fronds skittering along the pavement.

His cell phone rang. He yanked it from the cup holder and answered it.

"Daddy?" The voice on the line was shaky and weak.

"Sandy, honey. Oh, God, where are you? What happened? Are you all right?"

"Daddy?"

"Yes, honey. Where are you? We'll come get you."

"I don't know," Sandy said. She was crying.

"Inside? Outside? At a restaurant? In a house? Where?"

"In a house," she said between sobs.

"A house where?"

"I don't know."

"On St. Simons?" Impatience crept into Alan's voice.

"Yes, I think so."

"Do you have an address?"

"No. It's . . . it's . . . like to get here we had to cross like this little bridge with a gate and guardhouse and everything. Then we drove past like this golf course resort and down a street with lots of big trees and droopy moss and stuff."

"Did you turn off the main road anyplace?"

"No. At least I don't think so."

"Okay, calm down. I know where you are." The description Sandy had given him fit Sea Island, an adjacent, smaller island to St. Simons, populated with large, exclusive homes. It was five or six miles from where he was now, on the opposite side of St. Simons. "I'll be there as soon as I pick up your mom and Lee."

"Why? Where are they?"

"At the condo."

"Where are you?"

"Out looking for my daughter."

"Oh." A pause. "I'm sorry, Daddy."

"Don't worry about it. Where's the kid who brought you?"

"Alex?"

"Whoever. Where is he?"

"He left."

"Left?"

"With his parents."

"And they didn't take you?" He slammed his fist against the steering wheel.

"They didn't know I was here."

"How could that be?"

"We were in like this little house in back of the big house. And his parents came calling for him and he like told me to be quiet, that he'd be right back, and I waited and waited but he didn't come back so I went to the big house to look for him and there was like nobody there and the house was locked so I came back to this little house and waited some more and was afraid to call you cuz I like knew I'd be in trouble." The words rushed from Sandy like water careening down a spillway.

"But you're okay, honey, aren't you?"

"We didn't do anything, Daddy."

*Yeah, probably like I never did anything when I was a teenager.* "I'm coming, honey. As soon as I get Mom and Lee." He'd waste time going back to the condo, but at least he'd be going in the opposite direction of the molasses-like exodus. He checked his watch, ran a quick calculation in his head. "We'll be there in about twenty minutes. I want you to go out to the main street and wait for us. Okay?"

"I can't."

"Can't what?"

"Go out to the main street."

"Why?"

"Cuz there's like a gate across the driveway. It's locked. I can't get out. I tried."

"Jesus. Well, stand next to it; then jump up and down and wave when you see us. And keep your cell phone on."

"Daddy?"

"Yes."

"I'm scared."

"Don't be, Pumpkin. I'll give you a pass on this one."

"No, it's not that."

"What then?"

"The ocean's in the yard and it's like washing over the street."

# Chapter Eleven

## AIRBORNE, APPROACHING HURRICANE JANET
## LABOR DAY SUNDAY, 0730 HOURS

The Hurricane Hunter hit another patch of heavy turbulence two
hours out of Keesler. The WC-130 shook and rattled. A clipboard
slithered off the top of Karlyn's console and plopped onto a computer
keyboard in front of her. Startled, her hands fell instinctively—
protectively—to her abdomen. She glanced to her left to see if
Sergeant McKenzie had noticed. He hadn't.

She leaned her head against the back of her seat. *What a fucking
mess. Two months pregnant. The father with a previous commitment: a wife and
two kids. And me with a couple of jobs where being an unwed mom is like wearing
a sign on my back that says PASTE PINK SLIP HERE.*

The consequences were easy to picture:

Look, it's Kareless Karlyn the TV weather gal. Toting around her
own little high pressure mound. Bye, Karlyn. Come back when you're
slim and married. Just don't come back here.

Captain Hill, forget your pill? Not quite up to Air Force moral
standards, young lady. Besides, not a good idea to be bouncing junior
around in eyewalls. I think we can arrange for a quiet discharge.

*A couple of nights of passion and I get the shaft. Twice. First in bed, then
because I'm a woman. It's always the woman. Never the guy. But mea culpa.*

She'd been overeager that boozy Fourth of July weekend at the
beach to flaunt her sexuality, to make a run at a hunky thirty-
something who'd claimed interests in concert with hers. He said he
liked to race motorcycles and climb mountains, but his real talent
turned out to be that he was a blue-ribbon bull-shitter. After she'd
missed her period, a panicky phone call to his home revealed the truth.
A Mrs. Hunk answered. There probably was no Harley in the garage,
either, and the only peaks he'd ever scaled likely belonged in 36
Double Ds.

As the Hurricane Hunter had skirted the Gulf Coast, Karlyn had
glanced out the scanner window on her right. It was still dark, but

she'd been able to make out the lights of Panama City Beach below. The Miracle Mile of the Florida Panhandle. Where the indiscretion had taken place. And she had her own little miracle, her own little souvenir, to remind her.

"Hey, Karlyn?" The voice came through her headset.

"Sir?"

"Just wanted to confirm Janet's coordinates." It was the navigator, Major Best.

She had the numbers in her head but wanted to make certain. She pulled a notebook from one of the multitude of pockets in her flight suit and flipped through several pages until she found the tasking order from the Hurricane Center. "30.0 north, 78.7 west at eleven-z," she answered.

"Yeah. That's what I'd programmed in. We'll start our descent in about fifteen minutes."

"Roger that," she said. She closed her eyes. *I think I've started mine already.*

Abortion. The word seemed smeared in ugliness, as though a woman making such a choice was the moral equivalent of Adolf Hitler or Idi Amin or Pol Pot. *But it was still a choice wasn't it? A choice between life in-fact and life-presumed.*

*Why should I suffer the end of my career—careers, actually—because I made a shitty decision based on the lies some guy told me? How many other women have made the same dumb mistake but didn't end up pregnant? And how come the guy always skates? Even if he ponies up for an abortion, there's no stones cast at him. Damn the Right to Lifers. Let them walk a mile in my shoes before—.*

A tap on her shoulder. She looked up. Lieutenant Smithers and Hemphill stood next to her. She removed her headset and dismissed her angry musings.

"Mr. Hemphill is interested in getting the details on our flight pattern into the eye," Smithers said. "After that, maybe you could take him up to the flight deck." He paused, then added, "If we can manage to stay in smooth air for a few more minutes."

"Can do," she answered.

"I'll let Major Walker know you're coming up," Smithers said.

Karlyn nodded.

She took a pad of paper and set it on her drop-down desk where Hemphill could see it. With a pencil she sketched the Hurricane Hunter's flight plan for reconning Janet. "We basically fly an X-pattern through a hurricane," she said.

Hemphill knelt beside her as she drew.

"We'll drop down to 5000 feet and approach Janet from the southwest. We'll try to time our first penetration for twelve hundred-z, that's Greenwich Mean Time, or what's called Coordinated Universal Time now. Eight o'clock in the morning to you civilians."

Hemphill looked at his watch. "So, about half an hour from now?"

"Yes. We'll fly straight through the eye, Sergeant McKenzie will chuck a dropsonde into it, and we'll keep on going, out to the northeast side of the storm." She moved the pencil along her pad. "About 100 miles out we'll make a sharp left-hand turn and fly west along the northern edge of the hurricane."

Hemphill grunted his acknowledgment. He grasped the desk as the airplane shook again.

"When we get to the northwest side," Karlyn continued, still tracing the Hurricane Hunter's track on the pad, "we'll make another sharp left turn and fly southeast through the eye. This time we'll pop out on the southeast side of Janet. Then we'll turn left again and head north along the eastern periphery of her to the northeast quadrant where we'll turn—"

"Left," interrupted Hemphill, "and fly southwest through the eye. I got it." He seemed pleased with himself. "But why always left?"

"Winds blow counterclockwise around a hurricane—any storm, in fact—in the northern hemisphere. So, if we make all left-hand turns, we're always flying with the winds instead of fighting them."

"Makes sense," he said. "How many times will we actually fly through the eye?"

"Four times. We'll end up in the northwest quadrant. From there, it'll be a straight shot home, back to Keesler."

"A long day," he said.

"Most missions last ten or twelve hours. Sometimes as long as fourteen."

"What about food?"

"Box lunches." She wrinkled her nose. "I believe we ordered one for you."

"I don't know," he said. "My stomach has been doing an Irish jig."

"Sorry. Usually it isn't this bouncy on the trip out."

"Maybe I should stick with AirTran."

She smiled, her television best. "I'll convey your complaints to the management, if you'd like."

"Let's see how the rest of the trip goes."

Lieutenant Smithers returned from the flight deck. "They're ready for you up there," he said, inclining his head toward the front of the aircraft.

Karlyn stood. "You first," she said to Hemphill and motioned for him to walk in front of her. They entered a short, narrow passageway. Immediately to their left was the crew door. To their right, directly opposite the door, was a short ladder leading to the flight deck. "Be careful going up," she said.

Hemphill nodded and mounted the ladder.

Karlyn followed him.

**Through the panoramic,** multi-paned windshield of the Hurricane Hunter, Major Walker watched the first light of the dawning day spill over the eastern horizon. A thin line of steely brightness appeared, seeming to suck the blackness from the sky and replace it with a soft violet. He lifted his headset off one ear and listened to the growl of the turboprops. One, two, three and four. All solid. He scanned the myriad of digital avionic readouts in front of him and overhead, above the windshield. All normal.

"Everything looks good, Colonel," he said into his headset mike.

Harlow turned to look at him. "You were concerned?"

"Not really."

"Not really?"

*Let it go, Colonel.* "Everything's fine, sir." He felt a bit of the tension leak from his body, draining away like water guttering from a gentle rain. He settled back in his seat. Below him, the Gulf of Mexico was still locked in predawn darkness. Ahead, in the hazy distance, he could see the shimmer of scattered lights on the Florida Peninsula. Their flight path would carry them over Cedar Key, then, descending, across the peninsula near Ocala and Daytona Beach. From there they would turn northeast and make their first run into Janet.

"Guests," Harlow announced.

Walker turned as Hemphill and Karlyn clambered onto the flight deck. Karlyn flashed a grin at him, the same sort of easy, come-hither smile that had cast a spell over him during a layover in St. Croix earlier in the year. Their gazes locked, then lingered, as though the island magic were still with them.

**St. Croix. The Buccaneer Hotel.** The Terrace Bar. Palm trees. A soft, humid Caribbean breeze. And too many mai tais. The evening was indelible in his memory.

The rest of the crew had departed, but he and Karlyn had remained on the terrace. Whatever cologne she had dabbed on mingled in an odd nectarous manner with the sweatiness from a long day in the aircraft. The redolence was overpowering. It was as though they had already been intimate.

"Your wife's a bitch," she said. She took a little paper umbrella from her drink, placed it on the table and flicked it at him with her forefinger.

His head snapped up. It's not where their conversation had been going. They'd been talking about George Clooney movies and Nelson DeMille novels. "Karlyn, that's not—"

"Appropriate?"

"Yes."

"But it's not exactly a private matter is it? I mean not after the squadron party last week."

He stared into the depths of his almost-empty glass and didn't answer.

"The talk's been all over the base."

"Still . . . " He didn't know how to respond to her. Donna's behavior had indeed been mortifying, so why try to defend her?

"Come on, Arly, she was three sheets to the wind, minus her bikini top, floating tits-up in the pool and letting the world know her husband was a loser with two dead-end jobs, military and civilian." She paused, then added, "And that he had all the sexual prowess of an octogenarian in assisted living."

"She didn't say that."

"Oh, maybe I misinterpreted it when she said you were the poster boy for the old fighter pilot joke about firing a short round, an air burst, and a dud. That wasn't sexual?"

"It—"

"Or that if physicians were wondering what to do when someone taking an ED drug had an erection that lasted more than four hours all they had to do was grab a sample of your DNA to find a cure?"

"She's my wife." He couldn't think of another defense. He looked around the patio to make sure no one was sitting close to them, close enough to hear. Several couples sat at the far end of the terrace. He could hear their laughter, but not their conversations. The rustle of the palm fronds in the busy night-wind masked their words.

"I don't think your marriage values are being reciprocated," Karlyn responded. "Everyone in the squadron respects you, as an officer and a man. You don't deserve a dragon lady for a wife. She sure as hell doesn't deserve you."

"It doesn't make any difference whether the values are or aren't being reciprocated. They're not relative. They're absolute. At least for me."

"Well, maybe you should lay them to rest for a night. For God's sake, quit acting like you've got a dropsonde up your ass."

"Lay them to rest?"

She leaned closer to him and lowered her voice. "I'm offering you what your wife can't. Or won't. What you deserve." Under the table, she touched his knee with hers.

The night air began to hum; his heart ticked a little more rapidly. *What do I deserve?*

She reached across the table and took his hand. A puff of wind ruffled her short brown hair. Tiny flashes of colored light from bulbs strung around the eaves of the terrace reflected in her eyes. In another time or place, she could have been a fairy tale princess.

"It can be for one night. Or more," she whispered.

Do all fairy tales end happily? He tried to remember one that didn't, but couldn't. At least for the good people. Was he? Was she? Good?

She stood, teetered briefly, but regained her balance. She remained by the table, waiting, without speaking.

He didn't move.

"Don't make me look bad," she said, her voice not much louder than the rustling of the palms.

He nodded and rose.

In his room, the sound of the easy wash of breakers on the beach below filtered through an open window. Music from a steel band, distant and distorted, faded in and out on a fitful breeze. The faint odor of sea salt and Cuban rum drifted through the night, or maybe it was just the essence of desire.

Karlyn unzipped the top of her flight suit and undid her bra. She flipped it onto the bed. Walker stared at her, his heart rate accelerating. Raw animal response. He grasped at the last dram of self-control he could find. "This is a career-ender for both of us," he said, barely able to get the words out.

Karlyn stood with her hand poised on her zipper. She smiled, wistfully it seemed.

The spell had been broken and Walker damned himself for doing it.

"Up or down?" Karlyn asked quietly, evenly. Not challenging him, not calling his bluff. It were as though she sensed the battle raging within him.

The music ceased, the breeze faltered, and now only the soft lap of the sea riffled the silence that hung between them. Walker closed his eyes. If only he could decipher women. Was Karlyn's overture driven by the female imperative to comfort, or by unrefined sexual desire? Not that it made any difference. The passion, the lust, would be same. As would the consequences.

"Up," he said. He kept his eyes closed.

"Are you sure?"

He opened his eyes. "Yes, damn it," he answered in a scratchy whisper. He retrieved her bra from the bed and brought it to her.

She reached for it, but took his hand instead and guided it to her naked breast. He felt the firmness of her nipple rising from the softness of her bosom. His fingers explored it slowly and deliberately. He grew hard. They kissed. Prolonged. Tongues together. Bodies locked.

Karlyn broke the embrace and stepped back. "Still up?" Her fingers were on her zipper again.

Unable to speak, he nodded.

"Your wife's not only a bitch, she's a liar," Karlyn said. Her emotion was fierce. Her words, measured, controlled.

He opened his mouth to protest. But there was nothing to protest, and all he said was, "Liar?"

Karlyn's eyes flared. "She belittled your manhood." Her cheeks had turned an incarnadine shade of pink and her breath came in soft, choppy pants. She reached down and patted him where only his wife had, once upon a time. "ED? I don't think so. Not with that pocket rocket on its launch pad." She withdrew her hand and zipped up her flight suit.

Walker managed a weak smile.

She pointed at her bra, still clutched in his fist. "You want to keep that as a souvenir? Like 'I almost got lucky'?"

He tossed it to her.

"I promise, Arly, I won't try this again. Cuz I think you're the kind of guy I want to keep as a friend. Sometimes that's a hell of a lot more important than having a lover."

She stuffed the bra into a pocket on the leg of her flight suit, walked to the door, opened it and stepped into the hallway.

"She doesn't deserve you, Arly," she said, and shut the door.

**Karlyn made the introductions** on the dimly-lit flight deck. She placed her mouth next to Hemphill's ear so she could compete with the growl of the engines.

"Up front, on the left there is Major Walker, the pilot. You met him earlier. To his right, Lieutenant Colonel Bernie Harlow, the squadron commander, and today, the co-pilot."

Harlow gave Hemphill a thumbs-up.

The newspaperman nodded his acknowledgment.

Karlyn pointed to Hemphill's right. "And this is Major John Best. He's our navigator."

Major Best twisted around from his console, which faced the right side of the aircraft, to shake hands with Hemphill.

"So you guide us into the storm?" Hemphill said.

Best removed his headset. "What?"

"I said, so you guide us into the storm?"

"It's a cooperative effort. I set up the initial track to get us into Indian Country. Oops. Sorry. Not P.C. Don't write that. What you want to say is that I set up the course to get us to the periphery of the storm. When we get close enough to see the eye on radar, Karlyn and I will work together to give Major Walker the final vector through the eyewall into the eye."

"At that point," Karlyn said, "Major Walker takes the plane off autopilot and in we go."

"Major Walker steers and tweaks the throttles," Best clarified, "but he does keep the autopilot on altitude-hold."

Karlyn looked out the WC-130's windshield at the dawning day. Beneath the aircraft now was the Florida Peninsula. Ahead, on the east side of the peninsula, lay the Gulf Stream. The rising sun lit a line of towering thunderheads over the warm-water current. Their anvils, glowing pink and gold in the sun's slanting rays, flattened out as they bumped against the invisible upper limits of their growth—the stratosphere.

With a meteorologist's practiced eye, Karlyn noted the burgeoning thunderstorms. They reflected, she knew, the extreme instability of the atmosphere just offshore. Again, a transitory wave of unease swept over her. Hurricanes thrived on unstable air.

Janet was swirling toward a field of dreams.

# Chapter Twelve

## ATLANTA, GEORGIA—THE NATURAL ENVIRONMENT TELEVISION NETWORK LABOR DAY SUNDAY, 0730 HOURS

Obermeyer finished his broadcast segment and stepped away from the green key wall, the blank wall against which he gestured and pointed at images and graphics that weren't really there. To TV viewers, it looked as if they were, but it was only an electronically-produced illusion.

"Nice job," Sherrie said to Obermeyer. "Your fans are already calling in droves." She flicked her head toward a phone set on a nearby desk and pointed at the call buttons. All of them were lit. "The one that's the color of a nuclear explosion is Robbie," she said. "Second one from the right."

Knowing he had to address the executive VP's wrath first, he punched the button, picked up the handset and held it away from his ear.

"Goddamn ya, Obie," McSwanson roared, "I told ya to wait. Now you're about to make this network the laughin'stock of the cable world. Ya like stickin' your dick in electrical sockets? Mine, too?"

*Only yours, Robbie.* Obermeyer moved the handset closer to his mouth. "And if I'm right, Robbie, where's the network then? Where's Robbie McSwanson, in fact? On his way to corporate headquarters? On the cover of *Broadcasting & Cable?*"

"Don't condescend to me, ya son of a bitch. The issue isn't whether you're right or wrong or whether I'm a hero or not. The issue is whether ya can follow friggin' orders."

Obermeyer gritted his teeth and gripped the handset so fiercely his fingers ached—an involuntary response he thought he had put to rest when he'd stopped drinking, too late to save his marriage, and almost too late to save his career. But he had stopped, and at least salvaged his dignity. So where had this long-dormant emotion, this anger, come from? Could it be his outbursts of a decade ago hadn't been all

Tennessee sour mash-induced? Perhaps rage was something that always lived within him, held at bay and suppressed most of the time, but constantly wriggling around in his psyche, nibbling at his soul, looking for a weakness, waiting to be triggered. Booze was one of the triggers. But there were others, obviously. Incompetence, ignorance, insensitivity. All of which he saw in Robbie. *Or was it a looking-glass image?*

It didn't matter. His ire found a chink in his restraint and erupted. "The issue, you shit-for-brains, ignorant Scot," Obermeyer barked, "is whether people live or die. And yes, you're right, I was being condescending. But only because I thought it might appeal to your cretinous ego. A goddamn waste. Trying to reach you with either logic or flattery is like trying to teach Elmer fucking Fudd to slam-dunk a basketball. So you go your way and I'll go mine—"

"If ya go your way, ya self-righteous prick, ya goddamn well better leave a trail of bread crumbs, cuz ya ain't never gonna find your way back. Ya can crawl back inside your whiskey bottle and drown for all I care. Ya'd be doin' the world a favor. For now, you're off the air. That's an order, and I'll make sure the producer on duty understands it. I assume there's an OCM there."

"Yeah, Sherrie Willis."

"Let me talk to her."

*"Jawohl, mein führer."* He clicked his heels and handed the phone to Sherrie, but not before saying loud enough for McSwanson to hear: "Careful. It's hot. Guy's a flaming asshole."

She frowned in disapproval at Obermeyer's remark, then brought the phone to her ear. Cautiously.

Obermeyer moved to an adjacent desk and picked up another line. It was his friend Rick Keys at the Hurricane Center.

"What the hell are you doing, Obie? The director's screwing himself into the ceiling here. He's got calls from every emergency manager from Savannah to Jacksonville, not to mention the state EM in Georgia. You just stepped in a combination of dog shit and bubble gum, buddy. You're not gonna get your shoes clean after this one."

"Unless I'm right."

"You're an arrogant son of a bitch, you know that?"

"That's what my boss just said."

"Look, I agree Janet is strengthening, but to suggest it's going to intensify rapidly and change course, that's irresponsible. You've no basis for that."

"I do, and you know it. Thirty years of basis." Obermeyer's fingers, wrapped around the receiver, began aching again

"You could've waited. You should've waited. Until the recon bird reported. At least you would've had real-time data to defend your forecast. Why the hell didn't you wait?"

"Because under the best of circumstances it takes at least twelve hours to evacuate St. Simons and Glynn County. And this is the worst of circumstances. No warning, no preparation, and a holiday weekend with the coast full of tourists. Worst of all, the clock's started. They don't have twelve hours. So I figure every extra hour of warning I give is worth a thousand lives, maybe more. You want to buck me on that?"

Rick expelled a long, slow breath. On the other phone, Sherrie was yes-sirring and no-sirring Robbie.

Obermeyer didn't want to admit it, but for the first time in years he heard something deep within him calling for a rendezvous with old friends, acquaintances he had once counted on, not those who now berated and challenged him.

Old friends. From a distance, it was easy to overlook the fact they'd cost him his marriage and almost his livelihood. Easier still to recall the burn of a jigger of Jack or Jim as it slid down his throat, fuzzing the world, releasing his tensions, his anger. "For entertainment purposes only," he used to tell those around him as he tipped his head back and drained shot glass after shot glass.

He'd never considered himself as an alcoholic, only a boozer. He'd never gone through a twelve-step program or received counseling. He had just quit drinking. But now, it was as if his angry outburst had resurrected a nostalgic longing, as negative and pernicious as it might be: a desire—or was it a need?—for a drink. *You can't kill the boogeyman.*

**Keys' voice burrowed into** his introspection. "What do I tell the director? What do we tell the EMs?"

"Not my call."

"Yeah, in a way it is. You just woke up a sleeping giant. It's a little late to tuck him back under the covers."

"Maybe we can. I've been banned from going on the air again here. And my boss is on the phone as we speak intimidating a cute young lady who will appear on the network shortly to make things right. You know: 'We interpreted the data wrong, got carried away, blew things out of proportion. Sorry.'"

Keys didn't respond.

"What?" Obermeyer said. He sank into a chair and searched the cluttered terrain of his desk for another can of Dr Pepper.

"Dammit, Obie, it pains me to admit it, but there's a tiny part of me that thinks you might be right. If only we had the aircraft in there."

"But we don't. So what I think I might do, were I running the Hurricane Center—"

"God save us all," Keys blurted.

"What I think I might do," Obermeyer continued, ignoring the jibe, "is tell the EMs you got an eager beaver in Atlanta who might or might not be onto something. That the Hurricane Center, pending recon reports, is considering extending the hurricane warning south along the Georgia coast. That if the EMs want, they can order voluntary evacuations now, then go to mandatory if the warning is extended. At least you'll have your ass covered and will have heightened people's awareness—"

"I think somebody else already did that, buddy."

"Yeah, but the network's probably about to negate it."

"Maybe this isn't the time to start flip-flopping on your story. Can you stall the retraction?"

"Guerilla warfare?"

"Whatever. Just remember who started this. By the way, I'll deny it if I'm ever asked, but I like your idea of how to approach the EMs. Good luck."

"You, too."

Obermeyer hung up and saw Sherrie, her face the color of a stoplight, walking toward him. If she'd been a cartoon character, he guessed he would have seen steam jetting from her ears.

"Let me take a shot at this," he said, "Robbie the Wonderful said if you didn't go on the air and make nice for the network, you'd be on the street selling pencils for a living tomorrow."

"His exact words were 'peddling your sorry ass to buy soup for supper.'"

Obermeyer's jaw tightened. His hands balled into fists.

Sherrie saw it. "Let it go," she said. "I've got it under control."

He glimpsed a gunslinger steeliness in her eyes and knew what she was going to do. "I didn't ask you to be my spear carrier," he said. "Call Robbie back, tell him you're sick and need to go home. By the time he can get another OCM in here, we'll have the recon reports. We'll sink or swim then."

"No," she said. "The son of a bitch insulted and belittled me. And he was a whole lot less subtle about it than you were. At least you were kind of funny. I'm on your side now."

"That may not be where you want to be."

"The enemy of my enemy . . . I know where I want to be."

"Go home."

"I couldn't spit in the bastard's eye then."

Obermeyer inclined his head toward the main entrance to the studio area. "You know he'll come through that door like William Wallace charging the English."

"Braveheart? The guy wore a skirt. How much fear does that strike in you?"

"Did you play rugby or something in college?"

"I just don't like taking shit from people. Let's drop it." She pointed at a telephone that still had call lights lit. "EMs," she said. "You got some 'splainin' to do, Lucy."

# Chapter Thirteen

## AIRBORNE, PENETRATING THE EYE OF
## HURRICANE JANET
## LABOR DAY SUNDAY, 0755 HOURS

Karlyn, from her console aboard the Hurricane Hunter, sent a message, essentially an e-mail, that would be flashed to the National Hurricane Center via satellite. She wanted to find out if the Center had any new information on Janet.

The response came quickly. Forecasters thought Janet might be growing stronger, but that she was still just a cat one with max winds of about 80 mph.

"Looks like we're good to go at 5000 feet," Karlyn said over the intercom.

"Roger that." Walker's voice. "Cinch 'em tight, everyone."

The plane banked and gradually dropped, preparing for its first dash into the eye. On her radar monitor, Karlyn could see one of Janet's outer rainbands coming up fast. "Mr. Hemphill," she said over her headset, "we're going to hit some turbulence in a couple of minutes. It's just a rainband, not the eyewall, but it's going to get rough. You all set?" She stood up and peeked around her console, back to where Hemphill sat in one of the red canvas seats that ran along both sides of the aircraft.

Hemphill saw her and waved. "Yes," he said into his mike. He held up a small container of some sort for her to see.

His Dramamine, she assumed. She acknowledged his wave, sat down and pulled her safety harness tight. On her radar screen she could see several small red areas, color-coded to warn of heavy precipitation, in their flight path. "Got some nasty cells coming up, guys," she said into her mike, "hang on."

She glanced out the scanner window as a dark, rain-sheeted curtain enveloped the Hurricane Hunter. The plane rocked from side to side; big oscillations, not gentle little wobbles. She gripped the console with both hands, and watched the plot of wind speed soar on the screen adjacent to the radar depiction. Fifty, 60, 70 mph. More than she expected this far from the vortex of the storm. A healthy rainband. *Too healthy? What the hell is Janet up to?*

The engine note of the turboprops changed as the aircraft jumped upward, as if boosted by rockets. Then, as abruptly as it had lifted, it fell. Karlyn's stomach seemed to lodge in her chest as the WC-130 dropped. Over her headset, she heard someone say, "Uff," as if he'd been punched in the gut.

Then it was over. The plane steadied, the wind abated, and sunlight glinted through the window.

"Everyone back there okay?" Walker on the intercom.

Karlyn looked across from her at Sergeant McKenzie. He nodded. She leaned around the console so she could see Lieutenant Smithers and Hemphill. Hemphill sat with his arms wrapped around him and his head down.

"Mr. Hemphill's a little woozy, but he's okay," Smithers said into the intercom.

"Okay here, too," Karlyn added, so the flight deck would know she and McKenzie were unscathed.

"Nasty rainband," Walker said.

"Looks like Janet's kicking up her heels a bit," Karlyn answered.

Major Best cut in. "Is that another rainband I see on the scope ahead of us? Or is that eyewall?"

Karlyn looked at the radar readout. "Too soon for the eyewall," she said. "It's another rainband." She leaned toward the window to get a good look at what was outside. Stacks of imposing cumulus clouds billowed skyward as far as she could see, towering over the Hurricane Hunter. To the aircraft's rear, through layers of gray cloud debris, she could make out the rainband through which they'd just flown. Lit by the morning sun, a line of cirrus-capped thunderstorms took on the appearance of brilliant white cauliflowers mushrooming toward the upper reaches of the atmosphere.

She scanned the sky ahead of the plane. Another phalanx of thunderstorms guarded the ramparts of Janet—the eyewall that lay beyond. Lightning zigzagged out of the base of the clouds as if taunting the approaching Hurricane Hunter.

Karlyn spoke into her mike again. "Looks like a rough day at the office, fellas."

**The clouds in the** thunderstorm-laced rainband grew blacker as the Hurricane Hunter neared. Walker adjusted his safety harness and eased back on the throttles, searching for a break, a light spot, in the boiling clouds.

"Got a way through the Khyber Pass for us, Karlyn?" he asked into his mike.

"For you, my dashing Major, always."

Colonel Harlow looked over at Walker, smiled, then turned back to look out the windshield.

*Yeah, let your imagination run wild, boss. It doesn't matter now.*

"Turn left about twenty," Karlyn said. "I think we can squeeze between cells there."

Monitoring the aircraft's performance on the heads-up display projected onto the windshield, Walker banked the plane to the left until he had it on a new track twenty degrees west of the previous one. Within seconds the plane was in the band, swallowed by a barrage of rain that cracked against the cockpit's glass like volleys of rocks. Walker could see nothing, save for the cascade of water assaulting the windshield. It was like going through a car wash. At 180 mph.

Then sunlight. They were out.

"What'd we get for winds, Karlyn?" Walker asked.

"Around 80 at flight level. And I got Smurf readings of about 65 on the surface."

Walker stared ahead. "Oh, Jesus," he said.

"What?" Karlyn asked.

"Up ahead. Looks like the Great Wall of China." Intense pressure wrapped around Walker's head, like a metal band being ratcheted tighter and tighter. He felt himself being dragged back into the dimly-lit carnival tent with the gnarled chiromancer, her malodorous breath, her crenulated skin. Her warning: *do not go.*

*Here? Did she mean here?*

Once more he played back her words, and suddenly he understood. *Coliseum. Stadium. Trapped.* Mentally, he kicked his way out of the tent, attempting to reject the cheap circus act, but knowing now why it kept coming back to haunt him. He swallowed, once, twice, forcing saliva into his throat. "Here we go, guys," he said into the intercom.

The hard shaking of the aircraft abruptly ceased and the flight became strangely smooth, as though the Hurricane Hunter were gliding toward Janet. Five thousand feet, Karlyn had said. Walker had his doubts about that altitude, but they were committed now, too late to alter course.

Silently, he counted down the seconds until they hit the eyewall. Tennyson's words—"half a league, half a league, half a league onward"—rattled around inside his head like ricocheting bullets.

The Hurricane Hunter plunged into the eyewall. Walker's world went black. Rain thundered against the plane's fuselage with enough ferocity to drown out the roar of the turboprops.

"Left twenty. No, thirty," Karlyn yelled into the intercom. "We're gonna miss the eye."

"What the hell?" Walker said.

"The winds are pushing us right."

Walker crabbed the WC-130 to the left until its nose pointed just west of north, a "drift-kill" heading compensating for the tremendous sideways push of the eyewall winds.

A vicious gust slammed into the plane, pitching it steeply to the right, driftwood in heavy surf. Simultaneously, an express elevator updraft caught it, pinning Walker into his seat as the craft rose. It lasted only seconds before a sharp downdraft speared the plane and hurled it in the opposite direction. The plane sank, but Walker's body didn't. He hung suspended off his seat, restrained only by his safety harness. The plane nosed over, trying to dive, its autopilot attempting to keep it at a constant altitude. Impossible. It was calibrated using normal atmospheric pressure. But the pressure was falling so rapidly, the autopilot calculated the craft was way too high.

"Altitude-hold off," Walker said. "Help me here, Colonel." He fought to get the words out. It was like trying to talk while riding a rodeo bull.

Both he and Harlow tugged on the controls. But it was too late. Something snapped at the Hurricane Hunter. A dragon's mouth. The plane rolled left. Violently. Extremely. Walker found himself looking up at Harlow, still in his seat but now hovering above him. Wide-eyed. Pencils, a clipboard, someone's ring, a plastic water bottle careened around the cockpit like pinballs.

Over his headset, someone screamed.

Walker had never heard of a C-130 doing a barrel roll, but they seemed on the verge of being the first. A barrel roll directly into the Atlantic Ocean.

"Oh, God," he said out loud, not knowing if it were a plea or an exclamation.

The roll ceased. Suddenly. But Walker was no longer sure which way the plane was pointed. Up? Down? East? West? He tried to focus on the heads-up display, but before he could, the dragon attacked again, bashing the plane to the right, a punishing blow. The craft was way above the G-limits of a C-130. Walker looked down, past Harlow, at the right wing. It was flapping like a bird's. A piece separated from the tip.

He closed his eyes. He and the rest of the crew were just along for the ride now. Rag dolls in a clothes dryer. Is this how the last moments were for the men lost in Typhoon Bess? Violent? Hopeless?

Walker tried to picture Donna, to reach out to her, but her image turned its back on him and faded. No matter. Eternity was coming up fast and he could make that journey alone. He bit through his lip as shudder after savage shudder rippled through plane. The old soothsayer had been wrong. There was no coliseum in his future. He wasn't going to make it that far.

Something bounced off his face and tumbled into his lap. He opened his eyes and looked down. Down? He wasn't certain anymore. He looked into his lap. Teeth. Dentures. He turned toward Harlow.

Harlow, lips pressed together, pointed at his mouth. It would've been funny if they weren't about to die.

Walker had no idea how close to the sea surface they were. Pretty damn near, he figured. Maybe it was just as well if you couldn't see it coming. He had no visual cues. Just darkness and rain. He searched for the radar altimeter, but was too disoriented to find it.

"Bless me, Lord, for I have sinned." *Is that how it goes?* He wasn't Catholic.

The Hurricane Hunter continued to pitch and roll, but gradually the oscillations dampened. Then abruptly, ceased. Walker, still feeling as if he were churning in a cement mixer, struggled again to concentrate on the heads-up display, this time successfully. The readouts indicated the plane slightly nose-down and banked to the right. He leveled the aircraft, then glanced at the radar. They were near the inner edge of the eyewall, almost out of the turbulence. The calm of the hurricane's eye lay dead ahead of them. How in the hell had they managed to stay on track? A hole-in-one on a long par three. But they were very low, only five hundred feet above the surface of the ocean.

Into his mike: "Everyone still with us?"

"Wish I hadn't been." It was Major Best, the navigator.

"Sorry, guys," Karlyn said, as though it were her fault.

"What the hell was that?" Harlow asked.

"I think it must have been some kind of . . . well, what meteorologists call a mesoscale vortex," Karlyn said. "Like you'd find in tornadic thunderstorms. Sometimes in strengthening hurricanes."

"So we just flew through a tornado in a hurricane?"

"More or less."

"Mostly more, I think. You get a wind reading?"

"I had my eyes closed. Give me a sec."

"Louie, Van, you guys okay back there? Our guest?" Walker asked.

"Okay here," Sergeant McKenzie answered. "Something whacked into my forehead and left a little cut, but nothing serious. Sorry I couldn't get a sonde off."

"Understandable," Walker said. "Van?"

"I'm fine. Don't know about Mr. Hemphill. He's the one who screamed . . . just before he barfed. I'll need to move us to new seats as soon as we're in the eye."

Walker, trying to get a look at the right wing, peered past Harlow.

"What?" Harlow said.

"You didn't see? I think we lost a wing tip."

"Jesus." Harlow turned to examine the wing. "Yeah. Looks like a couple of feet missing off the end."

"The way those things were flexing, it's a wonder we didn't lose a couple of wings, not just a couple of feet. We must have been pulling six G's. The design limit's three."

"We'll have to drop Lockheed-Martin a thank-you note." Harlow's words came out in hisses and slurs. "Need my teeth." He pointed at the floor of the cockpit near Walker's feet.

Walker retrieved the dentures, gingerly, and handed them to the colonel.

Outside, the sky brightened. On the radar monitor, Walker could see they were about to break into the eye.

"Guess what, guys?" It was Karlyn.

"I give. Over." Walker.

"We just flew through a cat four."

"I guess you'll be kicking some Hurricane Center ass when we get back."

"The thought occurred. The data record showed 160 mph at flight level. We took one gust pretty close to 200. On the surface, we got 140 sustained. Solid category four."

The airplane burst into bright sunlight. The eye of Janet. They were a little off center, a bit to the right, but in the clear. A golf metaphor again: akin to being on the green but near the edge.

Below, Walker could see a chaotic, frothing ocean. Huge waves roiled the surface, leaping futilely at the Hurricane Hunter, as though trying to snatch it from the air.

"Wow," Harlow said. But he was looking up, not at the sea.

Encircling the airplane, which now flew through virtually cloudless skies, was a fortification of massive, seething clouds, billowing ten or twelve miles into the atmosphere. In the morning sun they shimmered with blinding whiteness, offering no clue to the black fury that dwelled within them. Beauty harboring a beast.

Walker had remembered the term just before they plunged into the eyewall: the Stadium Effect. The term used to describe the breathtaking environment, the feeling of being in a vast stadium, encountered by those who flew into the eyes of the most violent hurricanes.

Walker banked the plane away from the edge of the wall, not wanting to challenge its savagery again until they could climb. At the moment, the aircraft was no more than a speck at the base of a sprawling coliseum. A Christian surrounded by lions.

# Chapter Fourteen

## ATLANTA, GEORGIA—THE NATURAL ENVIRONMENT TELEVISION NETWORK LABOR DAY SUNDAY, 0810 HOURS

Sherri checked her clip-on mike and started toward the key wall.

"Hold it," Obermeyer said.

Sherri stopped. "What?"

Obermeyer stared at a text message on his computer. "A preliminary report from the Hurricane Hunter. Janet's winds are up to 140 mph."

"One-forty?" Sherri's voice sounded an octave higher than it had a moment ago.

"Preliminary," Obermeyer cautioned. "But if it's confirmed, Janet's on her way to a cat five." He called up a series of satellite images of the hurricane and studied them closely. He sensed Sherri hovering behind him, looking over his shoulder.

"She's already deviating course, isn't she?" she said.

Tracing his finger along the computer monitor's screen, he projected Janet's path. "Not very scientific, I know, but it's looking more and more like the south Georgia coast has bulls-eye on it."

"I've got thirty seconds before I go on the air. What do I say?"

He looked up at her. *Not what I would say.* "The data aren't confirmed yet," he said, "so do what Robbie told you. If you don't, he'll fire you." He knew he was spitting into the wind; knew that she was more than willing to throw herself under the bus.

"It'll look great on my résumé´." She stepped up on a platform next to the wall.

"Don't defend my forecast," he said. "This is my battle, not yours." *Who is this girl?*

"You need an ally."

"Damn it, Sherrie—"

She held her forefinger to her lips, telling him to shush, and watched as the red lights on top of the studio camera blinked out one by one, second by second, counting her down to live air.

The last light dimmed and Sherrie stepped toward the camera, simultaneously gesturing at the key wall. "Hurricane Janet," she said, "continues to strengthen. Preliminary information just received from Air Force Reserve Hurricane Hunters indicate winds have reached 140 mph, making Janet a very dangerous category four storm. Not only that, but the hurricane is deviating from its currently projected track toward southern South Carolina. Its new target appears to be coastal Georgia, perhaps somewhere around Sapelo Island or St. Simons."

Obermeyer's attention was snatched from Sherrie as the door to the studio area banged opened, slamming against a wall. McSwanson strode toward the Storm View set, then stopped abruptly. His gaze darted from Sherri to Obermeyer and back again; his weather-beaten face exploded into a crimson color pallet as he listened to Sherrie. Without saying a word, he pivoted and dashed down a hallway toward the master control facility.

Sherrie, in voice-over mode while a full-screen image of the locations under official warnings was displayed, turned to look at Obermeyer. Her eyes seemed to ask, *What's going on?*

Obermeyer drew his index finger horizontally across his throat.

Sherrie nodded, understanding.

McSwanson's reaction came rapidly. Sherrie's on-air monitor went blank briefly, then switched to a public service announcement about children and swimming pool safety. The studio lights went out.

The white-noise hum of the HVAC system was the only sound in the room. Sherrie removed her mike and stepped next to Obermeyer. Without speaking, they waited, elbow to elbow, for the return of McSwanson and his wrath. He didn't appear. Finally Sherrie said, "Where is he?"

"Probably getting an M-16," Obermeyer said.

She looked at him, her eyes betraying a wisp of uncertainty.

"I'm joking," he said. "I guessing he's gone for reinforcements."

As if on cue, McSwanson reappeared with a corporate security guard in tow, an elderly white-haired black man everyone called Uncle Fuzz. Fuzz, a retired Army first sergeant, was usually stationed at the main entrance to the network, and Obermeyer always made it a point to stop and chat with him when he came to work. Mostly it was small talk about the Braves or Falcons, but sometimes it was about Iraq or Afghanistan. Fuzz had two grandsons in the military.

McSwanson turned to Fuzz and pointed at Obermeyer and

Sherrie. "Escort them out of the buildin'. Now."

Fuzz, whose round head reminded Obermeyer of the cartoon character, Charlie Brown, pinched his lips together and hitched up his pants. He didn't move, his eyes registering confusion. He tugged at his pants again, but they remained stubbornly below his thick midsection.

"Now," McSwanson repeated.

"What the hell do you think you're doing, Robbie?" Obermeyer said.

"Firin' your asses. What does it look like?" McSwanson's face continued to roil in shades of red, as if seeking to complement his thinning, rust-colored hair.

"There's a procedure for that. Run it through HR," Obermeyer responded.

"I don't have to, ya son of a bitch. Insubordination. Both of ya. I'll not stand for that. You're through here."

"I'm not leaving, Robbie. And don't put Uncle Fuzz in the middle of things. His job is to man the front desk and monitor security cameras, not be a sheriff."

Fuzz, still behind McSwanson, nodded slightly. He was clearly uncomfortable in his role as a corporate bouncer.

McSwanson turned to Fuzz. "Go back upstairs and call the Cobb County Police," he said.

Fuzz hesitated.

"Ya do it, or I will," McSwanson snapped.

"It's okay, Fuzz," Obermeyer said, "go ahead." He didn't want to be responsible for a third person losing his job.

Fuzz shook his head, then walked slowly out the door.

"You can ease off on Sherrie, too," Obermeyer said. "I countermanded your order and told her not to back off of what I'd said earlier, about evacuating the Georgia coast."

Sherrie kicked his ankle softly. "He's lying," she said. "It was my idea to support him. Lives are at stake, Robbie—"

"That's not for certain, nor is it even the issue, lass," McSwanson interrupted, his words harsh and clipped. "I told Obie to wait. I told him to hold off warnin' people until the recon flight reported back and the Hurricane Center issued a new a bulletin. He chose to ignore me. That's insubordination." He started to walk away, but then turned and said, "And ya will be escorted from this buildin'. Both of ya."

**Obermeyer rested his finger** on the infrared image of Janet's cloud shield. The hurricane's eye, displayed as a black pin hole, had contracted dramatically in the last half hour. Around it, burgeoning bands of vermillion, indicating the presence of towering thunderstorms, swirled counterclockwise.

In counterpoint to that cyclonic twist, feathery streams of high, thin cirrus clouds pirouetted away from the storm in clockwise arcs. Obermeyer knew he was witnessing the awesome choreography of a hurricane about to become a monster. He turned to Sherrie. "Janet will be a category five within an hour," he said, "I'll bet anything."

"You've already bet everything," she said. "And lost."

He elected not to respond to her comment. Was it a dig at him or meant to make light of his situation? Checking his watch, he tossed some books and journals into a cardboard box sitting on the floor next to his desk. "I figure the cops will be here in another ten or fifteen minutes. If you've got some stuff you want to take out of here, I suggest you get it together. Once we're booted, we won't get back into the building."

"Why not fight it?" She tried to look defiant, hands on her hips, but the steeliness in her eyes had melted. Her words lacked the hard edge they'd carried earlier. "Couldn't we raise a fuss? You know, fall on the floor, kick and scream, turn blue in the face? The cops can't really toss us out of here can they?"

Obermeyer shrugged. "Maybe not, but I've had a long-standing policy never to argue with a guy with a gun. Besides, even if we stayed, what could we do? Robbie wouldn't let us back on the air. Look, I'm sorry I got you into this mess. It seems to me you're one of the few bright bulbs we've got left at the network."

"Not anymore."

"I've got a lot of contacts, I'll see what I can do for you."

"You don't owe me anything. I think you were right. My father was a stand-up guy, too. I've always admired that in men."

"Yeah, and look where it got you."

"I know all about that," she said. She plucked a pen from Obermeyer's desk, examined it casually, rolled it between her thumb and forefinger, then flipped it back onto the desk. "Dad was a lawyer in Boston. He had his own firm. It wasn't a big operation, but it was more than a one-man shop." She spoke quietly, seeming to sort carefully through her thoughts.

Obermeyer leaned back in his chair, locked his hands behind his head, and looked at her.

"He liked playing David against Goliath," she continued. "Liked taking on big corporations on behalf of clients with little or no means. He usually did very well. Then one day he grabbed his legal slingshot and flung a stone at a big Hartford insurance company. His client lived on social security and food stamps. It was a huge medical claims case that went on for three years. He lost." She looked away, covered her mouth with her hand and coughed lightly, attempting to hide a catch in her voice.

Obermeyer remained silent, waiting for her to finish.

"It cost him his firm," she said. "He went broke. He still practices law, but now it's mostly divorces and DUI crap. Still, he says he has no regrets because he knew he was right, that he should have won the case. And that was all that mattered to him. He just got overpowered by the deeper pockets of the insurance company and the ability of its attorneys to lay siege to his partnership until it ran out of resources."

Obermeyer studied her for a moment, then said, "So it's in your genes, this Don Quixote thing?"

"Yeah. As long as it's for the right cause. You know, sometimes the windmills really are the bad guys." She smiled, a sad smile. "Don't worry. Things will work out for me. What about you? What do you do now?"

He reached for the phone. "Let my friend at the Hurricane Center know his pain-in-the-ass bud in Atlanta has been drawn and quartered. That they won't have Dr. Obie to kick around anymore."

"No. I mean after that. What happens to you? Big picture?"

"I'll be fine." He punched in Rick's number. *Big picture?* What he saw, what he feared—though he would never say it to her—was tumbling into a Mariana Trench filled with bourbon and scotch, and drowning in great good cheer and anger. "I know how to handle this." *Sure I do.*

Rick answered the phone.

"I'm about to be run out of town on a rail," Obermeyer said.

"Tarred and feathered?"

"Probably."

"Why?"

Obermeyer explained.

"Piss poor timing, I'd say," Keys said after Obermeyer finished. "It looks to me like Janet's going crazy. Couldn't your boss have given you another hour?"

"Not when he can give me shit by marching me out of the building at gunpoint. The only thing that would make him happier is if he could squeeze the trigger."

"There're some guys down here who felt that way about you earlier this morning, but I think they're starting to have second thoughts. Mainly because it appears your intuition may be on target with Janet."

Obermeyer sighed. "It's a lot more than intuition," he said, "but without a confirmed recon report, as far as Robbie McSwanson is concerned, I might as well be reading tea leaves. You haven't got a corroborating message yet, have you?" He could feel Sherrie's soft breath on his neck as she leaned in close, trying to pick up snippets of the conversation.

"We should have one shortly."

Obermeyer felt a tap on his shoulder and turned.

"Guy with a gun is here," Sherrie said quietly.

"Sorry," Obermeyer said to Keys, "'shortly' isn't going to cut it. The SS has arrived." He hung up and arose from his chair. McSwanson, followed by a police officer, strode toward him.

"These two," McSwanson said to the officer, pointing at Obermeyer and Sherrie.

The officer stepped forward. Not a guy with a gun, a gal with gun. She was short and slightly overweight with hard blue eyes but a soft smile. "I'm Officer Donavon of the Cobb County Police," she said, all business. "I've been asked by Mr. McSwanson to escort you from the building. I understand you've been dismissed from employment here."

McSwanson, arms folded across his chest, focused his tiny green eyes on Obermeyer and grinned. His crooked teeth made him look like a six-foot-two piranha.

Obermeyer stared back, anger roiling deep inside him like a lava flow unable to find a vent. Sherrie nudged him and whispered, "Don't," nodding at his right hand which he'd clenched into a fist without realizing it.

He unclenched it and smiled at Officer Donavon. "That's what we understand, too," he said. He hoisted the box he'd been loading. "We're ready to leave."

"Put the box down," McSwanson ordered. "That's company property."

"No, it's personal journals and books."

"We'll have to make certain there's nothin' proprietary in there before ya take it out. Leave it until we can examine it."

Obermeyer stepped nose to nose with McSwanson. "No," he said.

McSwanson turned to look at Officer Donavon.

"I think you'd better leave it, sir," she said to Obermeyer. "Unless it's obvious it's personal stuff, like photographs or certificates, the corporation should probably take a look at it."

Obermeyer wasn't sure she was correct about that but decided to accede to his "guy with a gun" rule. He dropped the box.

McSwanson yelped and jumped back, yanking his foot from underneath the container. "Ya goddamn hooligan," he screamed. "Arrest him, officer."

Officer Donavon stepped forward quickly and put an arm between the two men. "Sir," she said to Obermeyer. "I think you'd better leave right now."

"Sorry," Obermeyer said, "it slipped."

"It was an assault. I want him arrested," McSwanson snapped.

Obermeyer felt himself being led toward the door by Officer Donavon. Her grip on his upper arm was surprisingly strong. "I've got things under control," she said to McSwanson. "Your foot will be fine."

Obermeyer turned his head toward McSwanson. "If it were an assault, Robbie, I would've packed an anvil iron in the box."

# Chapter Fifteen

## ST. SIMONS ISLAND, GEORGIA
## LABOR DAY SUNDAY, 0810 HOURS

After telling Sandy to hang on, that he'd rescue her shortly, Alan called Trish to let her know where Sandy was, that she was okay—*I think*—and that he was on his way back to the condo.

Although the creeping exodus was moving in the opposite direction he was, Alan found himself repeatedly stymied by cars and trucks from side streets sitting in his path as they attempted to bull their way into the line of evacuees. Several times he laid on his horn and flashed his headlights to intimidate vehicles into clearing a path for him.

Rain and debris filled the air as the relentless wind tore in off the ocean. Visibility at times was no more than a matter of yards. As he neared the condo, a small dog darted from the murk directly into his path; he stood on his brakes, but wasn't sure he avoided smashing the animal. He got out of the Range Rover to check. Apparently the dog had escaped. He glanced at his watch as he resumed his trip. Between the blocking cross-traffic and the runaway pet, he'd lost valuable time.

Twenty minutes after phoning Trish, he finally reached the condo. He should have been picking up Sandy by now.

Inside, Trish greeted him with hug, then said, "You'd better watch this." She pointed at the television. "I think we're in trouble."

A young woman, an attractive blonde, was saying: "To repeat, raw data just in from an Air Force Reserve Hurricane Hunter indicates that Janet is now a category four hurricane with sustained winds of 140 mph. This is a very dangerous storm and further intensification seems likely. In fact, our hurricane expert, Dr. Nicholas Obermeyer, is extremely concerned that Janet could become a rare category *five* before it strikes the coast."

Trish gripped Alan's hand with almost crushing force.

"To sum up," the woman continued, shifting to voiceover mode, "although these are the counties currently under official hurricane warnings"—a large map of coastal South Carolina and Georgia appeared—"there appears to be a growing risk of severe damage south of Chatham County and Savannah in Georgia, especially around Sapelo Island and St. Simons. Coastal counties, barrier islands in particular, have only a matter of hours to complete evacuations before movement becomes impossible. It's imperative that—"

The screen abruptly went blank, followed quickly by a public service announcement.

"What happened?" Trish asked.

"I don't know, but let's get moving," Alan said. He detached himself from his wife's hand and glanced outside. Sea spray coated the slider in what looked like salty hoar frost, but through the translucent glaze Alan could see that the ocean had overtopped the berm and inundated the pool area. It lapped at the decks of the first-floor units and slithered toward the parking lot at the rear of the building. "We'd better hurry," he added.

He looked back at Trish to find her glaring at him. "What?" he said.

"Maybe you should have taken Lee and me with you when you left for Epworth," she said.

"You mean it would have been better, we'd have saved time, if I hadn't ignored your recommendation to stick together and not leave someone here in case Sandy called or returned?" He spread his arms in front of him, a gesture of submission. "Everything's always clear in hindsight, isn't it?"

Silence. But he saw in her face she had more to say.

"Go ahead, Trish."

She continued to glare. "Your certainty can be maddening at times. As much as you've accomplished and driven yourself, as much as you've defined your own destiny, there are times you need to listen to someone else. Your wisdom, however much you may hate to admit it, is not all encompassing. Others possess it, too."

An ex post facto judgment. "I did what I thought was right," he said. "The jury's still out."

"Maybe not for long. Not if we get trapped on this frigging island."

A powerful gust of wind slammed against the condo causing the walls to shudder and pulse. Almost simultaneously the electricity went out. The building slid into a gray twilight and the background hum of the air conditioning ceased. The howl of the wind became piercing, whining through whatever tiny cracks and spaces it could find. The beat of the rain increased to the fierce drumming of a summer hail storm.

"Well, let's not get trapped then. Let's get Sandy and get the hell out of here." He led his family outside and downstairs.

In the parking lot, rain drilled horizontally into their faces as they struggled toward the Range Rover. They put their heads down and leaned into the wind, sloshing through ankle-deep surges of briny water.

Within moments they were on Ocean Boulevard, this time heading north, against the traffic. Even though a sheen of ocean covered the road, it was still visible.

"Where's Sea Island?" Trish asked.

"Out past that high-roller resort called The Cloister on Sea Island Road. It's a gated community."

"The place they call 'Millionaire's Island'?"

"Well, a millionaire probably couldn't cut it there anymore. A starter home probably goes for three mil."

East Beach Causeway was clear, but marsh water lapped at the edges of the raised road, seemingly gathering its forces for an all-out assault on the passage. Alan hunched forward in his seat, craning his neck toward the windshield, as though the effort would buy him better visibility through the sheets of rain. Tremendous blasts of wind slammed into the Range Rover, and as heavy and solidly built as it was, it shook and shuddered. He cocked the steering wheel to the right to prevent the vehicle from sliding into the marsh.

They reached the intersection of Demere and Frederica, only to find the turn lane north onto Frederica, the route to Sea Island, blocked by large orange barrels. Traffic coming south on Frederica was using all lanes. Alan leapt from the SUV and ran to a policeman who was directing traffic.

"I need to get to Sea Island," Alan shouted. "My daughter's there." He squinted against the stinging rain.

"No way," the policeman said as he continued to wave traffic toward the Torras Causeway. "All lanes are south-bound. Nobody goes north." He didn't turn to acknowledge Alan.

"It's an emergency," Alan pleaded, almost choking as the wind hurled a slug of water into his mouth.

The policeman, appearing bear-like in a bulky slicker and rain hat, persisted in his task, using his arms as semaphores to keep the vehicles moving. "Your daughter will have to find some other way out," he yelled. Then added, "you shouldn't be out here, sir. Please get back in your vehicle." Alan could barely hear him over the roar of the wind.

"She's trapped in an estate behind a locked gate," he screamed. "She can't get out. She's only fifteen." He staggered as another swirl of wind hammered him. The rain had soaked through his clothes and he began to shiver, perhaps as much from fear and anger as wind chill.

"Sir, please return to your vehicle."

"Send a patrol car. She was left there against her will."

"In case you hadn't noticed, buddy, we're a little busy at the moment. There aren't any units available to chase down people who haven't left yet. Now, I'm not going to ask you again to get back in your car."

"Shithead," Alan said and turned toward the Range Rover.

"What did you say?" the policeman demanded.

"I said I wish this shit would end." Alan stalked away.

Back in the Range Rover he considered his options. He could bust through the traffic barrels with the SUV but might damage the vehicle in the process, and if he didn't, he'd still have to fight his way up Frederica against a tide of cars and trucks.

He looked over at the policeman's car parked on the opposite side of the road. At the push-bumper on the front of it. The strobe lights on top.

"Don't even think about it," Trish said.

"It's Sandy we're talking about here."

"Keep talking. There's got to be a way other than stealing a police car."

"Let me see the map in the side pocket."

She handed him a road map of St. Simons.

He studied the map briefly. "Look at this," he said. "We can cut through this residential area off to our right and run parallel to Frederica. We'll have to get back on Frederica eventually, but at least we'll have only a mile to cover instead of two to get to the intersection with Sea Island Road."

He slammed the Range Rover into reverse and backed down Demere in a geysering spray of water until he found a road leading into the residential area. But the road was awash, the storm drains having been overwhelmed. Still, it was his only option. He drove cautiously, picking his way through downed tree limbs and floating debris. It seemed more like navigating a rushing river than maneuvering along an urban street.

Then, in one of those moments where a few feet or a couple of seconds can spell the difference between life and death, a towering pine crashed to earth immediately in front of the SUV. It seemed to happen in slow motion, the tree's roots launching huge chunks of dirt into the air as the evergreen lost it footing and toppled over. As it plunged, its thick, cone-laden limbs brushed the Range Rover's hood, almost as if seeking something to break its fall. Trish screamed as Alan hammered the brakes.

"Holy cow, Dad," Lee said.

"Yeah, holy cow," Alan answered, his breathing so spastic he could scarcely get the words out.

They sat silently for a few moments, hearing only the rapid thunk of the windshield wipers and the buckshot rattle of rain.

"Now what?" Trish said, regaining her composure.

Alan looked around. The road was blocked. But between the uprooted pine and the house it formerly sheltered, there appeared to be enough space to squeeze through. He slipped the Range Rover into low gear and steered it onto the lawn and toward the house. The tires gouged out great globs of thick-bladed St. Augustine grass as the four-wheel drive dug for traction.

"There's going to be some pissed off people when they come home and find their yard's been used for a truck rally," Trish said.

Alan cast her a sardonic look. "If the hurricane forecasters are right, there isn't going to be a yard here to come home to."

"Oh, yeah," she said, as though she'd really forgotten.

Alan reached over and patted her hand. Maybe she had drawn a blank. Similar to blocking out traumatic memories, perhaps she'd suppressed thoughts of the trauma to come.

He eased the Range Rover between the house and the gaping hole left by the tree, running the passenger-side tires over the front steps and through a flower garden. The driver-side wheels slid into the periphery of the root crater, threatening to drag the vehicle in after them. Alan gunned the engine and the SUV lurched forward, pulling itself free.

But as the Range Rover came around the base of the uprooted pine, Alan saw the only way back to the road was through another yard, one protected by a Cyclone fence.

He kept his foot on the gas and ripped through the barrier, mowing it down like an Abrams tank blasting through a cinderblock wall. The SUV bounced back onto the road in a spray of water, mud and pieces of metal.

"Woo hoo," Lee yelled from the back seat. "Can we do that again?"

"Once is enough, kid. That's really not what these vehicles are made for." He turned to Trish. "You okay?"

She nodded and smiled weakly. She had a death grip on the grab handle.

Adrenaline surged through Alan—a fix of rejuvenation that countered the rebuke of Trish's words back at the condo. It was time, as they say, to poke a finger in the eye of his adversary, Hurricane Janet. Time to rescue Sandy, to lead his family out of harm's way. "Let's go get our daughter," he said to Trish. He pumped his fist, the reassuring general in charge.

He sped down the street-cum-waterway with greater disregard than before for floating and semi-submerged detritus. The rain had morphed into a thick, wind-blown drizzle, and the visibility had improved slightly. Overhead, ragged legions of scud raced like great gray armies deploying for battle.

"Dad?"

"Yeah, Lee."

"What's that smoke coming out from under the hood?"

Alan shortened his gaze to the front of the Range Rover. "God—" He felt Trish lay a restraining hand on his thigh. "—bless America," he finished.

"What is it, Dad? Are we on fire?"

Alan glanced at the engine-temperature readout. It had soared. "No. I think it's steam." Alan pulled the vehicle to the curb and stopped. He stepped out into ankle-deep water and walked to the front of the SUV. A piece of Cyclone fence, like some sort of cubist spear, was lodged in the shattered grill. He lifted the hood. Steam spewed upward from a gaping wound in the radiator. A fatal injury.

His grandfather used to tell him: "Things are seldom as bad as they first seem, or as good as they first sound." But this was every bit as bad as it first seemed. And he didn't hear any good sounds. Only the incessant, powerful rush of the wind through the pines and oaks.

# Chapter Sixteen

## AIRBORNE, IN THE EYE OF HURRICANE JANET
## LABOR DAY SUNDAY, 0820 HOURS

"Let's try to get a fix on the center, Arly," Karlyn said. She judged they had enough room to maneuver. The eye appeared to be about five miles in diameter.

"Roger that. John?"

"Bring it around to about two-twenty, sir," Best said.

The plane banked sharply, turning hard left. Karlyn knew that Walker, once the new track was established, would work to keep the left wing of the Hurricane Hunter pointed into the wind, what little there was, and that that would lead them to the exact center of the hurricane.

"We're too low to shoot a sonde," Sergeant McKenzie said.

"We can extrapolate the surface pressure from flight level, Sarge, no problem," Karlyn responded. The aircraft leveled. Karlyn watched the wind speed numbers on her monitor slowly diminish. Fifteen mph. Ten. Eight. Five. Then steady. "Fix it here," she sang out, signaling Major Best to record the precise latitude and longitude of Janet's eye. She checked the pressure readout. "938 millibars at the surface," she said.

"How low is that? Give me a frame of reference," Walker said.

"I dunno. I think Andrew was pretty close to that pressure a few hours before landfall."

"And it came ashore as a five, right?"

"Down around 920 millibars, as I recall."

"So we may have just found Andrew's long-lost twin sister?"

"Let's hope not."

"Point taken. Okay, I'm going to start my climb now. We'll see if we can fly out of here at a more user-friendly altitude."

Karlyn leaned back in her seat, removed her headset, and wiped a sheen of perspiration from her forehead. Mountain climbing and motorcycles had never prepared her for what she'd just gone through.

No longer could she say in her briefings to Hurricane Hunter guests that she'd never been frightened on a mission.

She inhaled and exhaled slowly and deeply, and wondered if—hoped?—she might have miscarried. She dropped a hand to her belly and rested it there, resisting an instinct to stroke, to reassure, whatever life resided within her. If indeed, one still did.

Don't do that, she reprimanded herself silently. She withdrew her hand, jammed on her headset, and typed out a VORTEX message, a detailed technical report of the fury through which they'd just flown. It would confirm the automated data already transmitted to the Hurricane Center.

"I really am gonna kick your asses," she muttered and hit the send key.

**Walker inched the throttles** forward on the Hurricane Hunter and checked the engine power readouts. He wasn't reassured. "The power on three and four looks a little off," he said.

Harlow looked out the windshield to his right. "Damn. Something's leaking, too. Fuel maybe."

"Not surprising. That wing took a terrific beating."

"Both wings," Harlow corrected. "Time to head for home?"

"'Fraid so. Triple-A might be reluctant to deliver gas to us out here." Walker held the Hurricane Hunter in a circling left-hand bank inside the eye and began climbing. The alabaster wall of clouds, black-lacquered along its base, seemed to be edging closer to them, as if tightening a noose. Engines three and four, the turboprops on the right wing, continued to struggle, the instrumentation showing low horsepower on both.

Walker pointed at the readouts, and Harlow nodded. "Red sky in the morning . . .," he said.

"Whaddaya think?" Walker asked. "Fuel contamination? Bleed-air system? Bad sensors?"

"Any or all of the above. We just flew through a war zone. It's a wonder we're still airborne, all considered."

Walker nudged the throttles forward again, hoping for a little more muscle from the engines. Trapped in a stadium, the old woman had warned. No way. The Hurricane Hunter continued to climb, but the pace was leisurely, frustratingly slow. The craft was hurting.

Then the smell, an odor of burning rubber, hit him like a blindside punch to the head. Simultaneously, a flashing red light blinked to life and a warning siren began to whoop. He knew immediately what was wrong. And how much trouble they were in. The Hurricane Hunter's condition had just gone from guarded to grave.

A glance at the warning message flashing on a control panel screen confirmed his fears. "Bleed-air leaks," he said, his training keeping his voice calm. But his gut twisted itself into something that felt like a knot on a hangman's rope. 1100-degree air was trying to burn a hole through the wing.

"See if you can isolate the leaks, Colonel. Try the nacelle shut-off valves on three and four."

Harlow did, but turned and shook his head. "Negative. I can't isolate 'em."

"Shit. Okay, shut down three and four. I'll declare an emergency with Jacksonville Center." *Like that's going to do any good. We're on our own out here. In the middle of a cat five wannabe. Two engines feathered and leaking fuel like a cow pissing on a flat rock.*

He ran through their options, but it was a short list. There's no way they could climb to a safer altitude, and even if they could, no way they could challenge the eyewall with only fifty percent power and a busted wing. It would be a Kamikaze mission.

The old soothsayer's words echoed through his head with the reverberating rattle of a jackhammer: *I fear it does not end well.*

**The roar of the engines** diminished abruptly, and Karlyn felt the aircraft roll slightly to the right as though lift on the right wing had been lost. Simultaneously, the plane yawed in the same direction.

"Hey. What's happening?" she said into her mike.

Walker's voice came back immediately, his words directed to everyone. "We've got bleed-air leaks in engines three and four. For the benefit of our newspaper guest, those are the engines on the right wing. We've had to shut 'em down."

He paused, apparently searching for words, then continued. "Losing one engine is not good. Two is worse. We can't climb. And we certainly can't fly through the eyewall again. We took a hell of a beating coming through it the first time. Now there's no margin for error. Not only did we lose a couple of engines, but the right wing tip took leave of the aircraft, and we're spraying fuel all over the Atlantic."

"Pardon my ignorance, Major, but what's a bleed-air leak?" Karlyn asked. Her voice quivered. She hoped no one noticed.

"Bleed-air is extremely hot air pulled off the engines," he answered. "It's used to drive systems like the air conditioning and anti-icing. But a leak means we've got air hot enough to melt metal going someplace it shouldn't be. That's not a happy thought. So we shut down the engines, the bleed-air stops, and we avoid becoming a 75,000-ton Roman candle. We can live without the affected systems, by the way. Well, one thing. Half the hydraulics will be gone, so flying this thing will be a bit like trying to maneuver an elephant in quicksand."

Walker's announcement was followed by complete silence over the intercom. Dead air. As though everyone had been stunned into submission, trying to absorb the impact of what losing two engines in the eye of an intensifying hurricane meant.

Karlyn finally decided to ask the question she guessed no one else would, but probably wanted to: "If we sustained enough damage on the right wing to knock out both engines, what about the other—"

"If you don't ask the question, Captain, I don't have to answer it," Walker interrupted.

She looked down at her hands. She was gripping the drop-down table so hard her knuckles had turned bloodless white.


**Walker, with Colonel Harlow's** assistance, held the crippled Hurricane Hunter in a circling left-hand bank. It was demanding work and, with the air conditioning out, Walker was soon drenched in sweat. He and Harlow struggled to compensate for the tendency of the aircraft to pull to the right in response to the still-operating engines on the left wing. It was the same sort of reaction that would occur in a canoe if the person paddling on the right ceased, and the person stroking on the left kept working. The canoe would turn right. Walker cranked in a lot of left-rudder to counter the bias.

He punched the "private" button on his headset so he could talk to Harlow without the rest of the crew listening in. "I guess it's time to consider our options, Colonel. Not that we have any."

"Let's try 'Bernie,' okay? Like the rest of the guys."

"Yes, sir, Bernie."

Harlow looked at him, not a glare exactly, but a gaze that appeared rife with disappointment.

"I was hoping we were past that," Harlow said. "I thought I was up front with you about your performance report."

*Up front but unfair.* Harlow was right, though, he should be past it. If they got out of this fix, he was through with the Reserve anyhow. But gallows humor: he was through with the Reserve even if they didn't get out of this mess.

"You were up front," Walker said, "it's water under the bridge. Let's talk about how we get home."

Harlow turned to examine the broken wing. "Well, there's good news and there's bad news," he said. "The bad news, of course, is that we're losing fuel. The good news is, we don't have to dump any to stay aloft."

"How many hours do you figure?"

Harlow shrugged. "Five or six maybe. I don't know. It's just a guess. The leak might slow, or it could get worse. Maybe we'll spring another one. Who knows what kind of trauma that wing, and even the left one, suffered. It's a crap shoot."

"Ditching is out."

Harlow looked down at the boiling sea. "DOA," he confirmed.

"So, do we just continue to orbit, hope and pray for some kind of break in the eyewall?"

"The storm's intensifying, not growing weaker." A pointed put-down.

Walker didn't respond immediately. There was only one other option: a prison break. He stared at the bright bulwark of clouds surrounding them, the walls of the stadium now incarcerating them. But to attempt to escape, at least at the moment, would be just as foolhardy as ditching. Why not wait, see what Fate or God had in store for them?

The desiccating essence of fear crept into his mouth. It was nothing he could rid himself of or overcome, so he chose to merely ignore it. "Let's hold on for a bit," he finally said. "See what happens. At least we can keep track of Janet for the Hurricane Center until a replacement bird gets here."

Harlow squirmed in his seat and slowly shook his head. "No, I think not." He looked over at Walker. "Let's make a run for it while we've still got plenty of gas and two good engines. Who knows if we still will in an hour or two."

It was the Distinguished-Flying-Cross response Walker expected. Once a warrior, always a warrior, ready to attack. *Don't be so eager to die.* "Negative," he responded. "Let's give ourselves a chance. Keep orbiting. As they say, there's always hope."

"You afraid of dying, Arly?"

The words hit Walker like a bullet. He'd never thought about it. "We all die," he answered, stalling.

"That wasn't my question."

Walker tweaked the throttles and listened to the two good engines. They sounded solid. Still operating at optimum power. "I guess," he said, staring out the windshield, "I am afraid of dying. But not afraid of death. To me, they're two separate things."

"You mean, you've accepted your fate? Just not how you get there. The process."

Walker nodded. "And you?"

"We've gotta make a run for it, Major. Now. While we've got what little advantage we have. As senior officer aboard, I'll take responsibility for the decision."

"Damn it, Bernie, this isn't about taking responsibility. This is about the lives of six people. We haven't got a chance against the eyewall. Not in a broken bird. If we've got one ray of hope, it's that we might be able to slip out through a hole in the eyewall. But not now. There aren't any."

"And there won't be any," Harlow rejoined. "This thing is headed toward cat five, not cat one. I've made the call." He switched off the private button on his set. "John, plot an escape route for us. West. We'll try for Jacksonville. No point in waiting."

Karlyn interrupted. "The wall's solid, Colonel. No way out."

"Then let's hope we don't meet up with another one of your tornado-in-a-hurricane whirlwinds."

"Colonel. Sir. It doesn't make any difference, the turbulence will tear us apart. At this altitude, even with four engines, we might not make it." Walker could hear the desperation in her voice.

"If we stay in the eye, I'll guarantee you we won't make it," Harlow responded. "John, give me a heading."

Walker knew it was time to pick up a dueling glove and slap Harlow in the face. "No, John, don't," he snapped.

Harlow glowered at Walker. This time, there were no overtones of disappointment, only suppressed rage. "You've nothing to prove to me, Major." The words were sharp, clipped. "This isn't the time or place to try to convince me you can make a command decision under pressure. Let it go."

"I'm the aircraft commander, Colonel, and with all due respect the decision is mine. We're remaining in orbit. And I did let it go. I'm resigning from the Reserve. The form is on my desk at Keesler."

"You can't countermand my—"

"I can, sir, and you damn well know it. We're staying in the eye."

# Chapter Seventeen

## ST. SIMONS ISLAND, GEORGIA
## LABOR DAY SUNDAY, 0840 HOURS

Steam continued to vent from the Range Rover's holed radiator as Alan stared at the damage. They could press on in the vehicle, but what would be the point? Sooner or later the engine would seize and last rites would be due, perhaps in an unfavorable location or at an inopportune moment. Better to deal with the problem here. He signaled Trish to shut off the engine.

He stepped back and surveyed the neighborhood. Deserted. But maybe in one of the garages there would be a left-behind car. He didn't know anything about popping ignitions and hot-wiring vehicles, but he was willing to bet if he found a car he could turn up an extra set of keys someplace, in the garage, in the house, or in the car itself.

He leaned his head into the Range Rover. "You and Lee stay here," he said to Trish. "I'm going to practice my B and E skills."

"Your what?"

"B and E. Breaking and entering. We need a car."

"No way you're going to steal a car." She sounded incredulous.

"Okay. I'm not." He climbed into the SUV and shut the door. "So what's your idea? We know the police can't help. And I don't think we're gonna find a tow truck or taxi at the moment."

She stared at him, then turned away. "Okay," she said, "but leave a note if you take someone's car."

He snorted, not quite a laugh. "Of course. And a deposit, too."

Lee was leaning into the front seat. "This is so cool, Dad. We're gonna steal a car."

"Not *we're*, kid. Me. And it's not cool. It's breaking the law. Anarchy would be another term for it."

"Ann what?"

"Anarchy. You can use the word to help explain what you did during your Labor Day vacation when you get back to school."

"You need an accomplice, Dad. I'm coming with you."

"No, Son. You stay here with your mom. If you see another car, flag it down. Tell whoever is driving we need help."

"What if the cops come?"

"I don't think that's a concern right now. But if they do show up, tell them we need help or your dad's going to end up with five to ten in Reidsville."

"What's that?" Lee looked from Alan to Trish and back to Alan.

"It's the state prison." *And right now, the least of my worries.*

"Alan, stop it," Trish reprimanded.

Trish was right. The kid was probably already so uptight he couldn't breathe. "The cops aren't coming, Son. Don't worry about it. Take care of your mom. I'll be back shortly." *I think.*

Gusts of wind staggered Alan as he struggled, head down, across a spongy lawn. He moved toward a garage attached to what appeared to be an older home—common to the neighborhood—not one of the sprawling, flashy estates currently in vogue on other parts of the island. The windows of the house were boarded up with plywood, but there was an unshielded window on one side of the garage.

He cupped his hands on either side of his face, pressed his nose against the glass and peered in. There was no vehicle. He splashed into another yard and repeated his inspection. Again the garage was empty, save for an array of boxes, tools and trash cans. He continued his reconnaissance down one side of the street for about fifteen minutes, coming up empty at house after house.

Muttering a silent obscenity, he dashed across the flooded road and resumed his foray on the opposite side, working his way back toward the Range Rover. His clothes were saturated, and despite the tropical warmth he shivered nonstop in the wind-driven rain.

A large lawn umbrella blew through one of the yards, tumbling end-over-end like a giant metal-and-plastic tumbleweed. Shingles peeled from roofs and hurtled through the air in long, downward arcs. The rain, flying parallel to the ground, drilled into Alan with BB-pellet velocity.

He glanced at his watch. Time was running short. One last try, he decided, and then onto Plan B, whatever in the hell that was. He came back within sight of the crippled SUV and waved in its direction, but didn't know if Trish or Lee could see him through the thick curtains of rain.

He sloshed toward his final target, a garage detached from a weathered frame house. The garage door had a row of small windows across its upper half. He mashed his face against one of the panes. Inside sat a 1980s-vintage Ford pickup. He grasped the garage door handle and pulled upward. Locked. He considered the windows, but they were too tiny to smash and crawl through.

Moving along the periphery of the garage, he found a side entrance. Also locked. But the door had a four-pane window. He looked around for something to use to shatter the glass. Employing his bare arm and fist didn't seem like a good idea unless he wanted to risk cutting himself badly.

His cursory search turned up no loose items, like a shovel or rake or hose caddy, with which he could smash the glass. Evidently, in anticipation of Janet's onslaught, the conscientious homeowner had securely stowed everything.

The flower beds, however, were edged in short lengths of scalloped concrete. Alan bent and wiggled one of the pieces back and forth. It broke loose easily from the wet ground. He wielded it like a stubby club on the window. Over the roar of the wind, the breaking glass was inaudible. He plucked several jagged shards from the shattered frames, reached through, twisted the doorknob and stepped into the garage.

The pickup, though perhaps twenty or more years old, appeared in good shape. He opened the driver's door and checked the ignition. No keys. "Shit," he said. He felt under the floor mats, beneath the seat, opened the glove box. Nothing. He backed out of the cab.

"Don't move another step, cracker. Put your hands on top of your head." The voice was gravely and commanding.

Alan's stomach roiled. His breath caught in his throat. "I can explain," he managed to croak.

"I'll bet. But let's do it my way for now. Hands on your head. Never argue with a twelve-gauge Remington."

Alan turned his head slightly. He caught a glimpse of a bulbous face encircled in an explosion of thick, black whiskers. Bluto from the Popeye cartoon. Bluto holding a shotgun. Alan placed his hands on top of his head.

"I been tracking you for awhile, friend, watching you peep in all the garages. You probably figured this was a good time to score some nice wheels, huh, what with the hurricane coming and people scurrying for the mainland? Well, let me tell you, jerk off, you screwed up when you tried mine."

"Really, I can explain," Alan repeated. Water dripped from his clothes and puddled on the floor around his feet.

"Sure. Everybody's got an explanation. On your knees."

The barrel of the shotgun tapped Alan on his shoulder. His back was to Bluto, so he was in no position to make a grab for the weapon. He knelt. "Look," he said, "my car broke down, my daughter's trapped on Sea Island."

"This ain't the road to Sea Island, partner."

"I couldn't get onto Frederica. It's one way and—"

"Shut up. Now, lean over, put your elbows on the floor, then stretch out on your stomach."

"No."

"No?"

"You heard me. I'm going after my daughter."

Bluto chuckled, a deep, resonant laugh.

The blow came unexpectedly. Red and blue stars exploded in Alan's head as what must have been the butt of the shotgun cracked into the base of his skull. He toppled forward. He extended his arms reflexively to cushion his fall, but still hit hard, his face smashing onto the concrete. The coppery taste of blood filled his mouth. Red spatters from his nose mingled with darker stains already on the floor, oil and grease spills.

"Damn, you're dumber than Georgia clay, boy. Next time I'll hit harder. It'll hurt. We together on this?"

*Jesus, like that didn't hurt?* Alan spit blood then bobbed his head to indicate he understood.

"Good. Things always go better when you play by the rules. Now put your hands behind your back so I can truss you up."

A gust of wind shook the garage, found its way through the shattered windows and swirled around the interior kicking up a mini-haboob of dust and sand.

"You aren't just gonna leave me here, are you?" Alan said.

"I'll come back for you after the storm, buddy. I don't think there's much point in calling the cops right now."

"You can't be serious. This whole island may go under water."

"Not my problem is it? You should have thought about that before you decided to become a car thief."

"I'm not a car—"

The stock of the shotgun thudded into Alan's skull again and his world went black, punctuated by bolts of brilliant lightning. He sensed himself tumbling into a dark green sea filled with swarms of stinging red jellyfish.

# Chapter Eighteen

## ATLANTA, GEORGIA
## LABOR DAY SUNDAY, 0845 HOURS

Obermeyer and Sherrie stood in the parking lot outside The Natural Environment Network. The morning sun, shaded in tones of red and orange, spread a marmalade radiance over a layer of thin, gauzy clouds. Obermeyer leaned against his car, the impact of what had just happened to him only now beginning to register. He'd been thrust abruptly and unceremoniously into the ranks of the middle-aged unemployed. And he could forget about receiving a glowing job reference from Robbie. That was one of the downsides of working for an Asshole of the Year candidate.

"Up for some breakfast?" Sherrie asked, interrupting his thoughts.

"Actually, I was thinking of finding a bar." He wasn't sure if he were joking or not.

"You're SOL there, I'm afraid. It's Sunday."

"Damn."

"How about a Waffle House or IHOP?"

"Gag me with a spoon."

She laughed. "You're dating yourself."

"That's not hard."

"Well, I'd offer to take you back to my place, but the pantry is in pretty sorry shape. Breakfast bars and Slim-Fast." She smiled faintly, sunlight reflecting from her eyes like sparkles from smooth water.

Obermeyer guessed he'd misjudged her age. She seemed suddenly more woman than girl. She'd been solid and combative during their confrontation with Robbie; she hadn't panicked; nor had she lapsed into nervous, girlish chatter. A woman. Early thirties, perhaps.

"I'm out of ideas," he said.

"No you aren't."

He shrugged.

"I'm waiting," she said.

"Okay, I've got eggs and sausage in my refrigerator if you want to follow me home."

"This isn't going to be one of those 'have some Madeira, m'dear' deals, is it?" She leaned toward him, trying to look tough, but laughed instead.

"Good lord, I'm old enough to be your father."

"Doubt it," she responded. "Lead on."

Twenty-five minutes later, Obermeyer pulled his car into the double garage attached to his house, an upscale stone-and-stucco affair on a golf course—a waste, he didn't play—in the Atlanta suburb of Alpharetta. *Won't be able to afford this much longer.*

Sherrie, following, parked in the driveway.

Inside the house, she surveyed the kitchen. "Pretty neat for a bachelor," she said. "Neat and clean."

"I don't cook." *How many bachelor pads has she been in?*

"You don't cook! So you lured me here under false pretenses?"

"Lured? Not exactly."

"Really? What's on the menu then?" She opened the refrigerator door and peered in.

He ticked off some items on his fingers. "Frozen waffles, instant grits, bran flakes, milk."

"No Slim-Fast?"

"Bud Lite."

"What happened to the eggs and sausage?"

"Can I do eggs in the microwave?"

She let out a long sigh. "Well, far be it from me to be a stereotype-buster. Where are your cooking utensils?" She pulled a tray of eggs from the refrigerator, shut the door, and turned to face him. "Or do you even have any?"

"I'm not a cave man. Of course I do." He walked to an overhead cabinet and withdrew a bowl and frying pan. "There." He set them on a granite-topped counter.

"You're a smooth operator," she said.

He stared at her. Did she really think he was putting a move on her? That wasn't where his mind was at the moment. "What else?" he asked, perhaps a bit too sharply.

"I was yanking your chain," she said. "Relax."

"Sorry. Too much drama this morning." He forced a smile. "Let me try again. What else can I get you?"

"Spoon, spatula, whisk."

"Whisk?"

"Never mind. I'll find something." She began rummaging through drawers. "Why don't you take a bathroom break or something? I'll handle it from here."

"Okay." But instead of heading for the bathroom, he slipped into the living room.

"How do you like your eggs?" she called after him.

"However you like yours."

"I'm a Slim-Fast girl, remember?"

"Okay, sunny-side up."

"Don't need a whisk then. By the way, where are the sausages?"

"Bottom drawer of the fridge." He hoped they hadn't sprouted fuzzy, white growth like the last ones he'd kept had.

"Got 'em. Hey, what are doing in there?"

"In where?"

"Wherever you are."

"Looking for old friends." He pawed through a cabinet underneath a wet bar and hauled out two bottles: a fifth of Jim Beam, a fifth of Jack Daniels, each dusty, each virtually full. It had been awhile. He held the bottles up to the morning light. *Does bourbon go bad, like old wine?* He placed the fifth of Beam back beneath the bar. Using his hand, he wiped away the powdery film clinging to the bottle of Jack Daniels.

He carried the bottle into the kitchen and plunked it down on the counter. "Join me?" he said to Sherrie.

She looked at him, at the bottle, then back at him. "Little early, isn't it?"

"Never." He took a tumbler from a shelf and filled it halfway with the glowing, amber-colored whiskey. He set the tumbler back on the counter and stared at it. *How could something so efficient at numbing pain, so adept at slaying demons, unleash others? Was it that liquor itself was inherently demonic, or did it release its ogres only in the weak or flawed?*

"Never drink on an empty stomach." Sherrie slid a plate of eggs and sausage in front of him. "Where's the restroom?"

He inclined his head toward a hallway but continued to contemplate the Jack Daniels. *Why does it let go of some men after a sip or two, yet cling to others like a leech, sucking them dry of their dignity, their integrity, their self control? Shit, their life. But maybe I've changed. I'm aware of its dangers, I understand its insidiousness; I can control it. So, a quick pop, then back into the cabinet.*

He picked up the tumbler and swirled it under his nose, drawing in its pungent, boozy fumes, sharp counterpoints to the comforting breakfast smells of eggs and pork. *Goddamn you, Robbie McSwanson.* He tipped the glass to his lips.

The lights in the kitchen went out. He held the glass on his lips, not drinking, but gaping at Sherrie who had re-entered the room. She was backlit by sunlight streaming through a large, stained-glass window in the family room.

A kaleidoscope of subdued colors danced over her flawless skin as she stood naked, except for low-cut black panties, several feet from Obermeyer. Her broad hips, narrow waist and cantilevered breasts seemed exquisitely designed for, if not *Playboy*, then certainly an adolescent's soaring sexual fantasies. Or a middle-aged man's temptation. His heart beat stumbled over itself.

He set the glass back on the counter. "What are you doing, Sherrie?" The words came out a bit mangled.

In response, she merely motioned with her hand for him to follow her.

He stood and walked toward her, but stopped before getting within arm's reach. He shook his head. No.

"This isn't statutory rape, you know," she whispered. "I'm the one coming on to you. In case you're wondering, I'm out of my twenties." She reached for his hand.

For the first time in years, he blushed, blood rushing to his head so rapidly he doubted he could sustain his suddenly growing hardness.

Sherrie stepped forward and pressed herself against him, against his hidden erection, encircling him with her arms and moving her body in slow, gentle undulations, the tidal movements of a quiet ocean. She kissed him on the lips. Their tongues met.

She leaned back from him and their eyes met. "It's okay," she said. "I know what I'm doing."

His cell phone rang.

They continued to gaze at each other, neither one willing to be the first to laugh. Finally Sherrie said, "Bad movie." She broke away from Obermeyer and picked up the phone which was on a table next to her. Obermeyer extended his hand for it. She held up a finger and said, "Let me get it. I'm guessing it's our mutual nemesis calling to gloat."

He shrugged, now enjoying Sherrie's nudity, her brashness, her uninhibited sexuality.

"Hello," she said.

As she listened to the caller, Obermeyer saw in her eyes the mischievous glint of a silent poltergeist. When she spoke she said, "He's not available."

"Who is it?" Obermeyer asked quietly.

She covered the mouthpiece with her hand. "Robbie."

She put the phone back to her ear. "Sorry," she said after a moment, "not right now. He's busy." She listened again. A smile spread slowly across her face, then she said, "Because he's about to get laid, Robbie. I'll have him give you a ring when we're done." She held the phone away from her ear. "My, my. Maybe you'd better talk to him." She handed the phone to Obermeyer, kissed him on the cheek and padded off down the hall.

The moment was lost and Obermeyer knew it. He hated Robbie McSwanson more than ever. "What?" he snapped into the phone.

"I dunno what ya got goin' with the lass," McSwanson said, "but it can wait. Right now ya better haul your ass back into work. The Hurricane Center just extended the warnin's down the Georgia coast. They think Janet could reach category five."

"Bad shit, Robbie, but not my problem anymore."

"The networks are goin' nuts, tryin' to catch up with this story. But we scooped 'em. Now we need to stay on top of it. Get back here. Like now."

We *scooped* 'em? "You fired me, remember? Or didn't that register on your pea-sized brain?"

"I'm hirin' ya again."

"Same salary?"

"Yes."

"Wrong answer, dick head." Obermeyer hung up.

The phone rang again. Obermeyer answered. "Double my previous salary," he said.

"No way," McSwanson growled.

Obermeyer hung up.

The phone rang back.

Obermeyer punched the connect button and merely listened this time, waiting until McSwanson said, "Okay, damn ya."

"For a year, then we renegotiate," Obermeyer said.

"Okay, okay. Just get in here. We gotta get ya on the air."

"Sherrie, too."

"Sherrie what?"

"Gets hired back at double her previous salary."

"Not gonna happen—"

Obermeyer hung up again. And waited.

Robbie rang back and growled, "Twice her previous salary, then. Just get in here."

"Half an hour," Obermeyer said and disconnected.

"You're quite a negotiator," Sherrie said from behind him. She was dressed now, and holding the glass of Jack Daniels. "Shall I put this in the refrigerator?"

"Dump it down the sink. You heard the rumors, I guess."

She nodded.

"All true," he said.

She poured the whiskey out.

"Funny," he said, "I didn't know guardian angels used sex to protect boozers."

"I didn't," she answered.

"Would you have?"

She shrugged.

"Let me guess. Your father? He was an alcoholic?"

"No, he had reason, I guess, but it was my favorite uncle. Lost everything. His wife, kids, job. His freedom—got tossed in jail. Finally his life. Drove his car underneath an 18-wheeler one night on the Mass Pike when he was blitzed." She hooked her arm into his. "Let's go," she said. She leaned against him and put her mouth next to his ear. "Maybe it was a little more than just being a guardian angel," she whispered.

She still smelled bright, like roses and honeysuckle.

"Thanks for breakfast," he said.

"You didn't eat it."

"Maybe we can try again sometime."

"We should."

They walked to their cars.

# Chapter Nineteen

## AIRBORNE, IN THE EYE OF HURRICANE JANET
## LABOR DAY SUNDAY, 0850 HOURS

Walker maintained the Hurricane Hunter in a low, slow orbit, a marathon runner circling the track of an Olympic stadium. Every few circuits seemed to bring the wall of clouds closer to the aircraft as the diameter of Janet's eye tightened.

Harlow worked in tandem with Walker to keep the craft stable, but didn't speak or look in Walker's direction. Walker decided it was a good thing he was bailing out of the military; overriding a superior officer's directive, even though he, Walker, had command authority in this instance, was essentially career suicide.

But maybe he was cutting off his nose to spite his face. The only real happiness he'd found in recent years had been with the Air Force. Flying. He tried to remember a time when he and Donna had been happy—and they had been, at least briefly—before she became the abrasive, sniping shrew she was now.

His remembrances of the good times were essentially abstract, or perhaps manufactured from something he'd read in a novel or seen in a movie. He could recall images, but they had no texture, no emotion attached to them. He closed his eyes. He pictured Donna and him making love in the dark on the balcony of a condo overlooking the Gulf of Mexico on South Padre Island. Lying naked together on a fuzzy rug in front of a blazing fireplace after a day of skiing at Sun Valley. Laughing as they chased sanderlings through the surf on Hilton Head. All a long time ago.

What had happened to drive them apart? Something he'd done, or hadn't done? Or was it something so simple as substance-subsumed-by-sex in the early days of their marriage, the sex hiding a fundamental polarization in their expectations of life together? Did their frequent and often imaginative lovemaking conceal Donna's hopes for the future? The hopes that ultimately triggered her constant string of demands that he strive to be something different, reach for something higher? At least something higher in her eyes.

When marriage counseling failed, he assumed he had, too. Thus, willing to subordinate his own desires and goals in lieu of compromise, he acceded to her ultimatums. Probably a bad choice: deciding to give up the one thing he loved, for something he didn't any longer.

He opened his eyes. *There, I admitted it.*

He looked at the frothing ocean below, the wall of clouds above. *Who does a man reach out to in his final hours, when the person who is supposed to be closest to him, his soul mate for eternity, has abdicated that role? Is it better to die knowing there is no one to mourn you, or better to die knowing you'll leave a loving spouse with a sense of loss and sorrow that may never heal, that will always exist as an open wound?*

*Perhaps it is better not to die at all.*

He went back to work. "Karlyn, how's the eyewall looking?" he asked. It was a pro forma question. He could see on his monitor the ring of violent squalls was solid and tightening. A reticulated python coiling around its prey, squeezing life and hope from it.

"Nasty. All red and magenta on the radar returns."

"Pressure?"

"Dropping. Still."

"Okay. As long as we're parading around in here, we might as well do our job. Let's try for a fix on the center every fifteen minutes or so."

"I'm with you," Karlyn said.

Walker and Harlow turned the aircraft to set the left wing into the wind, then eased the plane toward the center of the eye, the fifty-yard line of the coliseum.

Karlyn called out, "Fix it," and Major Best punched a button setting the exact coordinates of Janet's eye in an electronic record.

"928 millibars," she said. "Down ten in an hour."

"Send a VORTEX to the Hurricane Center. Then send a separate message explaining our predicament and why they're going to be getting a VORTEX every fifteen minutes instead of once an hour. Tell them to lay on a tasking for another bird as soon as possible."

"Yes, sir."

Walker addressed the crew: "The fuel leak hasn't gotten worse. If anything, it seems to have slowed. So we still have time to buy. Maybe another four or five hours. When we're down to bingo fuel, if we're still in here, we'll make a run for it, no matter what the situation is. We won't ditch, that I promise you. I'll give us a fighting chance."

Harlow switched his headset to private. "You missed your opportunity to give us a fighting chance," he snapped at Walker. "The longer we fly in circles, the better the odds of something else going wrong. Not to overstate the case, Major, but you just signed a death warrant for us."

"You don't know that," Walker retorted.

"You don't know otherwise."

"Frankly, Colonel, all you're doing is betting on the negative. I'm betting on the positive."

"Tooth Fairy shit. What do you expect, a magic hole to appear in the wall? The bleed-air leak to miraculously repair itself? This is the real world we're in and we're in real trouble. Forget the ostrich approach and analyze the situation. You always claimed you were good at that. Deal with the knowns. Don't bank on unknowns. Stand up to the enemy."

"You see that as my failing? Lack of courage?"

"Yeah, lack of courage to face reality."

"With all damn due respect, sir—Bernie—the reality I'm facing is that I want to live. I think my decision gives us the best shot at doing that. And I have an additional motivation."

Harlow finally turned to look at him.

"To be able to poke a stick in your eye before I resign my commission."

**Karlyn leaned back in** her seat and massaged her head with both hands, a futile attempt to arrest the pounding within it. She didn't want to die, not yet. Funny how quickly, how unexpectedly, that defining ah-ha moment in your existence can sneak up on you, take you at knifepoint.

*Ah-ha. Maybe I should've done something a bit more redeeming with my life than tease men, scale mountains and straddle motorcycles.*

She looked down at her belly. *Look what it got me.* She sat up and spoke into her mike. "Major Walker, could I see you for a moment in the rear of the aircraft?"

"Kind of a two-man job up here," he replied.

"It's important. It won't take long."

He didn't respond immediately, consulting with Colonel Harlow, she assumed.

"I'll be back there in a sec," he said after a moment.

She took off her headset and walked toward the tail, passing Smithers and Hemphill on the way. Hemphill sat with his head back and eyes closed, his hands clutching the sides of the canvas seat. Smithers wrinkled his nose and pointed to where they'd been sitting earlier. A pool of semi-dried vomit puddled the floor. In the humid, tropical air that permeated the plane, the stench was overwhelming. She waved a dismissive hand at Smithers, pinched her nose, and rushed toward the massive cargo ramp at the rear of the plane.

She turned to find Walker behind her. He was fanning his hand in front of his nose. "Don't know how Van can stand it," he said.

"Me, either," she answered. "But I suppose that's the least of our worries."

He nodded. "What is it, Karlyn?"

They both shuffled their feet and leaned in the opposite direction of the plane's continuous bank. With only two turboprops operational, the noise in the interior was less deafening than previously. Still, Karlyn needed to raise her voice to be heard.

"I don't know if we'll ever get that cup of coffee you promised," she said.

He didn't answer.

"I need a friend," she continued. "I want a friend. I've made a tough decision. I just wanted someone to hold my hand. Figuratively, I mean."

"I'm here."

"I don't know . . ." *Maybe it didn't make any difference now.*

"Karlyn, what?"

"I'm frightened."

"Everyone is."

She dropped her gaze. "I'm sorry. There's other stuff, too."

He waited.

"Now's not the time." She lifted her head, smiled and stepped past him.

He reached out to stop her, placing a gentle, restraining grip on her arm. "You've got a friend," he said.

"When we get back, then."

"Yes. When we get back."

She laid her hand on top of his. "I wish I'd met you before Donna did. It might have worked out better for both of us." She thought she glimpsed in his eyes a flicker, a tacit message, an acknowledgment that said yes, but she wasn't sure.

"Life is full of 'might have beens,'" he said.

She withdrew her hand and stepped away from him. "And I know the only one that matters right now is what might have been if we'd penetrated at 10,000 feet instead of five. I shouldn't have taken up your time. I'm sorry."

"We'll meet at Starbucks. After we get back."

She stepped close to him again. "Just get us back," she said.

She watched as he as turned to go and wondered if this would be the last time she saw him. She uttered a silent prayer, but knew it came as part of a foxhole religion and thus felt vaguely embarrassed. Still, she'd been taught that God was forgiving and patient and loving, so maybe her entreaty had a chance. At least a tiny one.

**Walker returned to the** cockpit and settled into his seat. Harlow had struggled with the now-heavy yoke to hold the aircraft in a counterclockwise orbit. "I've got it," Walker said, grasping the controls. "Take a break."

Harlow leaned back in his seat and massaged his shoulders. "Everything okay back there?" he asked.

"Fine," Walker said. Then added, "Our weather officer's just a bit apprehensive." But there was something else, obviously. Something she wouldn't, or couldn't, confide in him, at least not now. But why had he become her chosen one, her confidante-to-be? Because of the one-night stand that wasn't? Because she felt compelled to act as an antidote to Donna? Because she, Karlyn, was genuinely attracted to him? Not likely, he decided. It probably was, for some reason, opaque to him, that she merely sensed he was someone she could trust. The trouble was, he was beginning to doubt he could inspire trust in anyone, including himself.

"Jacksonville Center called while you were talking with Karlyn," Harlow said. "They wanted to know our intentions."

"And you told them?"

"What you said. Fly in circles until we're on bingo fuel, then try to make it to the coast. They said they'd have a Coast Guard cutter standing by."

"For what it's worth."

"Yeah. For what it's worth. I probably should have told them not to waste the taxpayers' money."

With each circuit of the plane, the eye of Janet continued to grow tighter as the boiling mass of clouds that marked the storm's eyewall inched inward. Walker looked up, into the open hole of blue sky ten miles above them. Off the ramparts of the eyewall—the tops of the squalls surrounding them—he could see thin streamers of cirrus clouds descending into the eye, then evaporating. The descending air, warming and drying under its own compression, was what kept the eye devoid of clouds. It was also a sign of a mature hurricane growing ever more powerful. He checked his watch. "Time for another run into the center," he said.

"At your command, Major," Harlow answered. In contrast to the tropical warmth that permeated the aircraft, his words spilled out like chips of ice. He leaned forward and placed his hands on the yoke. "Ready here," he said.

The two men rolled the aircraft into a sharp turn, leveled it, and bisected the eye.

Karlyn again found the dead center of the storm, then called out, "919 millibars. I think it's safe to say we've been swallowed by a cat five."

"Jonah in the whale," Harlow muttered.

"Fuel?" Walker asked.

"Probably three hours at the outside."

"Two to bingo, then?"

"Something like that."

One of the two good engines abruptly skipped a beat, and both men simultaneously and quickly scanned the gauges for signs of a malfunction.

"I don't see anything," Walker said.

"Everything looks normal," Harlow confirmed.

They looked out at the left wing. "Looks okay," Walker said.

"Yeah, but we probably don't even have three hours anymore. Engines don't hiccup just because they swallowed too much foam off a Budweiser."

Walker understood now he'd painted himself, the entire crew, into a corner from which there was no escape. To put it bluntly, he'd fucked up. Big time. Harlow had been right. They should have made a run for it earlier, before doubts arose about the reliability of the two functioning engines. Before Janet's fury reached catastrophic levels.

But now it was too late. He alone bore the cross, shouldering responsibility for the lives, and now deaths, of six people. How could an old lady in a carnival tent have known?

He tried to recall the words to the Lord's Prayer. He'd known them once, a long time ago. All he could remember now, however, were the first few words: "Our Father who art in heaven, hallowed by thy name."

Three more times during the next hour, an engine—no one was sure which one—on the left wing sputtered, but always resumed a steady drone. The air pressure in Janet's eye continued to tumble. The storm was positioning itself with the great hurricanes of American history. Walker tried to find comfort, however cold it might be, in the hope their deaths would not be in vain. That the data they fed back to the Hurricane Center would save lives, even as they sacrificed theirs.

But the comfort would not come. All he found—or that found him—was an overwhelming sense of failure.

# Chapter Twenty

## ST. SIMONS ISLAND, GEORGIA
## LABOR DAY SUNDAY, 0950 HOURS

Alan fought his way to the surface of the swirling virescent sea into which he had been hammered by the blow from Bluto. He thought he heard Trish's voice, though he knew it couldn't be; Trish's voice saying, "Drop the gun, fatso, or I'll pull the trigger on mine."

He forced one eye open. Light. He listened. It was Trish. Now she was saying, "Real quick, buster, because I'm as nervous as a Sunni in a synagogue and this thing may go off accidentally."

*What the hell is she doing? She doesn't own a gun. Won't allow one in the house. Doesn't even know how to shoot one.*

The shotgun clattered to the floor. Alan rolled over, sat up, snatched the Remington and stood. Bluto swam in his vision, a roly-poly man with tiny pig-like eyes and an enormous tummy. Behind him, Trish held the tip of a large golf umbrella against the small of his back.

She gasped when she saw Alan's face.

"I'm okay," he said. Cradling the shotgun in his left arm, he wiped the blood from his face with his right forearm. He ran his tongue over his teeth, felt several loose. He stared at Trish and she read his tacit question.

She shrugged. "I saw you wave. I thought you meant for me to come."

He nodded. "You can put the gun down now, honey." He raised the shotgun and pointed it at Bluto's chest.

"Don't bother," Bluto said. "It ain't loaded."

Alan forced a weak smile. "Well, neither is my wife's umbrella." He checked the Remington's magazine. It was, as Bluto said, empty. He lowered the shotgun.

Bluto pivoted slowly and examined Trish and the furled umbrella she held in her hand, which shook spastically. Lee appeared in the doorway behind her. Bluto laughed, softly at first, then louder, the sound rumbling up out of his gut like some merry pyroclastic flow from a benign volcano. He clutched his stomach as his laughter subsided into wheezing chuckles.

"Fine cops and robbers we'd make," Bluto said when he finally ceased gasping.

Alan ran his fingers gingerly over his face. "You'd do okay with assault and battery, though."

Bluto responded, speaking slowly and deliberately, as if reprimanding the actions of a small child. "I wasn't the one who broke into the garage."

"Point taken. We'll call a truce, then." Alan reached out to shake the man's hand.

Bluto accepted it, then said, "Guess you'd better tell me what's going on here."

Alan did. When he'd finished, Bluto—it turned out his real name was Pete Pirwoski—said: "That tale's just goofy enough I believe it. Come into the house for a minute, get cleaned up, dry off a bit and we'll go fetch your daughter. I can't guarantee we'll get off this island before Janet arrives, but we'll sure as hell bust our butts trying."

They entered the house. Pete gave Trish and Lee a flashlight and pointed the way to the guest bathroom. Then he waddled beside Alan toward the master bath. "Sorry about your face," he said, "let's get you patched up. You know, you could have just knocked on the door."

"I assumed everybody had left."

"All the smart ones did, son."

"In that case, I'm glad you were dumb enough to stay behind. I appreciate your help. You don't know how much it means to me. To us."

Pete didn't respond immediately. Instead, he stopped and stared at a framed photograph on the wall of the hallway they were in. The ambient light was low and Alan couldn't see the picture clearly, but it looked like a woman and young girl.

Pete tapped the photograph. "My wife and daughter," he said. "My daughter was killed in a car wreck about ten years ago. Then my wife passed five years later. Collateral damage." He paused, then added, "So I do know how much it means to you."

Alan laid a hand on Pete's shoulder. "I'm sorry," he said.

Pete nodded. "We'll get your young lady, my friend. Don't worry."

A radio, obviously battery-powered, was playing somewhere in the house, the broadcaster announcing that hurricane warnings had been extended southward to the Georgia-Florida border and that evacuation of the entire Georgia coast was now underway.

"Janet has strengthened to a category five and the eye is now only 125 miles east-southeast of St. Simons Island," the radio voice said. "Landfall is predicted within eight hours, but evacuation routes from barrier islands are expected to be cut off momentarily. The National Hurricane Center expects a twenty-five- to thirty-foot storm surge near the eye of Janet when it comes ashore."

The words hit Alan as hard as the butt of Pete's shotgun had. At twenty-five feet, virtually the entire island would be underwater. He abruptly excused himself from his host and rushed to the bathroom. His stomach churned and he leaned over the toilet and vomited.

Afterward, he splashed several handfuls of cool water onto his face, then gazed at his image in the mirror above the sink. "Don't lose it," he whispered, "don't lose it." He yanked a towel from a wall rack and dried himself.

Now he saw it, perhaps too late: his hubris, his confidence, his cocksureness the island was hurricane proof, had been ill founded. He should have taken Trish and Lee with him when he set out for Epworth. He'd wasted time, delayed his daughter's rescue and placed his family in jeopardy. It was suddenly clear they had no chance of getting off the island before evacuation routes were submerged by the ocean. And if the storm made a direct hit on St. Simons, they probably had virtually no chance of escaping with their lives.

He stood, for once in his adult life riddled with doubt, not having a solution to a problem, unable to control his fate or his family's. He couldn't order the hurricane to change course, couldn't command his underlings to retrieve his daughter, couldn't throw money at the situation and have it rectified.

Outside, the wind had reached a steady low-decibel roar, and Alan could swear the walls of the tiny house pulsed with each powerful gust. Even within the home the air seemed to vibrate.

"Damn me," he said softly, "damn me."

# Chapter Twenty-one

## ATLANTA, GEORGIA—THE NATURAL
## ENVIRONMENT TELEVISION NETWORK
## LABOR DAY SUNDAY, 1025 HOURS

When Obermeyer and Sherrie arrived back at the studio, McSwanson was nowhere to be found. But he'd left a note for Obermeyer telling him to go on the air immediately. Obermeyer tossed it aside. "When I'm ready," he said.

On his computer, he typed in a command that allowed him to read the initial VORTEX message transmitted from the Hurricane Hunter just after he and Sherrie had got the bum's rush from the network. The Aerial Reconnaissance Weather Officer on the flight into Janet had appended a note to the report: "solid radar presentation, extreme turbulence in eyewall." The penetration had been made at 5000 feet, a death-wish altitude in a storm as strong as this one. Obermeyer shook his head. The crew obviously hadn't been aware of Janet's rapid intensification.

He tried to imagine what it must be like to punch through the eyewall of a strengthening hurricane. Terrifying certainly, even to those used to careening through the ring of violent squalls and thunderstorms that surround a hurricane's eye. He pictured medieval knights storming the rocky wall of a feudal castle as boulders, arrows and boiling oil rained down upon them. That kind of terrifying.

The most recent VORTEX report from the Hurricane Hunter indicated Janet's atmospheric pressure had plunged to 919 millibars. "Hey, Sherrie," Obermeyer said, "guess what? We got ourselves a cat five." A nascent urge to gloat welled up within him, but he knew with great certainty that people were going to die. It was inhumane to feel good about that.

He grabbed the phone on his desk and called Sally Ainsworth, the producer on duty. "Change the graphics," he said. "Janet's a cat five."

"How soon will you be ready to go on the air?" Sally asked.

"Let's say twenty-five minutes," he said. "I've got other business to attend to."

He hung up as Sherrie plunked the latest bulletin from the Hurricane Center onto his desk. "Hurricane warnings have been extended all the way to the Georgia-Florida border," she said.

"About damn time," he muttered. "Landfall?"

"The Hurricane Center thinks near Sapelo Island."

Obermeyer leaned forward in his chair, folded his arms across his chest and studied a looping satellite image of Janet's recent forward motion on his monitor. "No," he said, "it's going to be St. Simons, I'm sure of it."

"How strong?"

"She's already more intense than Andrew was at landfall, so it really doesn't matter at this point. However strong she ends up, the damage—and death toll—is going to be devastating, the worst in Georgia's history. The big problem now is the track." He pointed at a map stapled to the wall. "The coast south of Savannah is sparsely populated; just marshy islands and wildlife preserves with pine and oak forests. Not many folks to move out. Still, the only way off most of those islands is by boat. Like here." He tapped his finger on the map, against Sapelo Island just north of St. Simons.

He slid his finger up to Savannah. "People in and around Savannah are already leaving, so they've got a jump on things." Then he pointed at St. Simons. "But this place is in dire straits. St. Simons is filled with holiday tourists who think the hurricane isn't going to make a direct hit there. Yeah, evacuation is underway, but I don't think there's any notion of how bad things are going to get, how little time is left. There's no way everyone's going to get off that island in time."

He paused and looked down at floor. "Goddamn that Robbie," he said to himself.

Sherrie moved closer to him and he looked up. Their eyes met. He tried to read what was in her gaze, but couldn't. Was that his failure or her talent? It seemed to him women had an innate facility to be inscrutable. Back at the house, had she viewed him as anything more than an effete-willed middle-aged man who needed to be saved from himself? Or had there been at least a tiny spark of genuine attraction, romantic or sexual, rasped to life? *Yes, in my fantasies.*

On the flip side, did she worry about being seen by him as some sort of Ivy League chippy, an educated, articulate tramp looking for a clever way to add another notch to . . . whatever such women might add notches to? Or was she concerned she might be deemed by him as just a sophomoric twit, a silly girl who thought she could save him from the evils of alcohol by using sex?

As if reading his thoughts, she said, "Don't get yourself wrapped around the axle over it." She rested her hand on his shoulder. "It was both more and less than what you're thinking. Right now you've got more important things to deal with."

He couldn't help but laugh. "'Both more and less than what I'm thinking?' You've certainly blown away the mists of obfuscation." He used the big word knowing she would understand it.

Now it was her turn to laugh, though it was more of a giggle. "We women are good at that, aren't we?" She removed her hand from his shoulder and stepped back. "So what do we do about St. Simons?" she asked, her tone now dead-center professional.

He steepled his hands beneath his chin and gazed at her, the sexual tension now at least dissipated, if not totally buried. "In addition to the lack of urgency regarding evacuation there, there's an ingrained culture of hurricane immunity: if it hasn't happened, it can't happen. Nineteenth century history notwithstanding."

"So our resident hurricane hero does what?"

He reached for his telephone. "Calls the emergency managers of Glynn and Camden Counties and scares the hell out of them."

"You haven't done that yet?"

"Not even close." He inclined his head toward the satellite image of Janet. "See the cloud striations at the top of the eyewall? The ones perpendicular to the overall circular wind pattern?"

"Here?" she said, pointing at what looked like ripples in a stream.

"Yes. That's air venting out the top of the storm, literally flowing downhill over the outer periphery of the eyewall. It's a classic signature, a nightmare signature, of a rapidly intensifying hurricane. People will forget about Andrew and Katrina and Camille after this one."

He dialed the number of the Glynn County EM, Alfred Willis, a retired veterinarian whom everybody called Doc. When Doc answered, Obermeyer said, "Doc, this is Nick Obermeyer at The Natural Environment Television Network. You probably remember me. We've done business before."

"Yeah. Hey, Obie, good to hear from you again. So, Janet, huh?"

"Yes. And it's not looking good. I think you need to start—"

"I know, I know. We already got the word from the Hurricane Center. We're moving people off the barrier islands, but I think with the storm going in north of us, we'll be okay."

*No, you won't.* Obermeyer tapped a key on his computer that painted latitude-longitude lines over the image of Janet. "That's my point, Doc, it's not."

"Not what?"

"Going in north of you."

"The Hurricane Center said—"

"Listen to me. Carefully. Because I'm going to make my pitch only once. After that, you'll have to make up your own mind." He leaned in close to the monitor so he could see the latitude-longitude grid more clearly. "Janet already has deviated about ten nautical miles south of a track that would bring her over Sapelo Island. She's beginning to react to her own steering environment. If you extrapolate the deviation over the next six or seven hours, guess where ground zero is."

Doc was silent.

"St. Simons," Obermeyer said. "Get people off that island as fast as you can. One-way traffic over the causeway. Contraflow on I-95 going south. Not north. Not into the storm. South."

"All of that takes time to organize."

"You don't have any time. You gotta squeeze people off that island like they were coming out of a sausage grinder at warp speed. You've got Andrew's big sister coming at you."

"Worst case scenario?" Doc asked softly.

"You know, I really hope I'm wrong about this one. But . . . look, just get people the hell outta there."

"Come on. How bad?"

It was Obermeyer's turn to be silent.

"Obie?"

"Jesus, Doc. Worst case? Okay. There'll be nothing left standing. It'll become the St. Simons Island National Wildlife Refuge."

Doc didn't respond. All Obermeyer could hear was background chatter emanating from the emergency operations center.

Finally Doc said, "Nothing left standing?" The words came out cloaked in disbelief, as if he couldn't quite fathom what Obermeyer had said.

"If St. Simons takes a direct hit from a cat five, nothing but foundations and steel superstructures will survive within 500 yards of the shore. Even in the interior of the island, damage will be catastrophic. The surge will inundate everything. Five to ten feet of water over the very highest spots on the island. Twenty-five to thirty feet near the beach." As Obermeyer spoke, he felt a chill spread across his shoulders and neck, as if articulating his fears had called forth some cold, marmoreal breath of death. All he could add was, "Good luck, Doc. You've got a couple of hours, probably less, before low-lying evacuation routes are flooded. Seven, at most, before the eye hits."

"For Christ's sake, it'll take another four or five hours to finish emptying St. Simons. Plus we've got the Labor Day crowd to worry about."

"You've got a lot more than that to worry about."

"We can't finish St. Simons in an hour or two."

"You can't if you keep wasting time telling me you can't. And if you really can't, you'd better lay in a few thousand body bags for every hour you think you're going to fall short."

Their conversation ended abruptly.

Obermeyer called the Camden County EM next and repeated his pitch.

When he finished, he phoned his friend at the Hurricane Center and said, "Hey, Rick, just wanted to let you know I'm back in the saddle."

"I'm impressed, partner. How'd you manage that?"

"Three-beer story."

"I thought you weren't supposed to—"

"It's a metaphor. I'll tell you sometime when we don't have a cat five breathing up our ass. Look, I gotta run, get back on the air. But I do have a favor to ask."

Keys grunted, probably in resignation, then said, "Why do I always feel like I'm Charlie Brown and you're Lucy with the football when I hear those words?"

"It's not that kind of deal. It's just a phone call I want you to make if my forecast for Janet is on target, that she's going to blast St. Simons."

"Sapelo isn't good enough for you?"

"If Janet goes inland over Sapelo, St. Simons is spared, relatively speaking. Yeah, there'll be a lot of wind damage, but no storm surge. But if Janet landfalls on St. Simons, it goes underwater. The whole damn island. As simple and as deadly as that."

"You never can go with the flow can you?"

"Not when I think I'm right. Please, just make the phone call."

"To whom?"

"Someone I think of as an insurance agent."

"Insurance agent?"

"It's part of the three-beer story."

"This is sounding better all the time." Keys chuckled.

"You don't know the half of it," Obermeyer said, glancing at Sherrie.

She smiled at him and held up two fingers. Two minutes to air time.

Obermeyer gave Keys a name and phone number to call in Atlanta, and told him what to say.

As he hung up, Sherrie said, "One minute." She stepped toward him, and for the first time he noticed the color of her eyes, the blue-green of a pristine tropical sea. She handed him his clip-on mike and ear fob and tugged at his shirt. "Still a mess," she muttered.

"Ready for a long day?" Obermeyer asked.

"It's already been a long day," she whispered, smiling, the allusion clear: something secret between the two of them. But under the harsh glow of the fluorescent lights bathing the studio, and in its businesslike atmosphere, the events of an hour ago seemed suddenly distant and surreal, as if he'd just awakened from a dream.

The operations area had come alive, no longer a sleepy den of solitude on a holiday weekend. Two more producers, additional OCMs and extra meteorologists were scurrying around, gathering data, preparing graphics and rushing to apply makeup.

Obermeyer inhaled Sherrie's fragrance once more as she straightened his tie and brushed his lapels. She patted him on the shoulder. "Go," she said and pointed at the key wall.

Obermeyer stepped next to the wall and checked his monitor to make sure a satellite image of Janet would be electronically superimposed behind him. He watched the countdown lights wink out on the camera.

The last light blinked off and he said, "General William Tecumseh Sherman's march through Georgia took eight months. Hurricane Janet's march through Georgia will take a matter of hours. And will be immensely more destructive."

He displayed a large-scale map of coastal South Carolina and Georgia. "Hurricane warnings are posted from Isle of Palms near Charleston, South Carolina, southward to the Georgia-Florida border," he said. "But it appears the greatest risk for a direct hit from Janet will be along the south Georgia coast near St. Simons Island."

Obermeyer turned to face another camera which was framed to

shoot only his head and shoulders. "I can't emphasize too much," he said, looking directly into the lens, "the necessity of evacuating south Georgia coastal counties as rapidly as possible." He paused, wanting to swallow, wanting to slow his breathing, but forged ahead instead, unwilling to manifest his fears. "There are only a couple of hours left before weather conditions preclude evacuations, and perhaps six or seven before Janet makes landfall."

He paused again, this time for effect. "And wherever landfall occurs," he resumed, modulating his voice and measuring his cadence carefully, "damage will be catastrophic. Not *may be* catastrophic, *will be*. Let me explain it this way. In 1969, Hurricane Camille slammed into the Gulf Coast with sustained winds estimated at 180 mph. Camille, for all practical purposes, leveled virtually every structure along the Mississippi coast. Janet, I fear, will be stronger than Camille."

He switched back to the key wall camera. A composite image formed by the Charleston and Jacksonville Doppler radars popped up electronically on the monitor. It displayed the western-most rainbands of Janet. "The outermost squalls from Janet are pin-wheeling over the south Georgia coast already." Obermeyer swept his hand across the blank wall. "These squalls contain downpours and wind gusts to 70 mph, but consider them only a warning shot over the bow. Things will get much worse over the next several hours." *Unimaginably worse.*

He signed off and stepped away from the key wall. Sherrie handed him another VORTEX message from the Hurricane Hunter. "Pressure's still dropping," she said.

He studied the report. The barometric reading in the eye of the storm had fallen ten more millibars, down to 909, Camille territory. Janet was morphing into the Grim Reaper.

Sherrie delivered two more VORTEX messages during the next half hour. The data indicated the storm had continued to strengthen.

"But there's something else," Obermeyer said, "something weird."

"What?" Sherrie asked.

"The reports have been only fifteen minutes apart. Typically they're about an hour apart. The aircraft flies through the eye of the hurricane, then out to its periphery. There it turns, flies along the edge of the storm, turns again and penetrates the eyewall from a different direction. Usually that takes about an hour." With his finger, he traced the pattern over the radar imagery of Janet on his computer monitor.

"So what's going on?" Sherrie edged closer to him.

Her nearness was unnerving and slightly disorienting. On one level she emanated an aura that was youthful, innocent, fresh; on another, experienced, sensual, sexual. A strange amalgam of teenager and tigress. He had a difficult time focusing on Janet, not Sherrie.

He reached for the phone. "I don't know, but I'm gonna find out." Again he dialed Keys at the Hurricane Center.

When Keys answered, Obermeyer, skipping preliminaries, said, "Why isn't the Hurricane Hunter flying its normal track? It's been in the eye for over an hour."

Keys didn't respond. Obermeyer could hear him drumming his fingers on a table.

"Come on. What's happening? Something's wrong, isn't it?"

"Okay, just between you and me. Not for public consumption yet. The guys went in at 5000 feet thinking Janet was just barely a hurricane, a 97-pound weakling. Well, it wasn't. And it cost them. A wing tip and two engines."

"Jesus, Mary and Joseph. They're trapped in there, aren't they?" Obermeyer saw Sherrie's hand fly to her mouth after he said the words.

"They don't have enough power or lift to climb to a safe altitude to get through the eyewall again, to get out," Keys said. "And the plane's pissing fuel like a college kid after a beer binge."

"They can't ditch, can they? That'd be suicide."

"Yeah. They wouldn't have a prayer. Look, not a word of this on the air or to the media. Please. The families of the crew haven't all been notified yet."

"Okay."

"I just don't know . . . " Rick's voice trailed off, his words sounding flat and hopeless.

Obermeyer sensed he wanted to say something else, had a thought he couldn't quite articulate. "What?" he asked. "Tell me."

"I think we're gonna lose 'em."

# Chapter Twenty-two

## ST. SIMONS ISLAND, GEORGIA
## LABOR DAY SUNDAY, 1025 HOURS

Pete hurled his pickup north on Frederica Road, flashing his headlights, laying on his horn, and forcing the few remaining southbound cars that dared treat the road as one-way out of his path. The truck fishtailed back and forth on the water-covered street, scattering even more vehicles. Occasionally, Pete whipped the vehicle onto a winding sidewalk that paralleled the right side of the road, slaloming around thick-trunked live oaks that precluded the walk from following a straight course.

Alan and Trish sat beside Pete, Trish covering her eyes as the truck careened down the boulevard in an almost constant state of hydroplaning. Alan didn't bother, since he could see virtually nothing through the rain-streaked windshield anyhow. It was a wonder Pete could. Alan turned and looked through the rear window. Lee, huddled underneath a tarpaulin in the truck's bed, bounced from side to side with each violent slide of the pickup. The poor kid was a pinball. But that was the least of Alan's worries.

It would be only a short time before the roads became impassable, flooded by the surging Atlantic or blocked by fallen trees. If they couldn't get to Sandy quickly, there'd be no way off the island. They'd be trapped and at the mercy of elements so violent he refused to let their images linger. Still, in strobe-light milliseconds he caught flashes of submerged buildings and wind-shattered trees. Desolation.

"Sea Island Road coming up," Pete yelled. "Hang on." He flung the truck into a sharp right-hand turn. The results weren't good. The pickup continued straight, the rear end whipping around as the vehicle spun through the intersection. Cars scattered in various directions as Pete's Ford made like an out-of-control speed boat, nicking a Cadillac Escalade in the process. The pickup came to rest on a sidewalk, Pete looking unfazed.

"Well, if that wasn't piss poor driving, I don't know what was," he muttered.

The Cadillac pulled in front of the truck. The driver, a man decked out in a sou'wester and waders, jumped from the SUV and splashed toward Pete in a determined stride. Pete rolled down his window. Rain sprayed through the cab.

"S'matter with you, buddy?" the driver demanded. He sported a white mustache that twitched like a caterpillar tossed into a hot skillet.

"Nothing," Pete said. "I'm in a hurry, just like you."

"Well, you're gonna have to put your hurry on hold until we trade information and I call the cops. Let's see your driver's license and insurance info."

"Let's see how fast you can get that Detroit panzer out of my way," Pete snapped. He cranked the pickup's engine which had died in the spin.

"Don't get smart with me, buster. I'm a lawyer. If you wanna take me on, go ahead."

"I don't give a flying foobar about taking you on, Mr. Attorney, but I will take on your shiny new Cadillac with my dented old Ford unless you move said Cadillac in about five frigging seconds." He slipped the truck into gear.

"I've got your license plate, dick head," the lawyer said. He retreated, dashing for his SUV.

Pete whipped the pickup onto Sea Island Road in a geysering cascade of water as the Cadillac pulled back. He leaned out the window. "Name's not Dick," he yelled. "It's Pete Pirwoski. Give me a call sometime after you polish out the scratch and we'll grab a beer, talk about old times." He accelerated toward Sea Island, into the teeth of the wind and rain. The lawyer flashed him a hand signal.

Lee's face appeared against the rear window, his nose mashed on the glass like a pig's snout. He waved and said something. Alan smiled and tried to read his lips.

"I think he said 'that was cool, Mr. Pirwoski'," Alan said to Pete.

"I'm probably a bad influence on your kid, huh?" He fought the wheel as the truck settled back into its fishtailing mode.

"I would've done the same thing. But you didn't have to. Maybe you should've just dealt with it then and there."

"I did."

"Yeah, but that guy will come after you."

He shook his head. "That asshole? He's a lawyer. Windier than someone who just won a beans- and broccoli-eating contest. Besides," he continued, sweeping his arm in front him, gesturing at the rain-swept landscape, "in a few hours, how much do you think there'll be left to come after?"

They approached the mile-long causeway to Sea Island, and Pete slowed the truck. "Doesn't look good," he said. Wind-propelled surges of water from the salt marsh and Black Banks River, over which the causeway ran, flowed freely across the road in spots. At times, small, white-capped waves broke over the passage.

Pete brought the pickup to a stop. "Well?" he said.

"Don't go out there," Alan responded. "I'll go on foot from here. We can't risk getting the truck washed into the marsh. It's our only way off the island. If we lose it, we're as good as dead."

"And you, my friend. What if you get swept into the marsh?"

"I can swim. The truck can't." He reached across Trish's lap and opened the door. "You and Lee and Pete wait here," he said. "I'll get Sandy. Don't worry. It shouldn't take long." *It can't take long.* He kissed Trish.

"Please," she said. "Find her. Be careful."

It crossed his mind that the two requests might be mutually exclusive, but he didn't dwell on it. He clambered over his wife, pulling free, gently, from her viselike grip on his saturated shirt. He stepped out into the pounding rain, to the rear of the pickup to tell Lee what he was going to do. When he finished, he tousled his hair and told him to wait in the cab.

"But I wanna come with you, Dad."

"I know you do, son, but I need a really strong man to stay with Mom and keep her spirits up. Can you do that?"

Lee nodded.

"You're a good man, I'm proud of you." They knocked knuckles together and bumped elbows, a little "secret" father-son ritual they'd developed. Alan stood for a moment, studying his son: his big eyes, latent with mischief; his crooked smile, ready to disarm; his prepubescent muscles, poised to run and jump.

*How have I managed to put the people I love most in such jeopardy?*

He reached back into the bed of the truck, underneath the tarp, and wrapped his arms around his son in a water-logged bear hug.

"Dad," Lee exclaimed when the embrace lasted a bit too long.

"Okay, kid. Sorry." He relaxed his hug. "You know what to do, right?"

"Yeah, Dad."

Alan splashed back to the cab and motioned for Trish to roll down her window. He leaned into the interior of the pickup, out of the rain. "Listen," he said, "both you and Pete. Keep your eyes on the causeway. If the river starts to come up over it any more than it has right now, get the hell out of here. Even if I'm not back. Don't stop. Get off of St. Simons. If the causeway goes under water, that means the entire island is going under."

"You said it wouldn't take long," Trish retorted, her voice resonating with the tightly-strung timbre of a prosecutor reminding a defendant of his previous testimony.

"Just in case things don't well. Just in case it takes longer than I think to find Sandy. You can't afford to wait if the causeway submerges—"

"No."

He reached into the cab and took her hand. "If you wait—and I can't sugarcoat this—there'll be five people dead, not two." He gripped her hand even more firmly. "I love you, Trish. Take care of yourself, take care of our son."

Tight lipped, she nodded but said nothing.

"The right choices aren't always the ones our heart would make," Alan said.

She nodded again, still silent.

"Don't worry, Al," Pete said, "think of me as Moses. I'll lead your family out. Get going."

Alan released Trish's hand. Rain pelted into his eyes, masking his tears.

As he turned to go, a gust of wind hammered him sideways, almost knocking him off his feet. He recovered, crouched, and battled his way onto the causeway, the gale fighting him every inch of the way. The marsh itself was totally submerged. A capsized rowboat, pinned against the side of the raised roadway, jounced up and down in the waves that rolled across the swamp.

Alan reached the end of the causeway. There, a small, abandoned guardhouse marked the gated entrance onto Sea Island. Alan ducked under the gate, a thick, white crossbar, and crossed a short bridge onto the island. The rain drove into his eyes with such abandon he had to squint to see.

His cell phone rang. He snatched it from his pocket and answered

"Daddy, where are you?" Sandy's voice was infused with terror. "Water's leaking into the house."

"I'm coming, honey. I'm crossing the bridge now. We've had some problems, and I'm on foot, but I'm coming."

"Please hurry, Daddy. Please, please."

Alan, keeping the phone pressed to his ear, began to jog. Rain continued to machine-gun into his face. "Listen," he said, "after you passed the guardhouse, how long did you drive? A minute? Five minutes? Do you remember?"

"I don't know. I think a few minutes."

"Try to give me a number, Sandy. Please. Think back to the trip. Maybe you can remember how many cross streets you passed?"

"I think we drove for about five minutes. We passed lots of little side streets."

"And the house you're at is on the main street?"

"Yeah."

"Right or left?" A gust of wind almost knocked him down. He fought to regain his balance.

"Right, as you drive in."

"Okay, good. Let's see, I'm gonna guess you were driving about thirty mph. That's a half mile in a minute, so five minutes would be roughly two and half miles. Shit."

"What, Daddy?"

"I said 'sit, sit tight', I'll be there soon." Two and a half miles up Sea Island Road. At a brisk walking speed that would be over half an hour. But into a hurricane-force headwind it could take an hour or more. He broke into a trot, although it didn't seem to increase his forward speed materially.

"How long before you're here?" Sandy pleaded. "I'm so scared. The water's rising fast."

"Fifteen minutes," he lied. "Be out by the front gate. Watch for me. Wave and yell when you see me, honey. I love you, Sandy."

"Hurry, Daddy."

He felt like uttering a prayer, beseeching the gods for help, but it was not in his character. He was on his own. Whatever strength he could summon would come from within, as it always had. Yet deep down festered the fear that this time it wouldn't be enough. An hour to reach Sandy. Another hour, maybe a bit less with the wind behind them, to get back. Not a chance. The causeway would be under water by then.

He stopped and lifted his head into the pelting, wind-blasted rain and screamed. Bellowed really. And bellowed again. He could scarcely hear himself and knew with certainty no one else could, either.

He lowered his head and resumed his trot. He wouldn't allow his daughter to die alone.

# Chapter Twenty-three

ATLANTA, GEORGIA—THE NATURAL
ENVIRONMENT TELEVISION NETWORK
LABOR DAY SUNDAY, 1115 HOURS

Obermeyer sat staring at the hurricane's radar imagery for several minutes after he hung up with Keys. He attempted to imagine what it must feel like to know the hourglass of your life had been tipped for a final time. He didn't have to dig deep to find empathy for a group of men, maybe women, too, spending the waning moments of their existence in a metal coffin, orbiting within the tight, terrible eye of a violent storm.

He could see clearly the diameter of Janet's eye growing smaller and smaller, typical of an intense hurricane. It was like seeing a hangman's noose contract, slowly choking the life from its victim. And so it must be for those in the Hurricane Hunter: watching the wall of massive, boiling clouds as it drew ever tighter, squeezing hope from their souls.

Yet that was all the crew could do, all the pilot could do as he fought to hold the crippled aircraft in smaller and smaller orbits. Wait for the noose to close. For the last drop of fuel to drain from the tanks. For the two remaining engines to sputter to a final stop. The other options offered no hope, only a quicker resolution, a quicker death. Ditch? Even in the relative calm of the eye, the plane would break apart in the massive seas churned up by the storm's fury. Try to power through the eyewall? The broken craft would be tossed about like a bug in a whirlwind, unable to exert any control at all, spiraling down into the green-gray depths of a frothing hell.

So, do you wait meekly for death to come to you? Or do you draw your sword and rush toward it in a gallant but futile Pickett's Charge? Obermeyer had no idea which he'd choose. Wait, he supposed. Wait and hope. But hope for what? In the end, one way or another, the doomed crew would have to submit to a watery grave.

He looked again at Janet's looping image, and thought he saw something. He seized the computer mouse and brought the loop to a stop. He backed it up, then moved it forward again, slowly, examining it frame by frame. He repeated the process three times. No, he hadn't imagined it. There it was. Something. He could barely bring himself to think the word. Hope.

He grabbed the telephone and punched in Rick Keys' number so fast he missed a digit. His second attempt was successful. "Rick," he said when his friend answered, "set me up with a phone patch to the Hurricane Hunter. I've got an idea." He explained.

"Worth a shot," Rick said when Obermeyer had finished. "Give me about five minutes. By the way . . . "

"Yes?"

"If this works, I'm putting you up for the Nobel Peace Prize."

"Does that come with money?"

"Five minutes." Rick hung up.


## AIRBORNE, IN THE EYE OF HURRICANE JANET
## 1130 HOURS

Walker heard Karlyn's voice over his headset: "Arly?"

"Yes?"

"The Hurricane Center would like to set up a phone patch between us and the Natural Environment Television Network in Atlanta."

"Now's not the time for something like that. What the hell are they thinking?" Exhausted and irritated, he spit the words into his mike.

"It's not for broadcast purposes. It's something else. I think it's important."

"Like what?"

"Like maybe getting us out of here."

"Really?" It seemed highly unlikely, but . . . "All right then. I've got it." He switched frequencies.


## ATLANTA, GEORGIA—THE NATURAL
## ENVIRONMENT TELEVISION NETWORK
## 1135 HOURS

Obermeyer's phone rang. He checked the caller ID and snatched the handset from its cradle.

"I've got the phone patch to the Hurricane Hunter set up," Rick Keys said. "The bird's call sign is 'Teal Three-seven.' Yours will be 'O.B. One.'"

"Cute."

Say 'over' when you're done speaking each time so the pilot will know it's his turn."

"Okay."

"Ready?"

"Ready." Obermeyer listened as Keys called the WC-130.

A few seconds later he heard the pilot's voice burrowing through a soft fuzz of static. "O. B. One, this is Teal Three-seven. How copy? Over."

"Not too loud but clear, Teal Three-seven. Can you hear me?" Obermeyer waited, but there was no response. Then he remembered. "Over," he added.

"Loud and clear, O.B. One. Understand you might be able to show us a way out of this fun house? Over."

"No guarantees, Teal Three-seven. But I think I can give you a fighting chance. Over."

"That's all I'm asking for, O.B. One. Besides, I don't think these things were designed as PT boats. Lay it on me. Over."

How, Obermeyer wondered, can a guy carry a sense of humor and sound so damn stone cold steady when he's up there tooling around inside a cat five in a broken airplane? *And I always thought fighter pilots were the cool dudes.*

"Ever hear of something called the eyewall replacement cycle? Over," Obermeyer said.

"I've heard of it. But what's that got to do with the price of tea in China? Over."

"Long dissertation coming up, Teal Three-seven. Over."

"Ready to copy. Go ahead. Over."

"In very intense hurricanes with small-diameter eyes, a second eyewall, an outer one, often forms. And it does so at the expense of the inner, or original, eyewall. That is, as the new wall begins to take shape, the old one weakens. Over the course of several hours, the new eyewall becomes dominate while the original one collapses." Obermeyer paused and took a sip of a Dr Pepper. Was the pilot understanding where this was leading?

Obermeyer continued, "Eventually, the new eyewall becomes just as nasty, and its diameter just as tight as its predecessor's. *Voila.* The eyewall replacement cycle is complete. You with me, Teal Three-seven? Over."

"What I think you're saying, O.B. One, is that the best time for a prison break is during a changing of the guard. Over."

"Exactly, Teal Three-seven." *He got it.* Obermeyer leaned in close to his computer screen to study Janet's radar returns. Then he switched to a satellite image. He wanted to make certain. What he saw confirmed his belief.

"You probably can't see it on your airborne radar," he said to the pilot, "but a new eyewall is developing just east of the one that's got you surrounded. I'd guess that within about half-an-hour this new wall will begin wrapping around the storm. That's when the old wall will show some cracks. I don't mean it'll disappear, but there'll be some breaks in it. Watch for that to happen. When you see it, turn on the afterburners and get out. Over."

"O.B. One, I wish we had some afterburners to turn on. But I'll take a fighting chance. The alternative is that we become the first submarine ever in the United States Air Force, and nobody's gonna get a medal for that."

Obermeyer heard what sounded like a long sigh waft through the hiss of the static.

"So, we'll give it a shot O.B. One. Look, if this works, I owe you a steak dinner. And a Porsche. Thanks for your help, sir. Out."

"That's okay, Teal Three-seven. Forget the steak dinner. Just get me the Porsche. I'm counting on you. Out." His voice broke as he quickly added, "And Godspeed."

He hung up the phone and turned to look at his computer monitor again, but found that his eyes had misted over. He felt a hand on his shoulder.

"You okay?" Sherrie asked.

He shook his head and stared at the floor. "Two engines and half a wing. It'll be a Model-T in a tornado." He said the words so softly he himself could barely hear them.

"What?"

"Even in a dying eyewall . . . I don't know if they can make it."

Sherrie leaned down and brushed his ear with her lips. "You gave them hope."

He stood and patted her hand. "I guess that's all any of us can ask of life, isn't it?"

She smiled. "Your eyes are red. Put some drops in them before you go back on the air."

## AIRBORNE, IN THE EYE OF HURRICANE JANET
## 1145 HOURS

The muscles in Major Walker's forearms throbbed with searing intensity, so tightly was he gripping the yoke of the damaged Hurricane Hunter. But it wasn't just his arms; his entire body had gone rigid with tension.

He forced himself to relax, with only limited success, as he spoke into his mike: "Karlyn, John, when you see that break in the eyewall our friend in Atlanta thinks is coming, give me a heading for it, then to Mayport Naval Air Station in Jacksonville. It's the closest military runway and right on the coast. Plus, we'll have a bit of a tailwind going there. Given our fuel situation and flaky engines, the sooner we get down, the better. Just so long as it's on concrete and not in the water. I don't want to press our luck anymore than I have already."

Harlow bobbed his head in tacit, almost imperceptible, agreement.

"The Navy'll have their crash equipment ready for us," Walker continued, "but if our two good engines don't go Tango-Uniform, I'll get us down in one piece." *I hope.*

Harlow interrupted. "This is Colonel Harlow," he said, speaking to the crew. "If there's a pilot in the United States Air Force who can land this banged-up bird safely, it's Major Walker. I'm proud of how you all have handled yourselves today. Now let's go one more lap, finish the job, and call it a day."

Walker switched to private. "Thanks, Colonel. Bernie, I mean." He flashed Harlow a thin, guilty smile. "I'll need your help, you know."

"Truce?"

"Truce. Sorry about the stick in the eye comment."

"Whatever motivates you."

The Hurricane Hunter orbited for fifteen more minutes, including another run through the center.

"901 millibars. Smurf's got one-sixty-five on the surface," Karlyn called out.

"Way stronger than Andrew," Walker said.

"Near Katrina at her worst," Karlyn answered. "I think she hit

902 millibars in the middle of the Gulf."

Walker kept his eyes on the radar monitor as the aircraft continued in a race track pattern, but the computer-colored returns from the eyewall remained solid red and magenta. No way out. The frisson of hope that the tropical expert from Atlanta had dangled in front of them was rapidly disappearing into the maw of Janet's increasing fury.

The minutes oozed by, as though seconds had been redefined to measure eternity. God's little joke on those facing imminent death.

"We probably should make a run for it, Bernie," Walker said finally. "Regardless."

"Better to go down fighting than just standing here, you mean?"

"Something like that."

Harlow didn't speak for awhile, then turned to face Walker. "No, the charge of the Light Brigade didn't end well. Neither did the uprising of the Warsaw-ghetto Jews against the SS in World War II. But at least they were people who didn't await their fate. They went out to meet it."

Walker could see the resignation in Harlow's eyes, hear it in his voice. *Shit. Why does it have to end this way?* "John," he said, "give me a heading to Navy Mayport. We're going."

# Chapter Twenty-four

## SEA ISLAND, GEORGIA
## LABOR DAY SUNDAY, 1145 HOURS

Shortly after crossing the bridge onto Sea Island, Alan, through the storm-riddled grayness, spotted the exclusive Cloister hotel nestled among stands of sea palms and live oaks. The five-star resort, originally built in 1928, had been torn down in 2004 and completely reconstructed. He'd been invited to play golf at The Cloister once, then afterward to a round of drinks in the hotel's famous Spanish Lounge—

*Golf?* He ceased jogging. Head down, panting, he rested his hands on his knees. Water ran off his body and water-logged clothes in cascading rivulets. Powerful gusts of wind staggered him. He lifted his head to stare at the hotel. *Golf?*

Golf carts. Not for golfers, but for guests. The course was at the northern end of the island. Here the carts were used to ferry guests to and from their rooms, suites and villas.

He turned toward The Cloister's main building and broke into a dead run. The hotel, not surprisingly, was deserted. But several golf carts sat beneath the Mediterranean-style portico. He found one with a key still in its ignition. Apparently in the rush to evacuate, the key hadn't been removed. He hoped the electric cart was fully charged, but on a busy holiday weekend it probably would be, ready to carry The Cloister's multitude of guests.

He turned the key and stepped on the accelerator pedal. The cart lurched out of the portico into the blinding rain, but at least now he was shielded from the deluge, protected by transparent plastic sheeting draped around the cart.

Back on Sea Island Drive, the little vehicle plowed through water that in spots was above its tires. Overhead, tangled tendrils of Spanish moss suspended from an honor guard of live oaks danced a furious, wind-driven jig. Alan steered with his left hand and punched in Sandy's phone number with the thumb of his right. She answered immediately.

"The water's almost up to my ankles," she cried. "I'm at the front gate, Daddy. Where are you?"

"Almost there, honey. I'm in a golf cart. Watch for me."

"A golf cart?"

"Yes. One from The Cloister."

He tried to figure out how much longer it might take him. Two and a half miles. How fast does a golf cart go? Maybe ten mph? He wasn't sure. Then there was the headwind. But the close-knit trees lining the road seemed to be acting as a partial windbreak. And the oaks themselves appeared immune from toppling. It was the sea water washing over the road that slowed his progress more than anything.

"How much longer?" Sandy said, more pleading than asking.

"Maybe ten minutes." Optimistically.

"That's not 'almost there,' Daddy."

"I know, I know. I'm doing my best, Sandy."

"Please—" She stopped talking and screamed.

"What is it? What happened?"

"A snake. A big snake in the water."

"Climb up on the gate. Get out of the water."

"I'm standing on like the bottom rung, but I can't reach the next one. It's too high. It's a big iron gate with bars, like at a castle or something."

"Don't move then. Stay still. Don't attract the snake's attention. It won't bother you. It's probably just looking for dry ground." Odds were it was a harmless reptile, but it could be a water moccasin, a cottonmouth. Poisonous.

"Okay, Daddy. It's gone."

"Hang onto the gate, kid. Cavalry's on its way."

He kept the cart's accelerator pressed to the floor. Even on the semi-sheltered roadway, the vehicle shook and jiggled in the wind. When it hit a deep puddle or rushing water, it would wallow to a virtual stop. Palm fronds and pine branches tumbled down the street, occasionally ricocheting off the cart's vinyl windshield. Here and there, roof tiles arced through the air like mortar rounds.

After about ten minutes, Alan began checking driveways along the right-hand side of the street, looking for an iron gate, looking for Sandy. He tried to call her again, to let her know he was close. All he got was an out-of-service message. Her phone had probably gotten wet.

He pressed on, sluicing along a street that had become more a salt-water river than a road. The cart struggled, its progress like a tugboat pushing a string of heavily-laden barges upstream. Alan looked into the yards of the estates that lined the road. Many homes were no longer ocean front property. They were in the ocean. He was losing a race with the rising water. It would be perhaps only thirty minutes before the entirety of Sea Island was claimed by the Atlantic.

What had the radio broadcast warned of? A twenty-five- or thirty-foot surge? If Janet hit here, Sea Island wouldn't just be covered in water, it would be ocean bottom, fifteen or twenty feet down. Like New Orleans' Ninth Ward, but with multimillion-dollar homes. Not that there would be any homes left. The surge and wind would see to that.

He'd become a true believer in the omnipotence of Janet.

*Sandy, Sandy, Sandy.*

The rain continued to rattle furiously against the plastic sheeting of the golf cart, and the cart itself groaned and jerked as Janet's winds ripped at it like a wild animal. At one point, the vehicle lifted slightly, as if it were about to become airborne.

Then he saw her. Sandy, clinging to a wrought-iron gate, her arms wrapped around its black stanchions in a bear hug, water lapping at her ankles. Behind her, a sprawling two-story estate sheltered by wind-tossed live oaks stood silent watch. The architecture of the massive home was clearly Old South. For a fleeting moment, Alan pictured Scarlett O'Hara and Rhett Butler seated on the white-columned front porch, sipping mint juleps.

But all that mattered now was Sandy. Even as he approached the gate, she refused to let go and wave in acknowledgment. She merely flashed an ephemeral, dead smile.

He immediately saw her dilemma—and his. She was trapped inside the estate grounds surrounded by a stone wall. The only way out was over the wall or through or over the gate that spanned the driveway. There was no other exit. And since Sandy couldn't scale the wall or gate, he'd have to go in after her. He left the golf cart in the street and splashed over to Sandy.

"Daddy," she said.

"Sandy." He leaned through the vertical iron bars and kissed her. "Let's get you out of here." It appeared as if the wind and rain had whipped her shirt and jeans to tatters, but he remembered they'd looked that way when she'd bought them. He stifled a tiny laugh. Her hair was plastered to her head, wound around it in an auburn tessellation. She'd never looked more attractive, more grown up.

He stepped back from her to study the situation. Raising his hand, he shielded his eyes from the driving rain and looked up. The wall was roughly ten feet high. And the next vertical crossbar on the gate was almost eight feet up. He wasn't a rock climber, so scaling the wall wasn't an option. And while he might be able reach the crossbar, he probably couldn't do much more than hang there like a monkey.

He looked back at the golf cart. At the roof of the cart. There it was, an extra—what?—five feet, six feet? He got in the cart and maneuvered it next to the wall. He was sure the roof wasn't designed to support a 180-pound man, so he mounted it gingerly. It held, and he was able to peer over the barrier once he stood. He draped his arms over the smooth pieces of slate topping the wall and pulled himself up, his feet churning madly against its slick vertical side. He must have looked like the Road Runner trying to flee Wile E. Coyote.

He flopped onto the narrow top of the barrier and lay there for a moment, looking at his next challenge. Getting down. He could jump, do a paratrooper roll in the six inches of water that covered the estate's lawn, and hope for the best, or . . .

He slid along the top of the wall on his stomach until he reached the gate. Then, using its iron frame as a handhold, he eased himself to the ground.

Sandy stared at him. "You look like Robinson Crusoe," she said.

He looked down at himself. Not only were his pants in shreds, his golf shirt was ripped, and his arms, scratched and bleeding. "Thank you, Orphan Annie."

She laughed. A good sign. She released her death grip on the bars and hugged him.

Their attention was snatched from each other by the shotgun report of a pine tree as its top sheared off, snapped by a violent gust. The roar of the gale had become incessant, urgent, punctuated by the jet-aircraft thunder of even stronger squalls. Alan had heard such angry outbursts in summer thunderstorms, but they typically were transitory. A minute or two and they were gone. But here, now, they were becoming only more strident, more powerful, more persistent.

"Can we go, Daddy?" The fear was back in Sandy's voice, the apprehension, in her eyes.

"Yes." But how? She can't climb the wall or the gate. He scanned the yard, looking for something that might help. A ladder. A lawn chair. A garbage can. Anything.

Nothing.

A small wave rippled across the sea water sloshing through the yard. In its wake, the water level didn't recede. The ocean had gained another few inches.

"Snake. Snake." Sandy was screaming, pointing.

*Another one?* Alan wheeled, looking. "Where?"

"Over there. Where the other one was."

He followed the projection of her finger to the edge of the driveway, then waded toward it. He reached down and yanked a coil of garden hose from the water. "It's not a snake, honey." He held it aloft so she could see. *It's our salvation.*

He dragged the hose to the gate and looped it over the top. It was soft and supple, more like a rope than the relatively stiff vinyl hoses found in most hardware stores. He secured one end of it underneath Sandy's arms and tossed the other end over the top of the wrought iron barrier.

Reversing the procedure he'd used to get into the estate, he clambered out. Once back on the street side, he pulled Sandy up to the point where she, too, could scramble onto the top of the wall, then lower herself onto the roof of the golf cart.

"Neat idea, Daddy," she said.

You mean a teenager actually acknowledged that a parent can be smart? "Thanks, honey. But I have one request: please, never again put me in a position where I have to act like a Green Beret to get you home after a date. Well, sort of a date."

"I like screwed up, didn't I?"

"Big time."

"Sorry."

"What were you thinking?"

She looked at her feet. "I wasn't."

"Seriously. What?"

She continued to hold her gaze on her shoes. "Like you and Mom wouldn't let me go out with a kid older than me that you like didn't know."

"You were right. Come on, get in the cart. We gotta get moving."

"Am I grounded?"

"Forever."

She looked up at him. "You said—"

"I know. I said I'd give you a pass."

"Yeah." She sounded unsure.

*Good.* They clambered into the cart, and Alan steered it back onto the street. Small white caps knifed across the surface of the water filling the road, and occasional wavelets splashed over the cart's floorboard. He wasn't certain how much longer the vehicle would continue to run. But he knew it was just a matter of time before it crapped out, its electric motor falling victim to the ocean.

He tossed another question at his daughter, unwilling to let her transgression go undiscussed. "You didn't think you could have at least mentioned to your mother or me that you'd met someone online? Opened up a dialogue with us?"

"You're like never around, Daddy." She looked directly at him.

Bingo. An arrow through the heart. Change the subject. "This kid, why'd he leave you?"

"He wasn't suppose to be driving by himself. He only has like a learner's permit. He took his parent's car without them knowing. And if they'd found out he'd done that and then brought a girl home, they like would have sent him to military school or something."

"Good idea."

"Daddy." She said it sharply.

"So he left you alone in the guest house without telling his folks when they decided it was time to evacuate?"

"I guess."

"Nice guy."

She didn't respond, but instead looked out into the rain and wrapped her arms around herself.

He handed her his phone. "Call your mother. Tell her we're on our way. She and Lee and a friend are waiting for us."

She tried, but got no response. "Your phone's all wet," she said.

They passed The Cloister, crossed the short bridge, and reached the guardhouse. Alan halted the cart. He examined the causeway that lay ahead. River and marsh water, topped by wind-ripped foam and heaving gray swells, washed over the raised passage. Not good. Thick, pelting rain flew horizontally to the ground giving the air an almost gelatinous consistency. The drops hurled themselves against the windshield and plastic sheeting of the cart with savage intensity.

"What's the matter, Daddy?"

Alan leaned forward, trying to gauge the depth of the water flooding across the causeway. It wouldn't take much to turn the cart into a pontoon boat. And the wind would be much stronger on the exposed roadway. Even where they sat, the cart shook constantly, an inanimate object with Parkinson's disease. On the causeway, there might be nothing to prevent it from lift off.

"Just studying the lay of the land, sweetheart," he answered. Were Trish and Pete still waiting for them? His orders had been to leave if water topped the road. Now he felt ambivalent about that command.

"Will we be okay?" Sandy asked.

Alan detected a nascent tremor in her voice. "We'll be fine," he said. There's a time for dads to skirt the truth.

He pressed the accelerator and the cart surged through the standing water onto the causeway. The wheels remained in contact with the pavement. But the vehicle slowed in the rising tide of river, marsh and sea water. Powerful gusts herded the cart toward the left side of the raised road.

Alan cranked the steering wheel hard right, attempting to counter the force of the wind. But it was a mistake. A violent gust speared the cart, catching it abeam and flipping it onto its side. In an instant, Alan was in the water overflowing the road, Sandy sprawling on top of him. They were still in the cart, but it was sliding toward the edge of the causeway.

He wrapped his arms around Sandy. "Don't move," he said. "Wait until the cart stops." If it stops. There were no guardrails. "We'll get out then." Her body heaved against his in great, inaudible sobs. Unarticulated terror.

The swirling wind lulled. The little vehicle stopped moving. But probably not for long. Alan scrambled to his feet, lifting Sandy with him. The right side of the cart was now its roof. He punched the plastic sheeting out of the way and lifted his head into the gale. It was virtually impossible to catch his breath.

He ducked back into the shelter of the cart. "Okay, honey, I'm going to climb out. Then I'll help you out. We'll have to go the rest of the way on foot."

Sandy shook her head. "I can't, Daddy, I can't. I'm so scared. We're going to drown or get blown away or something."

"No. Listen. We won't. We will if we stay here. But if we get out, you can hang onto me. We'll keep our backs to the wind, crouch down, and side step, like crabs, along the edge of the causeway. Wrap your hands around my belt. Okay, G. I. Jane?"

She nodded. But her chest still rose and fell in soft, silent whimpers.

The hammering wind and powerful current fastened Alan and his daughter to the causeway's surface like insects pinned to an entomologist's display box. Alan, even in a crouch, fought to maintain his balance as he and Sandy edged sideways through the rising water. Almost blinded by the brutal, wind-propelled rain, he couldn't yet see the end of the causeway. He had no way of knowing if safety awaited them there. Or if following his behest, Trish and Pete had given them up for lost, and left. If they had, this would end very badly for Sandy and him. If they hadn't, it would end, ironically, very badly for everyone.

He lifted his head to appeal to a higher power. But he couldn't find the words, couldn't summon up the belief, couldn't surrender his sovereignty.

He looked down at his daughter. "We're almost there," he lied. He had to yell to be heard over the shriek of the wind.

But it wasn't just howling that assaulted his ears. It was something else, something mingled with the gale. Rushing, surging, rippling. He looked behind him. What used to be a marsh had become a salt water bay. Over it, a massive gray-green swell rolled toward them, rising from the dark water like a sea serpent of yore, a primordial monster come aborning.

He grabbed Sandy with both arms. Whatever happened, he wasn't going to let go of her. "Take a deep breath," he screamed.

Then the swell was upon them, over them, submerging them, pounding them, rolling them, spinning them. He refused to release Sandy. The swell passed and they bobbed to the surface, but no longer were they on the causeway.

They were in the marsh, the ocean, whatever the hell it was now. Alan flung off his shoes. He held Sandy to his chest and kicked frantically, trying to propel himself back to the road. Sandy was gagging, spitting salt water in his face. He only guessed he was going in the right direction. He kicked harder. Another swell washed over them. A surge of stinging water rammed its way down his throat. He felt himself losing his grip on his daughter. On everything.

"Oh, no, not this way," he whispered.

# Chapter Twenty-five

## AIRBORNE, IN THE EYE OF HURRICANE JANET
## LABOR DAY SUNDAY, 1235 HOURS

"Guys. Northwest quadrant. Look." It was Karlyn.

Walker glanced at his radar monitor. The imagery of the eyewall's northwest side had changed color, albeit across a very tiny arc. Where earlier there had been only vermilions and purples, now oranges and yellows appeared.

"It's weakening," Karlyn said.

Walker looked out at the eyewall. Against the white bastion of towering clouds that imprisoned them, he spotted a thin, gray crevasse. A gate in the ramparts of the stadium. He watched for half a minute as it rotated with the wall, folding, parting, reopening, changing shape. He studied the radar imagery again. The weakness was still there. A crack in the wall teasing them to flee. "Give me a heading, nav," he said.

"Three-two-two," Major Best answered.

"Jail break time," Walker said into the intercom. "Hang on."

He and Harlow banked the Hurricane Hunter toward the eyewall and hurtled toward the sliver of hope, the crew's fate tethered to the judgment of a weathercaster in Atlanta.

Again, one of the engines skipped a beat. Walker remembered a line in the prayer he couldn't find the words to earlier; he said it out loud. "Lead us not into temptation, but deliver us from evil."

"Amen," Harlow responded.

The plane plunged into blackness.

Again, as earlier when they'd flown through the eyewall, squalls hammered the Hurricane Hunter with relentless, blinding sheets of water. The aircraft shook constantly, the rattling of the fuselage challenging the automatic-weapon stutter of the rain.

Walker fixed his gaze on the heads-up display, making sure he and Harlow kept the craft straight and level. "Not so bad as before," he said to Harlow.

"Well, that trip set the bar pretty damn high."

Walker allowed himself a fleeting chuckle, the first in hours.

"John, got a vector for me to Mayport?" he asked.

"As soon as we clear the eyewall, sir, turn to two-four-eight. We should be in the good hands of our swabbie brothers in a little over half an hour."

"Thanks, John. Two-four-eight it is. Bernie, call Mayport and Jacksonville Center. Let 'em know we broke out of prison and are inbound. Tell the Navy guys the landing might not be a grease job."

"Arly." It was Karlyn's voice, tinged in panic.

"What?"

"That second eyewall, the new one the hurricane forecaster said was forming on the east side of Janet."

"Yes?"

"Look on your radar monitor."

Walker saw it instantly. The new eyewall had wrapped around the northern side of Janet's eye, outside the original eyewall, and was building toward the southwest, directly in their path. Deep orange and red returns already lit up the monitor. As he watched, they abruptly exited the old eyewall. The rain ceased and the sky lightened. The Hurricane Hunter stopped vibrating and settled into a smooth cruise. Walker knew it would last for only a minute or two.

He listened intently to the roar of the two functioning turboprops and scanned the engine readouts. Everything sounded and looked normal. He turned to Harlow, but didn't have to ask the question. Harlow merely nodded.

"Sorry, folks," Walker said into his mike. "We're gonna have to do this again. The new eyewall is wrapping around the hurricane pretty fast, so we've no choice but to fly through it. We're way past the point of no return. But engines one and two seem to be holding out, so I think we've got an excellent chance. Colonel Harlow and I will do everything we can to get us down safely."

Walker, out of habit, tightened his safety harness, although he already was firmly belted in. The straps bit into his shoulders as though punishing him for his disingenuousness. But there was no point in burdening the crew with his own fears, with what he knew: the two still-functioning engines were unlikely to make it through yet another penetration, this time of a healthy and strengthening eyewall.

The only visual cue Walker had that the Hurricane Hunter was nearing the replacement eyewall was deepening darkness: gray morphing to black. The aircraft was still in smooth air, but a glance at the radar suggested it had only seconds before it was swallowed by the fury ahead.

Walker began a silent countdown: Ten, nine, eight—

A pulse of lightning exploded around the plane. In that millisecond of illumination, Walker spotted, dead ahead, the cauliflowered exterior of a massive cumulonimbus—a soldier in the army of the new eyewall—boiling toward the upper reaches of the atmosphere. Walker glanced at Harlow, Harlow at him.

Harlow forced a sad smile. "'Into the jaws of death, into the mouth of hell, rode the six—'"

"Bernie, please. Enough with Tennyson," Walker snapped.

The Hurricane Hunter, for the second time within minutes, slammed into a dark palisade of slashing rain and murderous winds. The plane lifted sharply, a gut-wrenching rise, and Walker was slammed downward into his seat. Then, just as quickly, an unseen hand yanked him upward against the restraints of his harness. The plane fell, and once again an engine sputtered.

Walker and Harlow fought to bring the nose of the craft up, but at least one of the two remaining turboprops wasn't up to the job. Walker saw the horsepower reading plunge on number two. The WC-130, now barely flyable, sank toward the ocean, rocking from side to side as if it were a fishing trawler taking heavy beam seas.

"Not good, Bernie," Walker said, stating the obvious.

"If we can get out of this shit into smooth air, we should be okay."

"Don't know. Maybe. I think that was number two sputtering before. Some kind of fuel flow or contamination problem. If this beating doesn't stop, it's gonna give up the ghost for good."

As if on cue, it did. Another heavy-duty shudder rippled through the aircraft, and the engine stopped.

"Restart," Walker yelled. They were below 500 feet and sinking.

"Got it," Harlow responded.

Number two roared to life, coughed, then caught solidly. But Walker knew it had one foot in the grave.

Abruptly, the aircraft broke out of the clouds and the turbulence relented. Walker looked down. They were skimming over the ocean just a few hundred feet below. The seas were massive, chaotic. Foam and spray swirled through the air, splattering across the plane's windshield. Small speckles of crusted salt appeared on the glass.

"Let's try to gain some altitude before we lose number two for good," Walker said.

The plane rose, but the climb was agonizingly slow. They hit another squall. A powerful burst of wind got underneath the right wing and tossed the aircraft into a steep left-hand bank. Again the plane rolled toward the ocean. And again the engine coughed and sputtered.

"This isn't working," Walker said after they once more had leveled the plane and managed to climb a bit. "I don't think we can make it to Mayport. Two isn't gonna last."

"Yeah, but what are our options?"

"There's a 5400-foot runway on St. Simons Island that's used by small planes and corporate jets. It's plenty of runway for us. And we can be there in fifteen or twenty minutes."

"No ground control approach or crash equipment, though."

"Beggars and crippled Hurricane Hunters can't be choosers."

Harlow shook his head slowly. "A barrier island in the face of a cat five?"

The squadron commander had a point. Given St. Simons appeared to be a sacrificial lamb tied to a stake in the path of Janet, what would be their odds of survival even if they managed to land? Not good, but . . .

"The less time we're in the air, and the more time we're on solid ground, the better I like our chances," Walker said, "wherever."

"Well, you're the aircraft commander."

Harlow's way of agreeing, Walker decided. "John," he said, "change of plans. We gotta get this bird down. Give me a course to St. Simons Island, McKinnon Airport."

"Roger that," Major Best responded.

"We'll land on oh-four into the wind," Walker said. "Straight-in approach, no go around, cuz I don't think we're gonna have two engines much longer. Besides, this thing is a real load to handle."

"You can do it, sir, I know you can."

"Say a prayer."

"Any particular one?"

Walker twisted in his seat and looked back at his navigator. "One that works."

Best smiled weakly and nodded. "Not up to me, Arly."

Walker shrugged and turned away. Probably not. "Weather," he said, "can you get me an observation out of McKinnon? I think they have an automated station."

"Yes, sir," Karlyn said.

Walker addressed Harlow: "Let Jacksonville and Mayport know we're altering course, that we're going to be vacationing on St. Simons for awhile."

"Got it," Harlow responded.

"Arly," Karlyn cut in, "the winds on St. Simons are zero-six-zero gusting to 92 mph."

"Why me, Lord?" Walker said softly. His heart rate accelerated so quickly it felt as if a bottle rocket had been strapped to it.

"About 30 mph of cross wind," Harlow said after a quick calculation.

"Think we can land in that?"

"With one and half engines, a broken wing and muscle-bound hydraulics?"

"I was hoping for two engines," Walker said.

"Okay, two engines, et cetera."

"Piece of cake."

"I like your attitude, boy. You still gonna resign from the Reserve?"

"Ask me after we land." *Assuming we land. And assuming we land in one piece, more or less.* Walker's heart battered against the interior of his chest in a terrified staccato. He was certain everyone in the aircraft could hear it over their headsets.

*It's just another training exercise. It's just another training exercise.* He repeated the words to himself over and over.

# Chapter Twenty-six

## SEA ISLAND, GEORGIA
## LABOR DAY SUNDAY, 1240 HOURS

Alan Grant spit out a mouthful of acrid water, then coughed up a small bucketful. He felt his daughter trying to keep his head above water. Now she was acting as his savior, not he as hers.

"Daddy, you okay? We're drifting away from the road. Kick your legs." She was kicking hers, trying to push him with one arm, lifting his head with the other.

His muscles seemed to have given up, been sucked of their energy. He tried to kick, but he might as well have been a rag doll, so lame was the attempt. The day's travails had taken their toll. Too much, even for a young man. "Go," he said to Sandy, "let go of me. Swim for the causeway. I'll be right behind you." He knew he wouldn't.

White streamers of sea foam zig-zagged across the surface of the water. Above the surface, sheets of rain flew parallel to roiling whitecaps. In the middle distance, Alan could barely discern an object—a log?—drifting in the storm-tossed marsh. He tracked it closely until he could see clearly what it was: the corrugated silhouette of an alligator's head and back. A real-life Loch Ness monster. A dark eye swiveled in his direction.

"Go," he yelled at Sandy.

"Dad—"

"Right behind you," he said.

She released him and dog-paddled away, but then stopped and looked back. Her eyes said she knew what was going on. "Come on, Daddy."

He took a couple of ineffectual strokes with his arms, but only drifted farther away from her.

She headed back for him.

"No, Sandy, no." Another large swell rose behind her.

But there was something else, too, something lining out over the crest of the swell. It splashed down in the water beside him. A rope. From the direction of the causeway.

Sandy rose above him as the swell lifted her. Then he was above her. He flailed for the rope. Clutched it, but was unable to do anything else. Sandy swam to him, to the rope and wound it around his waist. Then she gripped its loose end.

Alan turned and looked for the alligator but couldn't spot it. Had it continued on its way, or was it stalking them? Probably, at the moment, it was more interested in saving itself than finding dinner.

The rope snapped taught and, like a boat battling its way upstream, he and Sandy began to furrow through the water toward the causeway. He blinked his eyes repeatedly, trying to rid them of the stinging salt water that had invaded them. Eventually he was able make out a stout form on the passageway, determinedly placing one arm in front of the other, leaning back, pulling, then performing the process over and over.

It seemed an eternity before they reached the raised roadway, but it probably was only a few minutes. Pete reached down and, one by one, lifted them out of the water. Alan sprawled into the saltwater coursing over the road. It sloshed into his mouth as fast as he could spit it out.

Pete knelt and lifted him. "Some friggin' hero you are," he said.

"Yeah," was all Alan could manage.

Pete, supporting Alan with his left arm, grasped Sandy's hand with his right. "Come on, little lady," he said. "Your mother's waiting for us."

"Is she mad?" Sandy asked.

"No, darlin', she's not mad. She'll be happy to see you. By the way, I'm Pete."

"I'm Sandy. Did Mom send you?"

"Pete's been helping us, Sandy," Alan explained. Even to him, his voice sounded tired and wasted. "We had some car problems."

"I saw you and Sandy on the causeway," Pete said. "I thought you were gonna make it. Then the swell came and swept you into the drink. That's when I grabbed a rope from the truck and went into my Coast Guard rescue mode."

"You must be like a guardian angel or something," Sandy said.

Pete nodded. "Maybe."

"Do you believe in that stuff?" Alan said. He slurred his words. Exhaustion.

"What stuff?" Pete asked. He released Sandy's hand as they neared the pickup.

"Guardian angels," Alan whispered.

Pete shrugged. "Ask me at the end of the day if we're still alive."

Alan saw Trish and Lee, sheltered behind the open doors of the truck, peering toward the causeway like visitors at a prison waiting for a glimpse of their loved ones. Trish waved. But Alan was too weak to lift his arm and return the greeting. Sandy broke from Pete and splashed toward her mother.

Pete leaned close to Alan's ear. "Before we get back to the truck, I gotta tell you, just between you and me, we're in deep shit here. I don't know if we can get off the island now. A lot of the roads are probably under water. And those that aren't may be blocked by fallen trees or power lines. If you're a praying man, Mr. Grant, now's the time to let 'er rip." Pete steadied Alan, withdrew his arm, then strode toward the truck.

Alan, silent, stared after him. Rain swirled around him in a tight, vicious whirlpool, smacking into his face with audible fury.


**With everyone in the** truck, Pete sped back over Sea Island Road toward the intersection with Frederica. There, he slowed. Tree limbs, palm leaves and pieces of shattered signs, driven by the battering wind, slithered along the wet street. Inoperative traffic lights danced a violent jig on dangling, overhead lines. There were no other vehicles in sight. No evidence of law enforcement.

Alan and Trish sat next to Pete in the cab of the truck. Lee and Sandy were ensconced under the tarp in back, even though Lee had protested loudly that putting his sister in with him was like forcing him to ride with "a wet dog."

"I'm gonna continue west on Sea Island Road instead of turning south on Frederica," Pete said. "The road runs out over another marsh, so there's less chance we'll encounter downed trees or power lines."

"What about flooding?" Alan asked.

"I think we'll be okay over the marsh," Pete answered. "The road's built up slightly higher than the one to Sea Island. After that, I'm not sure. There are some low spots closer to the Torras Causeway, the one leading back to the mainland."

"And the wind?"

"We'll just have to take our chances crossing the marsh. There aren't any good choices left, partner, only ones that aren't as bad as others."

Pete drove slowly along the road, easing out over the marsh.

"It looks like it's letting up a bit," Trish said as the both the wind and rain relented slightly.

"I wouldn't count on it lasting," Pete answered. "From what I know about hurricanes, we're probably just in between rainbands. The next arc of squalls could be even rougher."

"Thanks for giving me hope," she muttered.

Alan squeezed her hand. "We'll make it," he said.

She squeezed back in response, but didn't verbally acknowledge his hollow reassurance.

At the end of the marsh, the road turned left, south, and led into an area studded with trees. They'd driven only a short distance when Pete brought the truck to a stop. He didn't have to say anything. They all saw it. A massive loblolly pine laying in repose across the two-lane highway.

"Well, shit on a stick," Pete finally blurted out. He turned the truck around and backtracked over the marsh to the intersection with Frederica. There he turned south. "We'll try it this way," he said.

If Pete were nearing panic, Alan couldn't detect it in his voice. But he thought the guy should be. As he recalled, the only through roads leading south to where they could reach the causeway were Sea Island and Frederica. In other words, there were no escape options left after Frederica.

Within less than a minute, even that option seemed to evaporate as another fallen pine blocked their way. "I can get by this," Pete said. He slowed the truck to a few miles per hour and nosed around—in truth, partially through—the crown of the tree along the extreme right edge of the road. Geysers of dirt and gravel shot out from beneath the rear of the truck as it bulldozed its way back onto Frederica.

Another minute or two brought them to the intersection where Alan earlier had had the verbal run-in with the police officer. No police were around now. The area was deserted.

Alan's chest tightened as he looked to the right along Demere Road, the most direct route to the Torras Causeway. A downed utility pole and a spray of electrical sparks made it clear they weren't going that way.

"I'm running out of ideas here, folks," Pete said. This time Alan caught the slightest bit of a hitch in his words.

"So what's left?" Alan asked.

"Keep pressing south," Pete said, "to Kings Way. But Kings Way is low and there are lots of trees. I'm not optimistic, but we'll take a look."

They drove south, past McKinnon Airport on their left, to Kings Way. What they saw there was not rewarding. Water, perhaps two feet deep in spots, eddied over the road.

"Oh, no. Oh, no," Trish cried.

Alan and Pete exchanged a glance. Alan could see in that brief moment, in Pete's eyes, how dire their situation had become.

Pete leaned forward and rested his forehead on the steering wheel. When he spoke, his words were muffled. "The highest ground around is probably the airport. I suggest we go there. We might be able to find shelter in the operations building." His voice trailed off. "Maybe," he added.

Alan nodded, unable to speak. Trish's body trembled against his.

Pete pulled the pickup into McKinnon Airport a few minutes later. Though the rain came only in fits and starts now, the wind remained relentless, shaking the truck as though it were a toy in the fist of a toddler. Palms and pines bent toward the ground at acute angles, their tops seesawing wildly back and forth. With each toss they launched volleys of fronds and branches into the mizzling rain. Debris—chunks of wood, metal and plastic—tumbled and skittered across the runway. Overhead, ragged scud flew at near-NASCAR speeds.

Alan sniffed the air.

"What?" Trish said.

"Nothing," he answered. He thought he'd smelled fuel oil mingling with the salt-tinged mist, but wasn't sure. Even if he were, he had no idea where the odor might be coming from. A leaky fuel bladder at the airport? Or from someplace farther away, such as a service station or auto repair shop? It didn't matter, at least now.

"I don't suppose there'd be any planes around, waiting for the last moment to escape," Alan said as Pete maneuvered the truck next to the operations building, a single story structure with a gray-white tabby exterior. Dozens of vertical antennae sprouted from its roof, giving it the look of a scraggly wheat field.

"Doubt it," Pete said. "The airport's for private aircraft only. No commercial traffic. People fly Cessnas and Beeches or maybe a charter in for a weekend. Small jets, turboprops, stuff like that. I'm sure everybody beat feet pretty fast this morning."

The runway was separated from the airport's parking lot by a chain link fence. Behind the fence, in the shelter of a hangar, Alan saw several fuel trucks, but no aircraft.

Pete parked the Ford and ran to the front door of the operations building. He pushed and tugged, but it was obviously locked. He returned to the truck and pointed east, toward the Atlantic. "Another rainband," he said.

Alan looked. The sky over the ocean had turned pitch-black. The wind seemed to be gathering its forces for a renewed, even more furious assault. "We'd better hunker down someplace," he said.

"I'll move to the lee of the building," Pete said. "That'll give us a little shelter."

"What if the water comes up?" Trish asked. "All the way."

Alan looked at Pete. "How high are we here?"

Pete shrugged. "I don't know, twenty, twenty-five feet maybe."

"And if there's a thirty-foot surge?" Trish said, her voice sounding tiny, helpless.

Neither man answered.

# Chapter Twenty-seven

## AIRBORNE, EN ROUTE TO ST. SIMONS ISLAND, GEORGIA
## LABOR DAY SUNDAY, 1255 HOURS

Still deep in the clouds and being buffeted by downpours and bruising winds, Walker, with Harlow's help, fought to bring the Hurricane Hunter to a course he thought would line up with the northeast-southwest runway at McKinnon Airport. With no ground control approach, it was all dead reckoning as long as he couldn't see the surface. He knew in weather like this they wouldn't break out of the clouds until they were just a few hundred feet off the deck.

At least landing into the wind, the 30-mph cross component notwithstanding, their ground speed would be so slow they might even survive a crash. *Every cloud has its silver lining.*

The balky engine stuttered once, twice, then regained its composure. Just a couple more minutes, Walker urged, just a couple. He dipped the right wing into the wind so a gust wouldn't slither underneath and toss the plane into a violent roll as they neared the ground.

"See anything?" he asked Harlow.

"Nothing."

Rain thundered against the windshield, the wipers helpless to deter the onslaught. Walker strained forward, looking for a break in the leaden world that engulfed them. He needed a glimpse of the ocean, a marsh, a road. Something. A marker of any kind to get his bearings.

*Please, God, don't let me overshoot.*

"There, there," Harlow yelled, taking one hand off the yoke and pointing out the windshield.

Dead ahead, Walker saw it. A gray thread against a gray landscape. The runway. He drifted the Hurricane Hunter a little to the left, then crabbed it into the wind. To someone on the ground it would look as if the plane were cocked slightly sideways relative to the runway. Just before touchdown, he'd straighten it out.

He came in low, a couple of hundred feet above a frothing inlet, then over a pier being smashed into kindling by huge waves, then a golf course awash in sea water. All in slow motion, so strong was the headwind.

Harlow, unbidden, lowered the flaps, dropped the landing gear and switched on the landing lights. Walker continued to wrestle with the yoke in a grim, exhausting battle. His arms had become almost as unresponsive as the aircraft itself.

The closer to the surface they got, the more severe became the turbulence. The plane rocked from side to side in head-snapping lurches as the wind, deflected by trees and buildings, churned over the ground in violent loops and swirls.

The last few seconds would be the most dangerous.

The plane skimmed over a Cyclone fence, the outer boundary of the airport.


## ST. SIMONS ISLAND, GEORGIA
## 1305 HOURS

Lee hammered on the window of the pickup truck's cab. "What's that, Dad, what's that?" He was on his knees in the bed of the truck, gesturing at the horizon, just beyond the south end of the runway. He'd pitched the tarp off his body and was attempting to get to his feet. Sandy, still crouched in the bed, yanked the tarp even tighter around herself.

Alan stepped from the cab and looked in the direction Lee was pointing. He saw nothing. The rain had increased markedly again and came in thunderous, wind-propelled deluges. Using his hands, he shielded his eyes from the blinding precipitation. "Where, son?"

"There, Dad. It looks like a big balloon or blimp or something."

Alan squinted. He still couldn't make out anything.

"Look down the runway," Lee insisted. "Then above it, but farther."

Something loomed out of the scudding, rain-draped overcast like an ocean liner emerging from a fog bank.

"Oh, yeah. Yeah. Jesus. I don't believe it. Pete, look at this," Alan yelled. "What the hell's going on?"

Pete climbed from the truck and looked down the runway. "Good God. It looks like an airplane trying to land. That's impossible."

Trish followed Pete into the swirling downpour, clinging to the truck in an attempt to remain upright as the wind snatched and clutched at her.

Sandy popped her head out from underneath the tarpaulin. "What's happening?" she asked.

"Looks like a plane trying to land," Alan said.

"Impossible," Pete repeated.

"Maybe it's coming for us," Lee suggested.

"Nobody knows we're here," Alan said.

"Is it a bomber, Dad?" Lee was getting excited.

"No." Alan focused on the plane, trying to see what it was. Big. Bulky. High-winged. A huge vertical tail. Some kind of a cargo carrier. Military perhaps. What on earth was it doing here?

It moved at an improbably slow speed. Landing lights ablaze, it seemed suspended just beyond the end of the runway. Alan wondered why it didn't stall. Then he realized it was battling a headwind probably almost as fast as its landing speed. He guessed the plane's airspeed was over 100 mph, but relative to the ground, it wasn't moving much faster than a family out for a Sunday drive.

The craft, angled into the wind, pointed directly at where he and the others stood. But somehow it managed to stay lined up with the runway. Alan guessed that if the wind had been more perpendicular to the runway, the plane probably wouldn't have had a prayer. In all likelihood, it didn't anyhow.

He watched transfixed as the craft rocked violently from side to side, appearing virtually uncontrollable, its right wing dipped lower than its left. Both flexed wildly up and down, almost flapping, as if they belonged to a bird. But the right wing remained tilted toward the ground in what appeared to be a dangerous configuration.

As the airplane drew nearer, Alan saw why, though he didn't understand the physics. The props on the lowered wing weren't turning, and the tip of the wing appeared to have been sheared away. The aircraft was badly wounded. McKinnon was obviously its "any old port in a storm."

"Is it gonna crash, Dad?" Lee was unable to hide the youthful excitement in his voice.

"This isn't a video game or TV show. There're real people in that airplane. They're fighting for their lives."

"Oh." Barely disguised disappointment.

Even though the gunmetal gray of the airplane's fuselage blended into the sheeting rain, Alan could make out writing on the craft's side as it dropped to within a few yards of the runway: U. S. AIR FORCE. Big, black letters.

"It's a military plane," he said.

"Wonder what the heck they were doing flying through a hurricane," Pete said.

"Bad navigation? Bad weather forecast? Bad luck? I don't know," Alan answered.

"Well, whatever. At least we aren't going to be here alone," Pete said.

"Yeah," responded Alan. "A few seconds, they'll be down, one way or another. That pilot's about to earn a medal or a eulogy."

Alan had a flash of admiration—and a burning sense of empathy—for the pilot, or maybe pilots, trying to land the plane. Surely this was something they never had trained for. You either did it or you didn't. Skill? Certainly. Luck? A lot. Guts? Mostly.

The plane's wheels dropped to within a foot or two of the runway. It was like watching a landing in slow motion as the craft continued to struggle against hyper-hurricane-force gusts. Even though the plane was within a couple of hundred yards of them, Alan still couldn't hear its engines. The only sound was the thunder of the wind.

Almost down, the plane flared and veered, the pilot attempting to align the wheels with the runway. Its right wing remained low, barely off the ground. The rear wheels of the plane's broad landing gear channeled through pooled water on the surface, spewing out a huge rooster tail.

Alan held his breath. Now. Life or death. This moment.

It happened in a nanosecond. Trish screamed. Pete said, "Oh, shit."

A furious rush of wind hammered the right wing into the runway. The plane, responding to the lift generated by the operating props on the left wing, turned and rose into the air like a fat, pirouetting pole vaulter. Its right wing dug into the ground but couldn't take the force and snapped.

The aircraft slammed back onto the runway and spun sideways, its tires exploding soundlessly as it careened toward the edge of the landing strip. It canted over, collapsing onto its intact wing. The props stopped turning. Trails of sparks arced from the beneath the plane's fuselage as it continued its slow, now almost-lazy, skid. The sound of metal on asphalt finally overcame the wail of the wind.

Then it was over. The aircraft, now virtually perpendicular to the runway, came to rest on a grassy area overlooking Frederica Road. On its towering tail, the vertical stabilizer, was a blue banner with white lettering. HURRICANE HUNTERS. Alan pointed at it. "That explains a lot," he said.

"Yeah," Pete responded, "I guess they found one."

"Let's go," Alan said. "The crew might need help." Ignoring his fatigue, he started toward the chain link fence.

"Right behind you," Pete said.

The two men clambered over the fence and dashed toward the aircraft. The gale quartered in on them from the right, at times almost knocking them off their feet.

If the gusts had been behind him, Alan imagined he could have run a 100-meter dash in five seconds. He bent low and used his forearm to shield his face from the thick curtains of rain that swept across the runway.

The plane, resting on its left wing, was mired in mud and grass. Thin tendrils of smoke wormed out from underneath the aircraft. Alan saw no evidence of fire, so guessed the smoke was the result of the metal-on-asphalt friction as the plane slid down the runway.

He and Pete scurried underneath the left wing of the craft, maneuvering between the inert inboard prop and the fuselage. They brushed by a small door in the lower half of the fuselage and reached the front of the aircraft. There, sheltered from the fierce wind by the body of the Hurricane Hunter, Alan looked up at the cockpit.

He saw a surprised-looking face staring down at him. Whoever it was, waved. Alan managed a weak wave back. The face disappeared. Shortly thereafter, the small door opened. It was hinged at its bottom, not its side, and converted into a short set of steps as it touched down on the soggy grass.

A man in a flight suit appeared at the top of the steps. He held a small piece of cloth against his mouth, but pulled it away revealing a bloody gash in his upper lip. "I'm Major Arlen Walker, United States Air Force," he said. "I don't suppose you guys are the ground crew here." He pushed the cloth—it looked like a chunk of gauze—back against his lip.

Alan shook his head. "Sorry to disappoint you, Major, but we just happened to be passing by. I'm Alan Grant. This is Pete Pirwoski." He gestured at Pete.

The major removed the cloth again. "Just happened to be passing by?"

"Well ... we kind of got trapped here. We had some problems and couldn't get off the island before all the roads flooded."

"So then. It appears we're all in the same boat. No pun intended. But that's about all this bird is now, I suppose. Welcome aboard." He motioned Alan and Pete up the steps, and once more placed the gauze against his lip.

"Sir," Alan said, "there are more of us." His words were torn away by a heavy blast of wind that curled over the top of the aircraft.

"What?" Walker leaned his head out the door.

"My family's here," Alan said. He pointed across the runway. "My wife, daughter and son."

Walker shrugged. "Better go get them then," he said. "We've got a cat five hurricane bearing down on us." He raised his voice to be heard over the yowl of the wind.

More of the plane's crew, including a female, appeared behind Walker. They all wore looks of slight disbelief, staring at Alan and Pete as if having a close encounter of the third kind.

Alan turned to Pete. "Stay here. I'll go back."

"No. I'm coming, too. You'll need help with Lee and Sandy."

Alan decided not to waste time arguing. Besides, he was bone tired. He probably did need Pete's help. "We'll be right back, Major," he said.

He and Pete turned, hunched down, and struggled toward the truck, retracing their steps across the rain-slicked runway. From somewhere on the other side of Frederica, the loud pop of a tree or pole snapping challenged the roar of the wind. On its heels came the faint sound of shattering glass and the wail of a burglar alarm.

"There's a little shopping center over there," Pete said, explaining.

Alan nodded, then inclined his head toward the airplane. "You think we're going to be safe in that thing?"

Pete leaned close to Alan. "From what I've read and heard about cat fives, not much survives a direct hit by them. If you've ever seen pictures from the Mississippi Gulf Coast after Camille, all you saw were foundations. And the few trees left standing: snapped in two and stripped bare. So, I figure if we've got a chance, it's gonna be in something designed to fly through hurricanes."

Alan looked back at the wrecked Hurricane Hunter. "Yeah, but I don't think it's fared too well so far."

# Chapter Twenty-eight

## ST. SIMONS ISLAND, GEORGIA
## LABOR DAY SUNDAY, 1315 HOURS

Karlyn handed Walker a fresh piece of gauze for his lip. "That's probably going to need stitches," she said, looking at his mouth intently, "but keep pressure on it and that should stop the bleeding."

"Yes, nurse."

"What happened?" she asked.

They were standing in the cockpit and Walker pointed at the yoke. "Banged my face on that when we tried to do a cartwheel down the runway."

Major Best, joined them, the beginning of a grin frozen on his face. He held up a sheet of paper with a large bold "8" written on it. "I would have given the landing a ten, sir," he said, "but I had to subtract style points."

Harlow entered the conversation, attempting futilely to suppress a smirk. He, too, bore a sheet of paper and extended it toward Walker. "On the contrary," the colonel said, "I gave the effort a ten. I thought the major's touchdown was a real crowd pleaser."

They all laughed, Walker loudest of all. They were alive. Free of the specter of death that had stalked them for the past five hours. Relieved of the hopelessness and fear that had wrapped around them in Janet's eye. Unburdened from the doubts and recriminations that had burrowed into their psyches.

They'd been able to spit in the eye of the Grim Reaper, pull down his pants, and walk away—or in this case, fly away—chuckling.

"How're the others?" Walker asked.

"Louie smacked his head against the dropsonde console," Karlyn said. "Got a nice gash, but he'll be okay. Van's fine, but the newspaper guy is barfing up his guts again."

"Good Lord. I didn't think there'd be anything left after his first eruption. Make sure he stays hydrated."

"Major, with all due respect, I'm not going back there," Karlyn said. "It smells like an outhouse. And besides, I'm not a nurse."

"I'll check on him," Harlow said. He patted Walker on the back before he started down the ladder toward the rear of the aircraft. "Arly, if we had some champagne, I'd break it out now."

"Thank you, sir. But the day isn't done, is it?"

The words seemed to yank Harlow back into the reality of their plight. Whatever lightheartedness he'd projected seconds ago abruptly disappeared. His chiseled ebony features folded into a frown. He stepped back up onto the flight deck. "So what's the bottom line on our situation here?" he asked Karlyn. "Did we just step out of a frying pan into a grease fire?"

Karlyn looked away from Harlow, out the cockpit windshield. "The Swiss Family Robinson is approaching," she said quietly, ignoring the squadron commander's question.

"Karlyn?"

"Sir?"

"Janet. The no bull-shit bottom line?"

She continued to stare out the windshield, as though avoiding eye contact with Harlow might somehow soften the impact of her answer. "We're right in the path of the damn thing," she said. "Extrapolating its track brings the eye over us in about four hours."

"And the last winds?"

"One sixty-five."

"And going up?"

"Yes."

"There isn't going to be much left here, is there?"

"No, sir."

"So we haven't stepped into a grease fire then. More like an out-of-control forest fire." Harlow's voice was even, well modulated, but Walker caught a clear note of tension in it.

"I'm afraid so," Karlyn said. She had trouble getting the words out.

"So you're right, Arly," Harlow said, "the day isn't done." He descended the ladder.

Walker turned to Karlyn. "You okay?"

She tilted her head back and inhaled deeply before answering. "Sorry," she said. "Yes. I'm fine. The last damn thing I want to come across as is some limp-dick, whiney broad."

Walker couldn't help but smile. "Only you would come up with a description like that."

"Just one of the guys." She brushed a damp strand of hair off her forehead.

Their gazes met, but only briefly before Karlyn looked away. Yet Walker sensed in that fleeting moment that something other than Janet had ignited the edgy angst in her. Something she wasn't quite ready to articulate. Something she was preserving for a quiet discussion over coffee. When they got back. But he knew full well there was still an "if" attached to the "when."

He changed the topic. "The surge? How big with a cat five?" he asked.

"I'm not sure. I think it's like twenty feet or more. But there's something weird about the continental shelf here that makes surges higher. I don't recall by how much, though. I . . . I think it's a lot." She brought her gaze slowly back to Walker.

"So, at the very least, twenty feet?"

"At the very least."

"The elevation of the runway here is twenty feet. You knew that?"

She nodded and they both fell silent.

"Think happy thoughts," Major Best interjected. "The height of the cockpit gives us another six or eight feet."

"Yeah, John," Walker said, "but I don't know if these things sink or float. It's not like they've ever been tested for that. What if they float, like a car swept away in a flash flood? Then we end up as gator bait in St. Simons Sound. What if they don't float? What if they're a 155,000-pound stone, and the surge is thirty feet?"

"Okay, forget the goddamn happy thoughts then," Best said. He turned away from Walker and Karlyn, and sat down at his console without glancing back.

Once again, the sights and smells of the carnival, the dusky tent, the ancient palm reader swarmed over Walker. In her vision, somehow conjured from the creases lining his hand, the old woman had said she had seen him trapped in a stadium; the eye of Janet, he now knew. She also said it didn't end well. He assumed she had meant whatever happened in the eye, but maybe not.

Yes, the day wasn't done. And what was left of it would be compressed into four or five violent hours.

Perhaps it wouldn't end well.

**As Pete and Alan** and his family mounted the short stairs into the Hurricane Hunter, another rainband, angry and seething, swept over the runway. Low swirling clouds, unleashing torrents of rain, knifed through the gray afternoon at autobahn speeds. The wind smashed into the tops of the towering pines lining Frederica Road. The trees, bent over at alarming angles, spewed limbs and cones through the air like salvos of rocket-propelled grenades.

Palm fronds, from somewhere on the other side of the runway, tumbled across the tarmac like performing acrobats. As electric transformers fell victim to Janet's assault, blue and white flashes of light reflected off the rain-draped overcast like strobes in a discotheque. Yet Karlyn knew it was only a probing attack. That more would follow, quickly, each one growing in fury.

She extended her hand to a woman she assumed was Alan Grant's wife as the lady entered the aircraft. "Welcome aboard," she said, "I'm Captain Hill, but please call me Karlyn."

The woman gave her a wan smile. "I'm Trish," she said. Her clothes were damp and a steady stream of water cascaded off her long, dark hair. "Thank God there's somebody else here," she said. "I didn't know what we were going to do. We couldn't get off the island."

A young girl and little boy followed Trish up the stairs. "Sandy, Lee, this is Captain Hill," Trish said. "Say hello."

Sandy nodded but didn't say anything. She kept her arms wrapped tightly around her herself. Her clothes and hair were plastered against her body as though she'd just climbed out of a swimming pool. Karlyn noted Sandy's father looked the same way, and sensed there was a story behind that, but understood it wasn't her place to ask about it.

"Hello, Captain," Lee said. He reached out to shake her hand. "Is this a real Air Force plane?"

"Yes. It's called a WC-130."

"You almost crashed."

"Well, actually we did crash. But we were able to walk away from it."

"It looked neat."

Alan, coming up the stairs behind Lee, popped him softly on the head. "Don't say that," he said. "They could have been hurt."

"Oww, Dad. But they weren't."

"Come on, young man," Karlyn said. "I'll show you around the airplane."

"Do you have guns and stuff?"

"No guns, but other things you might be interested in." She led Lee back to her console.

Lee's head swiveled from side to side as he took in the stark interior of the plane: the exposed cables and wiring, the gray padding, the red canvas seats, the computer monitors.

"It smells funny," he said, "like someone puked." He wrinkled his nose, then pinched it.

"It does, doesn't it? Well then, maybe we'd better go up to the cockpit," Karlyn said. "Would you like to meet the pilots?"

"Yeah. Awesome."

"Okay, follow me. I think your mom and dad and sister are there." She went forward and climbed the ladder to the flight deck.

Lee followed her, his eyes widening as he reached the top rung. "This is totally cool," he said. "Wait 'til I tell the guys at school about this." He looked up at Karlyn. "Your kids are so lucky to have a mom like you," he said.

She started to reply, to tell him she wasn't a mother. But the words caught in her throat, blocked by a sudden lump. Instead, she merely nodded.

"Hello, young man," Walker said. "Why don't you sit in the pilot's seat here next to Colonel Harlow while I talk to your family. The colonel can tell you what some of this stuff does and—"

Lee was past him and into the seat before Walker could finish his sentence.

At the rear of the flight deck, Karlyn stood with Lee's family, Pete and Major Best, the small group leaning against the tilt of the canted aircraft, like passengers on listing cruise ship. But Karlyn was unable to draw her gaze away from Lee as he jabbered incessantly, pointing and gesturing at various instruments and controls as Harlow struggled to keep pace with the child's rapid-fire questions. *Your kids are so lucky . . .* Lee's words had been so innocent. Yet so accusatory.

She yanked her focus from Lee to Walker, and quickly buried whatever nascent guilt had attempted to burrow into the marrow of her soul. The next few hours were all that mattered now. Beyond that, her course was set.

The sharp rattle of heavy rain echoed through the interior of the Hurricane Hunter. Despite its bulk, the craft seemed to shiver ever so slightly as the wind rose into a relentless, low-pitched yowl. It was unlike anything Karlyn had ever heard; clearly a harbinger of something beyond the ken of humans.

# Chapter Twenty-nine

## ST. SIMONS ISLAND, GEORGIA
## LABOR DAY SUNDAY, 1340 HOURS

"I guess I should tell you how we ended up here," Walker said, addressing the small assemblage of newcomers on the flight deck. "The aircraft lost two engines and a wing tip on its first pass through Janet's eyewall and we ended up trapped in the eye for several hours. We couldn't risk trying to fly out on only two engines and a busted wing. But with a little help from a hurricane expert in Atlanta, we finally made a dash for it. We were lucky to escape. Trouble was, with a third engine about to toss in the towel, our only option was to land here. Ironically, right in the path of the storm." He paused momentarily, then concluded: "We're sitting in the bulls-eye of a category five hurricane."

The only immediate response to Walker's statement was a quiet shuffle of feet. No one spoke until Alan asked, "How much time?"

Walker turned to Karlyn. "Captain Hill is our weather officer. She can tell us better than I."

At the front of the aircraft, wind-driven rain continued to sheet the windshield as Lee sat with his hands on the yoke as Colonel Harlow pointed to different buttons and controls.

Karlyn's face seemed to have lost some of its youthfulness in the past ten hours, and as her gaze swept over Walker he could see her eyes were laced with fatigue and concern. Soft crow's feet radiated from their corners, and a purplish tint, like a hint of stage makeup, accentuated the area immediately beneath them.

"We've got a little less than four hours before the eye reaches us," she said. "Probably the last hour or so before it arrives will be the worst. That's when the eyewall will go over us."

"How bad will it be?" Pete asked. "The guy on TV said she might be stronger than Camille."

"We clocked winds in the wall at 165 mph when we flew out of it. And the storm was still strengthening."

"So, do you think we'll be safe in here?"

Karlyn looked at Walker.

"I think we can survive the wind," he said. "We're in a 75-ton airframe. What worries me is the storm surge, the water rise. Karlyn, Captain Hill, said she thought it might be more than twenty feet."

"On TV," Alan interrupted, "they were talking about twenty-five or thirty."

Twenty-five or thirty! The statement slammed into Walker as if he'd been told he had inoperable brain cancer. He deigned to respond immediately. The truth was, he didn't know how they'd fare. He looked through the rain-streaked windshield, out onto the airfield, the runway, the buildings, the nearby trees bent in the wind. They were on land, twenty feet above sea level, over a mile from the ocean. It seemed impossible that where they were could be inundated, turned into an inland sea.

Yet the mathematics, the facts, couldn't be ignored. Thirty feet trumped twenty by ten. If the aircraft shifted from where it sat now, to lower ground, it was in danger of becoming an Air Force version of Davy Jones's Locker. That is, unless it took off toward the mainland like some untested, unseaworthy Noah's Ark.

Walker outlined the alternatives and his concerns to the small group, which remained silent after he finished. Alan and his wife directed dead stares at him, but they seemed to be searching for something beyond him, distant and unseen. Hope, perhaps.

"Captain Hill," Walker said, "can probably give us a little more detail on what to expect and when."

Karlyn massaged her temples, as though fighting a migraine, before she spoke. When she did, her voice was uneven and almost inaudible. "I'm not an expert when it comes to storm surges," she said, "but I think within a couple of hours before the eye's landfall is when the water will come up most rapidly. Which is why they call it a surge, I guess. The strongest winds will be in the eyewall itself, so probably the last hour or so before the eye reaches us will be the . . . well, not something many folks have . . .," she appeared to search for the correct word. " . . .witnessed," she concluded.

"Lived to tell about" is what she meant, Walker knew.


**Alan gathered his family** around him on the flight deck. He knelt down so he could be at eye-level with Lee.

"We'll be okay," Alan said to his son. In fact, he hated speaking those words. He felt uncomfortable not being in control of events, having to rely on others, being at the mercy of a force over which no man had dominion. "Even though the airplane got broken up a bit when it landed, it's still solid."

"What if the water comes up like they said?" Sandy asked. She continued to hug herself, and stared at the floor of the flight deck as she spoke.

Lee looked at her, then at Alan. For the first time, Alan saw uncertainty in his son's eyes, as though the seriousness of their situation had finally awakened a fear response in his immature brain. "Dad?" he said, seeking an answer to Sandy's question.

"We'll deal with that if and when it happens. No one is sure it will. And if it does, these Air Force people are trained to deal with emergencies. We're in good hands here." *Making it up as I go along.* "Look, I'm sorry," he continued. "I should have gotten us off the island earlier. I screwed up, but we'll get through this and you'll have some great stories to tell your friends when you get home." He reached out to Sandy and Lee and drew them to him, hugging them tightly. "I'm not laying the blame on you, honey," he said to Sandy. "If I'd listened to your mother and not taken off by myself this morning, we might have had a chance to get back across the causeway."

Trish remained silent. Alan looked up at her and could read the latent anger—or was it disappointment?—in her eyes. He stood and embraced her. As much as he detested not being in command of things, having to apologize for his shortcomings and misjudgments was worse. He'd rarely had to do it. But now an admission of guilt was in order.

"My fault," he whispered in Trish's ear. "I made a bad call. But we'll make it through the next few hours, I promise."

He felt her nod, her head buried in his shoulder.

"You with me?" he said.

"Of course," she murmured.

She inhaled and exhaled in jerky little breaths, but the sound of her breathing was overwhelmed by the thunder of the wind as it hammered at the plane in great pulsing gusts.

**"Arly, better come look at this,"** Major Best said. He was looking at the drop-down crew door, the entrance and exit to the aircraft.

Walker climbed down from the flight deck to the door. It was closed, but not sealed.

"It looks like it may have gotten warped or bent when we landed," Best said.

"Crashed," Walker said. "It's okay to say it. We crash-landed." He examined the door, running his fingers along the top of it. The wind whistled through a small separation between the door and the frame.

"That's as tight as I could get it," Best said.

"You smell something?" Walker asked.

Best sniffed the air. "Yeah, salt spray and something else: fuel oil."

"Me, too."

"Us?"

Walker stepped back from the door. "I don't think so. We were flying on fumes. It must be coming from someplace on or near the airfield, though. Maybe a cracked storage tank or feeder line. I don't know."

"So much for my smoke break," Best said.

"Chew gum," Walker said. He knew his navigator didn't smoke.

Best gave a one-snort response through his nose.

A spray of rain blew through the unsealed gap. Walker again reached his hand to the top of the door, this time sticking his fingers into the narrow opening. "Good news, bad news, I guess," he said.

Best looked at him.

"The good news is we won't set sail like an unmoored tramp steamer."

"And the bad news," Best said, picking up on the thread of Walker's dark humor, "is that we could become a steel aquarium."

"Maybe we should have tried for Jacksonville after all."

"No. You got us down here in one piece—well, more or less—and that's all that counts. One crisis at a time. No looking back."

Walker climbed back to the flight deck and retrieved his cell phone from his flight bag. He dialed squadron operations at Keesler. He feared the relay towers may have been toppled by the wind, but to his amazement, the call went through. He told the captain who answered they were on the ground safely, but that the bird was busted. "You'll probably have to bring it home in a bag," he said.

"You're where again?" the captain asked.

"On St. Simons Island."

"Shit."

"Yeah. I know. If the hurricane were a blowpipe we'd have a poison dart up our ass."

"The last bulletin from the Hurricane Center pegged the winds at 175 mph. You guys gonna be okay? I heard the whole island may go under water."

Walker cupped his free hand over the phone so the others on the flight deck couldn't hear him. "You may have to bring *us* home in a bag, too," he said. His throat tightened as he said the words.

"I don't want to do that, sir. Take care of yourselves. We'll get some folks there as soon as we can. Look, is there anyone I can contact for you, you know, like family or friends, to let them know you're okay?"

Walker gave the officer the names of the crew, and asked him to get in touch with their spouses or whoever was listed in squadron records as next of kin. "Call the Atlanta Journal-Constitution, too. Tell them their reporter is fine, just a few pounds lighter."

The captain forced a laugh, then asked, "How about your family, Major? You got a wife or somebody I should call."

*Not anybody who cares.* "I'll handle that on my own, but thanks for asking." Walker said goodbye, flipped the phone shut, and slipped it back into his bag.

A furious blast of wind, a pile-driver gust, hammered the plane. A pulse of air, almost as if it were alive, rippled through the craft's interior.

# Chapter Thirty

## ATLANTA, GEORGIA—THE NATURAL ENVIRONMENT TELEVISION NETWORK LABOR DAY SUNDAY, 1535 HOURS

Nicholas Obermeyer slumped in his chair. He'd been on the air almost continuously for five hours, but now was taking a half-hour break as another OCM covered for him. He reached for an open can of Dr Pepper resting on his desk and tilting precariously against a stack of journals from the American Meteorological Society. He tipped the can to his lips, started to swallow, but instead spit the contents into a waste basket. He slammed the container onto the desktop.

"Go bad?" Sherrie asked.

"Warm."

"You need some fresh air. Let's walk up to the patio."

"I'm old. I'm tired. I need a nap."

"You seemed pretty frisky for a while this morning, old timer."

He felt himself color. "Yes, I think I do need some fresh air."

She laughed lightly, her tropical eyes dancing.

They walked up the stairs and out onto the patio. The wind was busy, rustling the leaves—still mostly green—of surrounding sweetgums and oaks. The air bore the scent of crushed pine needles and holiday barbecues. Overhead, the sky had turned milky with dense cirrus. He pointed at it. "Battle streamers from Janet," he said. He leaned his elbows on the concrete railing of the patio and stared at the Atlanta skyline.

"I think you may have saved a lot of lives today," Sherrie said.

"Probably not enough."

"Hugs and kisses from Robbie, though."

"Sure. He loves getting his nuts squeezed in a vise."

"You called his bluff."

"He knows how the game is played."

"We got new contracts out of the deal, didn't we?"

"Did we?" He turned to look at her, gave her a tight-lipped grin.

"Well, he said—"

"My brother was an adherent to the 'paper bag theory',"
Obermeyer interrupted. "He sold used cars. He said a deal was never
closed, despite the assurances and sincerity of a customer, until the
customer drove off in the car and my brother had his money in a paper
bag. So to speak."

"And we don't have a paper bag let alone a paper contract,"
Sherrie said. She kicked at an empty plastic cup tumbling across the
patio. "So now what?"

"I know how the game is played, too," Obermeyer answered.
Overhead, a halo, shimmering dully in the high, translucent overcast,
encircled the sun. He looked up at it. "But first we need to deal with
Janet."

"How bad will the next few hours be? On St. Simons, I mean."

"The water will start to come up fast now. The eyewall is only
about thirty miles offshore. I'm guessing roads near the beach are
already under water, but even the highest points on the island will be
submerged within another ninety minutes. And the winds . . ." His
voice trailed off.

Sherrie touched his arm lightly.

"Roofs will be the first thing to go. And windows without storm
shutters. Then, when the eyewall hits, entire buildings and homes will
be leveled, assuming there's anything left to level after the surge.
Clapboard, cinderblock, brick—it won't make a lot of difference. This
will be equal opportunity destruction."

"And the people, those who didn't get off the island?" Sherrie's
voice was soft, a bit of a catch in it.

Obermeyer didn't answer for a while, then said, "I understand
drowning is a pretty horrible way to die. Maybe the lucky ones will just
take a flying billboard to the head or two-by-four through the heart."
He paused and looked away from Sherrie. "Let's get back to work." He
trudged toward the door, head down, hands jammed in his pockets.


## ST. SIMONS ISLAND, GEORGIA
## 1630 HOURS

Frederica Road, adjacent to the runway at McKinnon, had become
a small river. So had other access roads to the airport which, for all
intents and purposes, was rapidly becoming an island. An island on an

island.

Pete stood next to Walker. They stared out the windshield of the aircraft, watching the Atlantic Ocean claim St. Simons foot by vertical foot.

"Can't be much more than thirty or forty percent of the island left above water," Pete said.

Walker nodded. He looked across Frederica where earlier he'd seen a copse of pine trees. It now lay in horizontal repose, leveled by the wind. Broken, bent and shattered limbs littered the ground as though a great battle had taken place.

The electric-blue flashes of dying transformers and shorting power lines continued to refract off the dark scud and sheets of rain that swept over the airport. The flickers were becoming more intermittent, however, as though the hurricane's gusts were running out of viable targets.

Debris of all sorts—garbage cans, beach balls, shingles, lawn chairs, pieces of sheet metal—bounced and cartwheeled across the runway.

Pete nudged Walker's shoulder. "Look." He pointed at something in the direction of the strip mall on the other side of Frederica Road.

Walker strained to see through the water-streaked glass of the cockpit, but quickly spotted what Pete was pointing at. A long section of roof over the shops in the mall was being torn away, as though someone were using a knife to peel an apple. The roof rolled back, flapping up and down. Then it separated from the rafters and lifted off into the storm like a great, soaring bird.

"God," Pete said, "that was like watching a Space Shuttle launch."

**Karlyn stood with the** others, peering out the cockpit windows, as the ocean surged around them, not quite over the runway, but flowing freely on all sides of them. Spray and foam filled the air, mingling with the thunderous cascades of rain. She checked her watch. Four forty-five. Several hours before sunset, yet the late-summer daylight had disappeared, swallowed by Janet. Four forty-five. The eyewall had to be almost upon them.

The minutes dragged by in a slow-motion countdown. Then the waiting ended as a blast of wind rocked the aircraft, sending a palpable shudder rippling through its fuselage. And even though she was used to the reverberating thrum of the Hurricane Hunter's turboprops, the bellow of the wind became overwhelming, unnerving. It was as though she were hunkered down behind the blast shield at the end of a runway while dozens of jets simultaneously spooled their engines to takeoff thrust.

Even the crash-damaged crew door contributed to the cacophony. Gusts of wind screamed through the gap around the door, filling the interior of the aircraft with a relentless, high-decibel ululation. The wail of dead souls, it seemed to Karlyn. She placed her hands over her ears.

No one spoke, each mesmerized by the violence that surrounded them.

As the wind rose, so did the water. White-capped waves and volleys of foam ripped from their crests swept across the runway. A swelling oceanic surge, like a tidal bore filling a narrow harbor, submerged the airport. The surge slapped against the sides of the Hurricane Hunter and the craft shifted slightly. Trish screamed, then clapped a hand over her mouth in embarrassment.

"Oh my God," Walker said. His face was pressed against the port-side cockpit window, his hands cupped on either side of his head, trying to block out whatever dim light there was in the interior of the aircraft.

Karlyn scurried next to him, followed by Harlow. "What?" Karlyn said.

"Someone's out there."

She mashed her face against the glass. In the dusky, storm-swept light, she saw two figures on the opposite side of the runway near the operations building. A man and a woman, perhaps, judging by their relative heights. They struggled over the fence, one of them falling heavily into the water that by now was two or three feet deep on the tarmac.

The figure stood, but was immediately knocked down by the wind and sent plowing through the surge like a human surfboard. The other person tried to help, but he or she was cut down by the wind, too.

Both figures flailed in the rising water. One managed to stand, tried to grab the other, but was pounded back into the ocean, for that's what it truly was now, once more.

"We need to help them," Karlyn said "They're trying to reach us."

Walker placed his hand on her arm. "We can't," he said. "It's too late. You can't even breathe out there, let alone stand."

"What the hell is matter with those people? Why did they wait until now?" Karlyn screamed. They were perhaps a hundred yards from the aircraft. Under the circumstances, they might as well have been a hundred miles.

Karlyn continued to watch, tears misting her vision. The figures managed to steady themselves by crawling through the water on all fours. Again, one of them attempted to stand, the man, Karlyn thought. He wore a loose-fitting jacket that bulged upward in the wind, molding itself around his head. He clawed at the jacket, ripping it away, tossing it to the wind as if it were some sort of atoning sacrifice. Hands covering his mouth and nose so he could breathe, he bent into the teeth of the hurricane and took a labored step forward. But a blast of wind snapped him backward and he hit the water spread-eagled, like a watery snow angel. The other figure managed a weak wave in the direction of the Hurricane Hunter. *Help me.*

But it clearly was hopeless. A long green wave washed down the runway, a six-foot swell capped by flotsam and jetsam. It picked up the couple, just more debris, and swept them toward the south end of the airport. But they wouldn't stop there, Karlyn realized. Maybe in St. Simons Sound. Or on Jekyll Island, the next island south. It didn't make any difference. They wouldn't survive the trip.

She released an audible sob.

"You can't always save people from their own folly, young lady." Pete stood next to her, staring out at the eyewall's violence. "There are always folks who insist they can ride out a hurricane. Probably most of the time they can. But they aren't allowed any mistakes. Zero. No second chances. I'm sorry. They just waited too long before they realized they weren't going to make it. I'm guessing they must have seen the plane come in earlier and decided to try to reach the airport."

Karlyn wiped her eyes and nodded. "Life sucks," she snapped. She realized it was as much a commentary about her own problems as it was about the drama she'd just witnessed.

"It can be harsh at times," Pete responded. His words were gentle and almost lost in the din filling the aircraft.

Karlyn bowed her head and uttered a silent prayer—for the people she'd seen carried away, for herself, for the crew. It felt awkward, praying. She hadn't done much of it recently. She'd kept God at arm's length, a mere life preserver. In essence, she'd placed Him on a shelf behind glass. *BREAK IN CASE OF EMERGENCY.* She was breaking it now, but she understood it probably was too late.

The plane shifted again, a sudden jolt that sent the people on the crowded and already-slanted flight deck piling into each other.

Best was standing near the rear of the flight deck, peering down at the crew door. He turned around, his face drawn taught. "Water's coming in," he said.

# Chapter Thirty-one

## ST. SIMONS ISLAND, GEORGIA
## LABOR DAY SUNDAY, 1705 HOURS

Seawater streamed into the Hurricane Hunter around its ill-fitting crew door and flowed freely toward the rear of the fuselage. As yet, it was no threat to the flight deck, but Walker knew that might not last. In addition to the water itself rising, the aircraft kept edging toward lower ground, pushed along by the storm surge. Another six or eight feet and the Atlantic Ocean would be in the cockpit.

A strong essence of seaweed and shellfish permeated the airplane. And mingled with it was the pungent odor of gasoline. Walker had no idea where the fumes were coming from, but they seemed to be water borne, and that wasn't good. It meant they were sitting in the midst of an open fuel dump. With transformers and electrical lines arcing out all over the place, they were a holiday barbecue waiting to happen.

He walked to the front of the cockpit and once more stared out at the scene unfolding around them. He couldn't quite comprehend it, couldn't quite believe it. The island was flooded. Underwater. There was no bare ground visible. Only the superstructures of shattered buildings and isolated live oaks poking above the surface of the water, like cypress stumps in a black swamp, suggested they were still on an island and not in the middle of the Atlantic.

In the distance he could see the red glow of something burning, flames flattened against the water by the eyewall winds. He surmised it was a blaze fed by a rupture in a natural gas line.

Harlow nudged him and pointed in a different direction. Entire roofs were floating by, riding the storm surge, looking like migrating flotillas of A-framed rafts. A broken-hulled shrimp boat, capsized and propelled by the wind, knifed across the end of the runway like a tiny humpback whale.

A Volkswagen Beetle, wheels in the air, and appearing for all the world like an oversized bathtub toy, spun in circles on the swirling tide. It bumped against the nose of the Hurricane Hunter, recoiled, and kept going.

"Dead Bug!" Harlow exclaimed. Air Force humor. Walker got the reference. An old fighter pilots' game. Someone in an officers' club bar would yell "dead bug" and everyone would fall to the floor, rolling on their backs and flailing their arms and legs in the air like dying insects. If you didn't join in the juvenile fun, you bought the house a round.

Days of yore. Good times. "We'll have to educate the rest of the crew about that when we get back," Walker said. Positive thinking.

"Just in case," Harlow said, "I want you to know, I've never flown with a better pilot." He extended his hand to Walker.

*Just in case? How had it come to this?* "Thank you, sir." He accepted Harlow's hand. "But you don't mind if I store your accolade in my over-dramatic hyperbole file, do you?"

"Not if you promise never to remind me of it."

"It's goddamned ironic, you know. You earned a medal in combat, I flew through forest fires, and we end up like this, trapped—"

"In a boat that don't float," Harlow interjected without humor. "Yeah, goddamned ironic."

The plane shuddered and Walker fought to keep his balance on the tilted flight deck. A wave broke over the windshield and the angry wind continued to fill the fuselage with a thick, brain-numbing whine.


**Ocean water gradually filled** the lower six feet or so of the Hurricane Hunter's interior, sloshing back and forth in the fuselage as the plane rocked unevenly in the heavy surf washing over the airfield. The water lapped at the top of the ladder leading to the flight deck, only inches from invading the last dry refuge in the craft.

Waves broke relentlessly over the plane giving Walker the feeling he was beneath the surface of the sea in a diving bell. It was virtually impossible to see anything outside. He checked his watch and looked at Karlyn.

"How much longer before the eye?" he asked.

"Maybe ten minutes."

"The surge is still coming up." Nothing she didn't know.

A stream of silty water snaked onto the flight deck's floor. "As soon as the eye gets here, the surge will cease," she said.

"I know, but it's already over the nose. Another two or three feet and it'll be over the cockpit. Good thing the door isn't warped worse than it is, or we'd be up to our knees in water already."

Karlyn moved closer to him so that their bodies touched. "Ten minutes," she said. "Maybe fifteen."

He didn't move away from her, sensing they shared an awareness of their mortality and thus sought a semblance of reassurance in the touch of another human being. A touch that signaled you weren't alone, hadn't been cast adrift, hadn't been offered as a random sacrifice to the inherent violence that inhabits the natural world.

Most of the time, it seemed to Walker, the savagery was merely there, lurking quietly and benignly beyond the horizon and so allowing people to forget about it and live their lives in peace and normalcy. But when loosed, it reminded them of their fragility, driving them to seek strength through the presence of others. He leaned against Karlyn, ever so slightly.

"Something's on fire," she said.

"Buildings in town, I think. I saw something burning earlier."

"No, closer. Look to the right."

It was hard to see, but through the rain- and wave-sheathed windshield he could make out a line of flames snaking across the top of the water in the direction of the aircraft. He tracked the fire for several minutes as it rode the foam-flecked surge and slowly fanned out into a broad, fiery front, weaving and dancing toward the crippled airplane. It hugged the surface of the seawater, flattened by the unrelenting wind.

The orange-red glow of the blazing assault attracted the attention of everyone on the flight deck.

"Where did that come from?" Alan asked.

"Probably a fuel leak someplace nearby," Walker said. "A tank, a truck, a line. I don't know. I'm guessing a power line fell into some gasoline and ignited it."

"But we'll be okay in here?" His voice was strained.

"We should be. We didn't have much fuel left when we landed, and C-130s aren't exactly made of kindling sticks." In fact, he had his doubts. He was thinking of the wing they'd sheared off on landing and wondered what kind of exposed fuel and oil lines might have resulted from that. All the flames had to do was find a severed line and it would be like piranhas discovering Porky Pig floating in the Amazon. A feeding frenzy. If fire chewed its way into whatever residual fuel or fumes the Hurricane Hunter harbored, the craft could become a funeral pyre in the midst of a cat five storm surge.

"Life's burlesque," he said, more to himself than anyone else.

But Karlyn heard him, looked at him, her eyes shiny with trust, or maybe doubt, and slipped her hand into his. "Yeah," she said.

The blaze, ebbing and flowing in chaotic whirlpools and still leveled by the wind, crept closer to the airplane, ever so often sending fingers of fire darting toward it. Walker tried to gauge the distance between the flame front and the plane. Thirty yards perhaps.

Everyone watched in silence. Tears glistened in the eyes of the young girl, Sandy. Her bottom lip began to quiver. Lee buried his face in his mother's thigh, his arms wound tightly around her leg.

Twenty yards.

Pete lowered his head. Was he praying, or did he just not want to watch any longer? Hemphill, the newspaper columnist, wrote furiously, almost in anger it seemed, on a water-logged pad.

Ten yards.

Walker had to make a decision: whether to have everyone remain on the flight deck or send them down the ladder into the water that filled the lower part of the fuselage. He looked at Harlow and Best, and pointed down. Both men nodded.

Five yards.

At least if the airplane exploded—unlikely—the water would act as a buffer. If it caught fire, it might act as a shield.

The ruddy shimmer of the blaze filled the Hurricane Hunter, refracting through the thick glass of the windshield, reflecting off the panels of the instrumentation. The flames flickered and pirouetted, dipped and darted in a *Danse Macabre*.

"Listen up," Walker said. "We need to get into the water in the lower part of the aircraft. The fire's too close. If it gets into a broken fuel or hydraulic line, it might ignite the airplane. The water should offer us safety." He turned to Sergeant McKenzie and Lieutenant Smithers. "Louie, Van, you guys go down the ladder first, get your footing in the water, then help the rest of us down. Start with the family, then Pete, then—"

He stopped talking. His voice had become strangely loud. Why?

The wind. The wind had dropped off, its thunderous roar replaced by a softer wail. It was a mere gale now, and seemed to be losing its punch: a hurricane with emphysema.

"The eye?" Walker asked Karlyn.

"Must be. It's about time."

Walker turned toward the windshield. The continuous onslaught of rain and spray had ceased, and he could see more clearly through the salt-flecked glass. The fire riding the surge had stopped its advance, the flames shooting skyward now, no longer pressed against the surface by the wind.

But the surge itself had not relented. Seawater still covered the nose of the aircraft, the runway, the airport, the city itself. It was as though the airplane had crashed on a submerged atoll marked only by the skeletons of man-made structures and the silhouettes of denuded trees. St. Simons Island had become part of the Atlantic Ocean's seabed.

Walker felt pressure in his head, as though he were on climb-out in an airplane. He swallowed hard and heard his ears pop. He glanced at the analog altimeter, essentially an aneroid barometer. Even though the Hurricane Hunter rested at sea level, the altimeter showed its elevation to be over 4000 feet, the anomalous reading dictated by the rock-bottom low pressure in the hurricane's eye.

Walker heard a small intake of breath behind him. It was Trish, Alan's wife.

"There's nothing left out there, is there?"

"Not much."

"I mean nothing living."

"I don't see how there could be."

"The fire?" She pointed.

"It won't come any closer. The wind's dying. Then it'll blow from the opposite direction after the eye passes."

Overhead, the clouds parted, leaving only scattered puffy cumulus drifting in a light breeze. Above the cotton-ball clouds, the deep turquoise of a pure tropical sky offered a false sense of serenity, that is, if one looked up and not out.

But Walker looked out. Trees, parts of homes, signs, automobiles, golf carts, small animals, birds, garbage cans, barbecues—an endless tally of debris—floated on the surface of the surge, as if it were a filthy harbor in some environmentally derelict third-world country. A flotilla of mobile homes, a dozen or more, looking like a defeated armada of tin cans, bobbed in the shallow sea.

In the distance, black smoke chimneyed skyward from whatever had been burning earlier. The fire seemed to have spread, found new fuel, more oxygen.

"My home used to be here," Pete said.

"I'm sorry," Walker answered. He didn't know what else to say.

"Poor fellow," Pete said. He was staring at something in the water.

"What?"

"There, looks like a black lab." Pete pointed to the left.

A dog, looking tired and shell-shocked, if that term could be applied to animals, paddled aimlessly through the surge. It looked as if he'd given up hope, for he, or maybe she, made no attempt to scramble aboard the pieces of lumber and tree limbs that accompanied him as he floated down Frederica Road, or what used to be Frederica Road. It was now part of the Atlantic surf zone.

# Chapter Thirty-two

## ATLANTA, GEORGIA—THE NATURAL ENVIRONMENT TELEVISION NETWORK LABOR DAY SUNDAY, 1715 HOURS

Obermeyer, Sherrie seated next to him, couldn't tear his eyes from the radar imagery on his monitor as Janet made landfall. The hurricane's tight, violent eyewall, its torrential rain color-coded in angry reds and magentas, swirled over St. Simons in a furious ballet; a dance of death choreographed in tornadic violence, spectacular atmospheric beauty, and cruel death for those unlucky enough to have front row seats.

"Awesome," Obermeyer said quietly.

"Yes, to us. As meteorologists," Sherrie said.

"I know. We view it too clinically, too objectively. We think, 'Wow, this is the strongest hurricane on record in the Atlantic Basin, the greatest storm in recorded history to hit the United States.' And yet in reality we're witnessing a tragedy. The destruction of an entire city, the death of hundreds." He turned to look at Sherrie. "Thousands if the evacuation got screwed up."

"You did your part," she said. She rested her hand on his.

He shrugged. "I tried. But who knows, maybe I was just lucky. What if my forecast had been wrong? I don't think I have a corner on the market when it comes to attempting to figure out what the atmosphere is going to do."

"But today you did. Today you were right. Your experience and study paid off."

"You sound like my mother."

Sherrie smiled. "It's not a mother-thing, it's a woman-thing. Don't you know it's a female prerogative to comfort, to soothe, to give approbation?"

He took both her hands in his and studied her face, as if it might reveal a hidden truth. "It seems to me you were ready to give more than that this morning."

She cast her gaze downward. "Was I?"

"Were you?"

"Maybe that's one of life's questions that will go forever unanswered."

Her way of saying nevermore? Her way of cutting it off? "I'm sorry," he said. "It was inappropriate of me to bring it up." He released her hands.

Someone walked past them—looking askance at them, it seemed—and said, "There's food in the break room. Better get it while it's hot."

The smell of pizza and barbecue wafted through the studio.

Obermeyer shook his head. "Not hungry," he said.

"A little too much like Nero fiddling?" Sherrie asked.

"I suppose." He reached for his fifth Dr Pepper of the day.

She pointed at it. "Well, better Dr Pepper than Mr. Daniels."

He popped the tab on the can's lid. *The question may go forever unanswered, as she said, but apparently she's going to keep reminding me I asked it, at least indirectly.* She was an enigma to him. Weather, he could figure out. Women, he couldn't. Was she really older than she looked? Her intellect and words suggested maturity far beyond someone in her twenties. But her actions at his house . . .? Calculated or impulsive? Sacrificial or sexual? Did she see something in him besides the avatar of a booze-riddled uncle? Probably not. He knew he didn't exactly rank on the high side of the good-catch barometer. Divorcee. Boozer. Opinionated. And apparently a pink-slip magnet in his job.

He turned back to the monitor and, on the Doppler radar image, switched from precipitation mode to wind-speed measurement. Due to power outages and equipment failures, regular weather observations from St. Simons and nearby Brunswick on the mainland had ceased long before Janet's eyewall hit. Although he knew the Doppler measurements, taken at sites remote from St. Simons would provide only estimates, they would still be reasonable indicators of the fury sweeping the island.

"Bad?" Sherrie asked.

"Very." Obermeyer tapped his finger on the velocity scale. "It looks like we've got 240 knots at around 5000 feet." He heard Sherrie suck in her breath. "That's almost 170 knots, or 195 mph, at the surface. Sustained. Figure gusts well in excess of 200 mph. Not much is going to survive that."

He spun in his chair to face her. "The force of the wind increases exponentially with its speed."

She nodded.

"So imagine a small room turned on its side with a Hummer sitting on its outside wall. That's the force a category one hurricane would exert. With Janet, figure seven Hummers. As I said, not much is going to survive."

## ST. SIMONS ISLAND, GEORGIA
## LABOR DAY SUNDAY, 1725 HOURS

Alan stood beside Walker and Pete staring out at the bleak scene. He was appalled by how close he'd come, how close he'd allowed his family to come, to being part of that scene—statistics in the morning paper and evening newscasts.

Something caught his eye and he lifted his gaze toward the sky. Flights of egrets, the evening sun glinting off their alabaster wings, circled in the eye of Janet. There seemed to be hundreds of them, like heavenly hosts, hovering over the destruction below.

Heavenly hosts? Biblical fantasy. And yet, what were they there for? Merely seeking refuge from the storm, most likely, cruising along in the calm of the eye. But in their stately, slow-motion orbit, he sensed a larger meaning. Or perhaps willed himself to sense a larger meaning. As unreligious as he was, he knew with great certainty something new had been awakened within him.

The egrets dipped and soared in effortless flight, harbingers, perhaps, of good fortune. Alan knew the winds on the other side of the eye would blow from the opposite direction, pushing the water back out to sea. But they would also unleash renewed fury. Janet's last, violent hurrah.

*So then, the birds; prophets of doom? Mocking us? Mocking me? My folly?* He could have lost everything. He turned to look at Trish, Sandy and Lee. Everything.

His father had once told him that life-changing events should be life changing. Alan stepped next to Trish and hugged her, then tilted her face up so that their eyes met. "St. Simons will be rebuilt," he said. "Buildings can be put back together, resurrected. You guys can't. Help me remember that next time I say a project will tank without me, that I need to spend twenty-hour days on the job; that I don't have time to go to Lee's ball game, or Sandy's dance recital."

"Daddy," Sandy said, overhearing her father, "I gave up ballet two years ago."

A little twist of the dagger. "So what do you do now?"

"What do you mean?"

"For fun, recreation. What do you do?"

"You don't know?"

"I plead guilty, honey. I really want to know."

"I write a column for the school's newspaper." She cocked her head at him, as if she knew she'd one-upped him. "And I like don't write like I talk. I won an award last year."

The dagger twisted deeper. He didn't have a comeback.

"I brought my stuff home so you could read it, but you never had time."

*Can a grown man cry?* He didn't, but bent down instead so that he was face to face with his daughter. "I'll read everything you write in the future," he said. "And may I suggest a topic for your next column?"

She nodded, her gaze fixed on his.

"How about 'The Failure of Fathers'?"

She blinked. Something glistened in her eyes. "No," she said, "I don't think so. What you did today was pretty . . . awesome. I was thinking more along the lines of 'My Dad, My Hero.'"

They stared at each other for a long while without speaking further. Then Alan said simply, "Okay."

**Walker squinted into the** sunlight glinting off the now-ebbing surge. The burning fuel oil that had advanced on the aircraft was slowing retreating, but something else caught his eye. "John," he said, "do you still carry field glasses in your flight bag?"

"Yes, sir. I'll get them."

He handed Walker a pair of Nikon binoculars. Not military issue, but a powerful commercial set. Walker adjusted the right eyepiece and focused on an object floating in the water, a humped, bloated shape that he couldn't identify for certain with his naked eye. But he had an inkling what it was even before he looked through the field glasses. "Christ," he said softly.

"What?" Best asked.

Walker put a finger to his lips. "Shhh. Don't let the kids hear us." He handed Best the binoculars. "Out there, just to the right of that red golf cart, the one that's floating upside down."

Best brought the field glasses to his face. "Dear God," he said. He took the binoculars away from his eyes. "A man or woman, you think?"

"Hard to tell."

Best handed the binoculars back to Walker. He lifted them to his eyes and studied the form, a body, spinning in-place in the water. Spread-eagled and floating face down, its clothes were in tatters. Its nearly naked rump, a startling patch of white in the green-gray surge, offered a convenient perch for a crow, a survivor of the storm, that pecked disinterestedly at the buttocks.

Walker moved the field glasses slowly over the shallow sea. "There are more," he whispered. A black man, his arms twisted at awkward angles, floated face-up, bobbing like dark seaweed. At least two more bodies were discernible beyond him. One looked as though a blow to its head had nearly decapitated it. The other appeared to be a child.

An emptiness dug into Walker's gut like nothing he'd ever felt. He'd known there would be death in a storm of this magnitude, but to see it, to sense the reality of it, the finality of it, was soul-rending.

He continued scanning. Movement in the limbs of a fallen pine tree caught his attention. The huge tree, several hundred yards away, was drifting slowly, but almost at a dead stop, along with the rest of the debris field. Along with the bodies.

It looked as if an animal, maybe a squirrel or large bird, had found refuge in the downed tree. Walker adjusted the focus of the field glasses, then worked them slowly back and forth over the broken limbs. The movement again. Subtle. It wasn't an animal. He steadied the binoculars and held them where he's seen the motion. The tree gradually rotated in the ebbing surge. Now he saw it clearly, and caught his breath.

A woman, half-naked, her arms splayed wide and motionless, lay entangled in the branches. Her head was twisted toward Walker and he could see the dead stare in her eyes. She lay on her back. On top of her, an infant, perhaps five or six months old, clung to her breast.

# Chapter Thirty-three

## ST. SIMONS ISLAND, GEORGIA
## LABOR DAY SUNDAY, 1725 HOURS

Walker's arms trembled as he fought to hold the field glasses steady, looking for some sign of life from the baby. Then he saw it, a slight twitch of the little legs, a half-hearted kick. The child seemed to tighten his grip on the dead woman, probably its mother, and buried its face in her bosom.

Walker spun toward Karlyn. "How much more time before the eye passes?" he said. He could barely get the words out.

"What's wrong?"

"How much time?"

"I don't know. When we were in it, the eye was maybe four miles wide, moving at 15 mph. So . . . " She checked her watch. " . . .maybe another ten or twelve minutes. Why?"

Not enough time. But it didn't matter.

"Help me open the crew door," Walker said to Best.

"What?"

"There's a baby out there. It's still alive. I'm going after it."

Harlow overheard Walker. "I'm coming with you," he said.

"It's a one-man job, Bernie."

"Better with two."

"No."

"You aren't going to pull that aircraft commander crap on me again, are you?"

"If I have to."

"Good. Because we aren't flying anymore. I'm boss now. Louie, grab a couple of PFDs for us."

Walker knew that valuable time would be lost by arguing the point, and acquiesced.

Sergeant McKenzie scrambled down the ladder and waded back through the fuselage, neck deep in seawater, until he reached a submerged locker. He took a deep breath, dipped below the surface of the water, came back up, went down again, and surfaced with a handful of PFDs—inflatable life jackets.

While McKenzie was retrieving the jackets, Walker, Best and Harlow forced the crew door open. The drop-down stairs, like a diving submarine, disappeared beneath the surface of the water as the door fell away from the side of the aircraft.

The sergeant splashed back to where the officers stood and handed Walker and Harlow each two PFDs. "I thought you might need extras," he said.

Each man donned a jacket, inflated it, and slung the spare over his shoulders. Walker went out the door first, swimming away from the airplane instead of trying to find his footing on the stairs.

As he dog-paddled off, kicking lightly, he heard Harlow plunge into the water behind him. Pieces of wood and plastic, Walker had no idea from what, bobbed in the water all around him. The fetor of garbage, oily smoke and marsh mud mingled with what he presumed was the stench of death. It was more than he was prepared for, and he gagged, covering up the reflex by pretending he'd swallowed a mouthful of seawater.

Harlow swam along side of him. "I don't think our Air Force training covered this, did it?"

"If I'd known we were going to be doing shit like this," Walker rasped, "I would have joined the Navy."

Harlow held up his hand and stopped paddling. "Listen," he said.

Walker stopped, too, treading water silently with a slow frog-kick.

"The wind," Harlow said.

Though only light zephyrs wafted through the air immediately around them, a subdued roar, like the greatly amplified rumble of traffic from a distant freeway, thrummed over the surface of the surge. Somewhere, not more than a few miles away, the winds of the eyewall continued to level whatever stood in their path.

"Sounds like a jet engine test facility," Walker said.

"Dragons," Harlow said, "the dragons are coming for us." He resumed swimming, a little more frantically it seemed to Walker.

Walker set out beside him, he, too, employing an adrenaline-enhanced kick. But he'd lost his bearings. At water level, everything looked different than it had from the elevated perspective of the cockpit. "Wait a minute," he said. He ceased kicking. "I need to get a fix on the tree. I can't see it anymore." When he quit swimming, his legs dropped and his feet touched solid ground. "Hey, Bernie, I think it's shallow enough here we can stand."

Both men rose from the water and found themselves only chest deep in the surge. Walker scanned the surface of the water. He could see several large pines floating within a hundred yards of where they stood. He looked back at the aircraft, trying to line up the cockpit with the correct tree. Wasting time, he realized, but it made no sense to race off toward the wrong target.

"I think it's that one," he said, pointing. The limbs of the downed pine he'd identified seemed to rise out the water more prominently than those of other trees.

"About a three-wood shot," Harlow said. "Let's go."

They strode off through the water, plowing through the surge with the determination of tiny tug boats. Fields of debris, including the offal of small animals, continued to bob in the seawater that surrounded them. Walker covered the lower part of his face with his hand to prevent the dreck from splashing into his mouth.

Pushing through the water was physically demanding and he found his legs growing wobbly, but refused to relent in his drive toward the stranded baby. He could see Harlow's chest heaving as he fought to draw in deep lungfuls of air.

"Should have worked out more, huh?" Walker said.

"We're not supposed to be goddamned SEALs," Harlow gasped. "We're supposed to be sitting on our butts flying airplanes, not acting like snake-eating Special Forces on rescue missions."

"We may have to rescue each other before this is over," Walker panted. "Thanks for coming along, boss."

"Wouldn't have missed it for the world. But next time—" He stopped in mid-sentence. "Hold it!" He extended his arm in front of Walker's chest.

Both men halted.

"There," Harlow pointed. "Walk softly and carry a big stick."

A water moccasin, its body moving in an easy sinusoidal weave, sliced through the water a short distance ahead of them, apparently oblivious to their presence. Walker turned slowly in the water, a 360-degree pivot, looking for more. "Clear," he said, as the snake slithered away. The men moved off.

Above them, the azure sky, dotted with tiny cottonball clouds, gave no hint of the fury that surrounded them. The sun, sinking in the west, dropped toward the tops of the anviling thunderheads that marked Janet's western eyewall. Walker turned to scan the eastern horizon. No different. A fortress of black-stemmed clouds mushroomed into white explosions ten miles overhead. The eastern eyewall. They were back in the stadium. Trapped again.

The low-pitched yowl of the wind, heard but not yet felt, grew louder. Walker didn't have to look at his watch to know they had only minutes left to get the baby and race back to the aircraft. He also knew time would run out before they could do that. That the dragons, Harlow's metaphor, would catch them.

The two men plowed on, narrow wakes trailing behind them in the surge. Walker could see the tree clearly now. It no longer was moving, apparently hung up on higher ground beneath the surface of the water. The woman, her skin torn and ripped, probably flayed by the prickly pine branches at the height of the storm, lay motionless. The baby on her chest squirmed.

Fifty yards to go. A breath of wind out of the southwest rippled the surface of the water. A phalanx of gray scud, the shock troops of the eastern eyewall, knifed into the puffy cumulus overhead, sending them scurrying away.

"Almost there," Harlow wheezed.

Walker reached out and grabbed Harlow's arm. Ahead of them, the jagged, scaly back of an alligator slid through the water, then stopped adjacent to where the woman and baby lay enmeshed in the pine branches.

"Well, a dragon for real," Harlow whispered.

The gator lifted its snout out of the water and turned toward the tree. It slithered closer, nosing into the branches that hung into the water. It was perhaps six feet from the woman and baby. Six feet from prey.

Walker and Harlow were thirty feet from the reptile.

"Any ideas?" Harlow asked.

"Only bad ones."

"Let's try one."

"Okay. We walk abreast, making as much noise and kicking up as much water as we can. Maybe the gator will think it's a bigger gator coming after him and he'll get the hell out of Dodge."

"You think they're that smart? That analytical?"

"No. But maybe they're that dumb."

"What if he decides to attack instead?"

"He can only go after one of us. The other guy grabs the kid and runs."

"You know, Arly, you're a great pilot, but that's the dumbest frigging idea I've ever heard. Let's go."

Now only waist deep in the surge, they strode toward the alligator shoulder to shoulder, splashing, yelling, waving their arms. Walker bellowed at the top of his lungs, terrified if he didn't, the fear that coiled around his chest like a crushing spiral of barbed wire would totally paralyze him, leaving him unable to scream, unable to move. He hoped if the animal attacked, its bite would be swift, sure, and fatal, though he knew that probably wouldn't be the case. He'd read somewhere that the reptiles usually just locked onto their prey and dragged it under water to drown it.

The gator backed away from the tree as the men approached, turned to face them, opened its jaws and snapped them shut with a clack that reverberated over the water like a gunshot. It repeated its warning, once, twice. It stood its ground. Guarding its prey.

"This isn't working," Harlow shouted.

"Yeah, well big fucking surprise," Walker retorted, using his unfocused anger to flail at the panic that was about to consume him. But he knew time was up, that neither man nor beast was going to back down, raise a white flag. Without dwelling on the consequences—because he knew if did, he wouldn't act—he stepped in front of Harlow. "I'll take the charge," he said. "You get the kid."

Harlow started to protest, but the alligator moved first, launching itself at the invaders. It disappeared briefly beneath the water, then broke the surface, jaws wide open, its rip-saw teeth glinting in the fading sunlight.

In one motion, Walker yanked the spare PFD that draped over his shoulder and flung it into the gator's mouth. He dove to his left and saw the reptile sweep past him, its jaws clamping shut, slicing the life jacket in half. The animal plunged below the surface again, leaving only a wake of white, foaming bubbles to mark its trail.

Walker sat in the water, unable to catch his breath. Harlow stood over him, not speaking. If a black man's face could said to be drained of color, Harlow's was. Finally he said, "You crazy sonofabitch," and extended his hand to pull Walker up.

Walker shook his head. "Can't," he said. His legs wouldn't support him. He could barely speak, but managed to ask, "Is that thing gone?"

Harlow turned to look at the fading wake. "I think so," he said.

A gust of wind rattled the branches of the pine. A soft whimper escaped from the tangle of broken limbs.

"Time's up, Arly," Harlow said. "Stay here, rest a few seconds, I'll get the baby."

"No. I'm coming." Walker rolled over so that his hands and knees touched the ground, and pushed himself up. A gust of wind riffled the surface of the water and sent a sharp chill rushing over his drenched skin. A purple twilight had settled over the wrecked landscape as the advancing eastern eyewall of Janet flung a ragged blanket of thick nimbostratus across the sky.

Harlow reached the tree first. Walker was right behind him. Together, they pushed through the branches and prickly needles until they reached the woman. Her body was badly scratched and bruised. It looked as though a shard of wood or metal had been driven into the side of her chest, through her rib cage, probably into a lung. Slowly coagulating blood leaked from her mouth and nose. She had not been unattractive: blond, freckled, slightly overweight.

"Poor kid," Harlow said. Walker didn't know if the colonel was talking about the woman or the baby.

Harlow stripped off his life jacket, stepped onto a sturdy limb and reached for the child. The baby, a boy, whose head was turned away from the men and thus oblivious to their approach, reacted with a jerk and sharp cry as he was plucked from his mother. His tiny body, naked, was water-wrinkled and criss-crossed with shallow lacerations from the pine branches.

Walker continued to stare at the woman. Her green eyes, unseeing, dull in death, stared back. They seemed to convey the terror, the pain, the despair she must have experienced in her last moments as she clung desperately to her child. "He'll be okay now," he whispered, and reached to shut her eyelids.

He stepped away from her, wondering how she'd made it to the tree, but seeing manifest in her effort a mother's love and determination; the spirit of self-sacrifice that is the essence of love, the essence of the only constant in the world.

"Bernie, should we—"

"No," Harlow interrupted, obviously knowing what he was going to ask. "She's dead. There's no time. The recovery teams will get her."

"What if she's carried back out sea?"

"She's dead, Arly. The kid's alive. Let's get him back. Let's get us back."

Walker couldn't argue the point. He waded behind Harlow, back toward the Hurricane Hunter, scanning the surface of the surge, looking for the alligator, or at least its telltale wake. The wind rose steadily, the roar filling his ears, subsuming his thoughts. A heavy squall blitzed across the water, the rain laying out horizontally. The men lowered their heads, leaning into the renewed fury of the gale. The downpour, its drops stinging like killer bees, attacked their exposed skin. Harlow clutched the baby with both hands, wrapping his forearms around it and pulling it against his stomach like a running back protecting a football.

As quickly as the water had calmed, it became chaotic again, laced with whitecaps and foam. Walker decided the gator was probably the least of their worries. Getting back to the plane was now their biggest challenge.

Harlow stumbled over a hidden obstacle beneath the roiling surface of the water, and Walker reached out to steady him. But before he could fully extend his arm, a violent gust wrenched it backward. Instantaneous pain. He cried out as the limb separated from its socket and fell limply against the side of his body.

Harlow glanced at him but kept moving, or attempting to move. The strength of the wind bordered on epic. Walker realized they were no longer moving forward, that all of their energy was being expended merely holding their ground. A step forward, if it came at all, gained only inches.

Walker gasped for breath. Wind rammed into his nose and mouth faster than he could exhale. Seawater, whipped from the crest of sudden waves, drained into his throat, gagging and choking him. It seemed as if he'd become the object of some sort of bizarre end game: to see whether asphyxiation or drowning would kill him first.

He thought he heard Harlow yell something, but couldn't make it out. He glanced up, attempting to locate the aircraft, but it had disappeared from view in a leaden Mixmaster of rain and spray. He felt Harlow bump him, and saw that he was turning around, putting his back to the wind. Walker did likewise, and though he was unable to make any greater progress in the direction of the plane, he was at least able to breathe again. He spit out a mouthful of salty water, then raised his uninjured arm and signaled a thanks to Harlow.

Yet all considered, they were in a bad situation, trapped in no man's land, probably two hundred yards from the safety of the Hurricane Hunter. The depth of the water had steadied, and if anything, was beginning to recede. But debris, some of it sharp and serrated like chunks of deadly shrapnel, continued to lance through the air. And if one were to consider the worst-case scenario, out there someplace lurked a hungry and probably very pissed-off alligator.

Walker resumed his ponderous backward struggle against the wind. "Don't quit," he told himself, "don't quit."

**In the cockpit of the** Hurricane Hunter, Karlyn lifted the field glasses to her eyes. "I can't see them," she said, raising her voice to combat the renewed fury of the wind. "They got the baby, but then the eyewall hit. Now everything is just spray and sheets of rain out there." Her chest tightened, and a faint tremble rippled through her arms causing the binoculars to shake and lose focus.

Major Best, now the ranking officer on the plane, stood beside her. "How much longer for the eyewall to pass?" he asked.

"An hour, maybe longer."

Neither Karlyn nor Best spoke for a moment, allowing an unarticulated conclusion, an ugly deduction, to hover in the air between them: the odds of anyone being able to survive that long in the maelstrom that swirled outside were virtually nil.

Karlyn lowered the field glasses and turned to Best. "Can't we do anything?" she pleaded.

He shook his head slowly, conveying a sort of infinite sadness. "If we sent people after them, they'd only get into trouble, too. Like Bernie and Arly, they'd be fighting a 150-mph gale to get back to the plane. They wouldn't have a chance."

"Damn it, we can't just let them die out there." She brought the binoculars to her eyes again, mainly to hide the incipient tears that misted her vision. She knew Best was right, that any rescue attempt would be futile, but she couldn't accept it. Though rational thought argued against it, her heart told her not to surrender hope.

"How much rope do we have on board?" she asked.

"Karlyn—"

"How much rope?"

"Not enough. I know what you're thinking. We cinch a rope around somebody and tether it to the plane. Then whoever the lucky hero is slogs off into the storm and finds Bernie and Arly and the baby. He ropes them up, and everybody in the plane tugs them back to safety."

"Maybe *she* ropes them up."

"You've never lacked for chutzpah, Captain. But beyond the lack-of-rope issue, there are a couple of other problems. You wouldn't know which direction to go. And even if you did, it would be like wading through a free-fire zone with all that shit flying around out there. You'd get cut in two before you ever reached them."

"Yeah," she whispered, and tossed the binoculars onto the pilot's seat.

As if to emphasize Best's last point, something solid whanged against the body of the aircraft and sent a ringing vibration echoing through the fuselage, a noise that challenged even the caterwauling gale.

Karlyn sat down heavily in a canvas bunk at the rear of the flight deck. She buried her face in her hands and allowed the tears come. She didn't sob, but merely let the anger, frustration and sadness flow out of her.

She sensed someone sit next to her and felt an arm come around her shoulders. "If it's okay, I'll sit with you awhile," a woman's voice said, softly.

Karlyn nodded without looking up.

**Walker and Harlow crouched** in the surge as waves smashed into their backs, and wind-propelled debris from the ruined island continued to assault them. Harlow held the baby tightly against his chest, trying to keep from smothering it, yet at the same preventing seawater from splashing into its mouth.

The men attempted to scuttle backward, like ungainly crabs, in the general direction of the airplane, but made no progress.

Something smacked Walker in the back of his skull, filling his brain with red and amber flashes: stars and darts and lightning bolts. He blacked out. But a vague awareness of water stinging his eyes and throat, and pain arcing through his head as if it were a battered piñata, awakened his consciousness.

Choking, spitting water, he lifted himself from the surge and saw a shattered window frame, devoid of glass, floating in front of him. To his right, another large object, possibly a broken door, pitched wildly up and down in the surf. He looked for Harlow, but couldn't spot him. He attempted to stand, only to be knocked flat and driven back into the water by the wind.

Something hidden in the water bumped against him. Reflexively, thinking alligator, he leaped backward. A desperate attempt to escape. But it wasn't the gator. It was the baby, floating face down. He snatched it from the sea and drew it to his chest. It wasn't breathing. He held the child out, away from him, and looked into its tiny face. Contorted. Turning blue. Walker struggled with his right arm, the good one, to turn the baby over. He wanted to slap its back, to clear its lungs of water, but with only one functional arm, that was impossible. He felt the edge of panic knife into his psyche. What should he do? Turn the kid upside down? Shake it?

He snapped his head around, left, right, behind him, looking for Harlow. "Bernie," he bellowed, "Bernie!" But he couldn't hear his own cries over the wail of the wind.

The water seemed to be receding and he discovered he could sit down, draw his knees toward his chest, and have them just above the choppy surface. He placed the infant, stomach down, against his right knee, head resting against his kneecap, and slapped its back gently. Nothing. Again. Nothing. So, harder.

A little stream of gray water flushed from the child's mouth. Walker slapped again. More water. Another slap, followed by another. Finally, no more liquid. The lungs cleared. He turned the baby on his back. Still not breathing.

"Bernie," he screamed again. But there was no Bernie. "God," he yelled, "what do I do?"

Missiles of glass, wood, and metal, a fusillade of death, rifled past him on a wind fit only for the ride of the Valkyries. Its roar filled his ears and forced its way deep into his brain, suppressing his ability to think the problem through.

So, the Nike approach. Just do it. He placed his mouth over the child's mouth and nose and blew his breath into the infant. Still, the boy didn't stir. He blew again and again, setting up a rhythmic pattern. Finally, a half-hearted cough, more seen than heard.

Then a cry, torn away by the wind. The baby's eyes opened. Big and shiny, green like his mother's. He stared at Walker, whimpering, his arms and legs moving in jerky little motions. Walker drew him against his chest, pressing him into the life jacket. He turned the child's head to one side so it could breathe.

"We're just going to have to sit here awhile," he said into the baby's ear. "Just you and me. Help me watch for alligators. You know what those are? Like dragons, only they live in lakes and lagoons. Well, you probably don't know what those are, either." Walker looked around him, searching for help, for shelter, for Harlow, but the relentless onslaught of rain made it impossible to see more than a few yards.

"Okay," Walker said, continuing his monologue to the infant, "tell you what. How about helping me watch for an old friend instead of an alligator?" Walker thought the boy smiled, but maybe it was just a random facial expression.

"His name's Bernie," Walker went on, "the friend, not the alligator." The baby looked up and seemed to smile again. "A funny line, huh? Well, Bernie's the guy who pulled you out of the tree and carried you for awhile. I don't know what happened to him. I think he got hurt by flying debris—you know, junk—and dropped you in the water. He didn't do it on purpose. It was an accident, you understand."

The broken hull of a yacht half slid, half floated along Frederica Road.

"We're in kind of a bad fix here, so I hope you don't mind if I keep talking. It takes my mind off the situation." The baby reached a hand toward Walker's mouth.

"No? You want me to stop talking? Well, maybe it's your turn. What's your name?"

Walker waited, as if really expecting an answer. He began to shiver, the wind wicking away his body heat through his saturated flight suit as he remained seated in the shallow water.

"My name's Arlen," Walker said, "but people call me Arly. If it's okay with you, I'll call you 'Stormy' for the time being. That's what Air Force guys call weather officers, by the way. But considering the circumstances, I think the name probably fits you, too."

*Keep talking.* "We must look pretty weird, you and me, sitting out here in the middle of a hurricane. A couple of little stumps in a wind-whipped lake. Kind of lonely, isn't it? So I'm glad we've got each other." Even though the water level continued to drop, the wind made it impossible to stand. Walker realized he and the infant remained in extreme danger: exposed targets for the de facto weapons hurtling through the air.

Accentuating his concern, a piece of sheet metal, its rattle barely audible over the thunder of the wind, whizzed past his ear.

"I think I'm going to have to fit you into this life jacket somehow, Stormy," Walker said. "If I get sliced and diced by something out here, you'd be on your own. And you've been through enough already. So bear with me. I'll try not to drop you in the drink again, but I've only got one good arm."

Walker struggled to extricate himself from his PFD while holding Stormy, but it was an awkward, frustrating process. Whenever he tried to rise from the water to give himself more leverage, the wind leveled him with fire-hose fury. After minutes of battling the wind, the surge and the life jacket, he managed to wriggle free of the PFD and get it draped over his right forearm.

He rested Stormy against his chest and released his grip on him. Acting quickly, Walker raised his arm and shook the life jacket loose so he could transfer it to the baby. He wasn't quick enough. A tornadic gust snatched the PFD and swept it away over the white-capped water. Straps and flaps fluttering like the wings of a shot-gunned duck, the life jacket disappeared into the gray, wind-driven rain.

"Shit," Walker said. "Oops, don't say that, Stormy. That's a foo-foo word." Sitting again, he nestled the boy to his chest. "Bad Day at Black Rock," he muttered. "In case you're wondering, that's a movie title. From the '50s, I think. Spencer Tracy and Lee Marvin. You'll probably see it on TV reruns someday."

A tiny hand grasped Walker's flight suit and tugged it toward his mouth with more strength than he would have guessed a baby could have. "Hope you're not hungry, Stormy. I'm a bit short of the necessary equipment." The baby began to fuss, tiny stuttering cries, virtually lost in the wind.

"I've got an idea," Walker said, "maybe when you get a little older, we can go fishing together someday. I don't have any kids of my own, and it doesn't look like . . . Well, no need to go into that. At any rate, how's that sound? Just you and me, grabbing a charter boat to stalk the wily pisces?"

Stormy broke into a high-decibel wail.

A wave slapped a foamy surge of seawater onto Walker's neck. "Okay. I understand. Given our present circumstances, I can see where deep-sea fishing would be out. So maybe a nice mountain brook someplace. Far away from oceans and hurricanes. Colorado or Montana. We'll go after German browns or rainbows. With a fly rod. Just us guys. A few beers maybe. That work better for you?"

Stormy continued to cry.

Something thudded into Walker's back. A chunk of roof tile splashed down next to him.

"Okay, Stormy. We gotta move, gotta find shelter. We're gonna get killed if we sit out here much longer." Walker ran through his options. The plane probably was only a couple of hundred yards away, but against the wind, it might as well have been on the other side of the moon. To his right, he recalled seeing several small buildings, including flight operations, but they were just hollow shells now. Besides, that's where the fuel oil had spread from. Probably not a good choice for an escape route. To his left, across Frederica Road, the wreckage of a strip mall. Lots of debris. Another bad choice.

Back to the pine tree then, assuming it's still there? At least he'd have a tail wind. At least there'd be some protection among the branches. "Okay, here we go, kid. Hang on." Walker made no attempt to stand, instead, holding Stormy firmly against his chest, he began to duckwalk through the water.

Several times, the wind drove him to his knees. But he managed to keep from pitching forward, into the roiling surge, and falling on top of Stormy. The baby, almost as if sensing their dire situation, stopped crying and clung to Walker with the tenacity of a leech.

Walker lost track of time. The bellow of the wind was unrelenting; the assault of airborne debris, relentless. Each squatting step became agonizing. The muscles in his thighs and calves, strained far beyond the limits of their normal use, rebelled, burning with welding-arc intensity. Bullets of pain shot through his separated shoulder. And it felt as though a sixteen-pound shot put were rolling around in his head. The journey seemed endless.

But at last, the tree. Absent the baby's mother. Maybe a different tree? It didn't matter; it was a tree, a tall pine, prone in the water.

Walker reached its shattered branches and placed Stormy on a broad elbow where a large limb extended from the trunk. "Stay here, kid," he said. "Gonna make you a little bed." He was panting, riddled with pain, barely able to get the words out.

He unzipped his flight suit, front and legs, then stripped it from his body. A difficult task using only one arm and fighting wind gusts bent on hurling him into the next county. He wrapped the suit around Stormy, forming a U.S. Air Force-issue cradle, then tied its arms around a tree branch to secure it.

"There," he whispered. "Done."

He sat back in the water and toppled onto his side, half of his face settling into the surge. He closed his eyes. Just to rest.

# Chapter Thirty-four

## ATLANTA, GEORGIA—THE NATURAL ENVIRONMENT TELEVISION NETWORK LABOR DAY SUNDAY, 1830 HOURS

Phones at the network rang incessantly as radio stations and newspapers called for interviews, and emergency managers of inland counties in Janet's path sought additional information. Obermeyer and Sherrie allowed other staff to field the calls. A handful of previously off-duty meteorologists, lured away from holiday cookouts and golf games by Janet's sudden ferocity, had spontaneously materialized in the operations center during the course of the afternoon.

In contrast to the mausoleum-like silence that had permeated the work area twelve hours ago, a constant murmur of voices, punctuated by occasional shouts, now filled the floor, as did the odor of necrotic pizza and dried-up barbecue—pork, not beef. Obermeyer felt his stomach rumble—*great, now I'm hungry*—and turned to see if Sherrie, seated across from him, had heard it.

Her eyes were closed and her head rested on a desk as she breathed in and out of her mouth slowly and steadily, but softly. She'd done well, Obermeyer judged, stepping into a whirlpool of a day when she probably was expecting only a lazy float down a quiet river. She'd been a good soldier, a surprise ally, willing to take on the enemy, Robbie, without even a bayonet.

Over the past few hours, Obermeyer's objective, scientific mind had rallied and beaten back any middle-aged romantic fantasies he may have briefly harbored about her. He was what he was, and because of that, she'd been able to tempt him, play him, for motives other than sex. But he hoped he would keep her as a friend.

She opened one eye. "I heard that," she said.

"What?" he exclaimed, caught off guard, fearing he'd somehow verbalized his thoughts.

She opened her other eye and sat up. "I'm hungry, too. Let's go find a McDonalds or something and clog our arteries."

"Wait a minute," he said, shifting his gaze to the far end of the sprawling room, "I think something else is about to clog our arteries."

Robbie McSwanson, his gangly, scarecrow frame moving at a determined gait, strode into the ops area. Brushing a tangle of stringy red hair from his eyes, he came to an abrupt halt where Obermeyer and Sherrie were seated. "Nice job today, both of ya," he said. A reptilian smile followed his words.

Obermeyer started to rise from his chair.

"No, no, Obie. Please. Stay seated. Ya must be tired. A long day, I know, what with all the broadcastin', ballin' and blackmailin'."

An adrenaline-fueled rush of anger surged into Obermeyer. "Balling?" he said.

"Unless I misunderstood the lass, here, I think her words to me this morning when I asked about ya were 'he's about to get—'"

Obermeyer sprang from his chair, drawing his fist back for a shot into the Scotsman's face.

Sherrie was quicker, launching herself between the two men. "'About to' doesn't equate to 'did,'" she snapped at McSwanson. She turned to Obermeyer, grabbing his arm. "Don't," she said. "That's what he wants. An excuse to fire you."

"He's going to anyway," he replied.

"What?" Her mouth remained open after she spoke, as though she wanted to say more.

"Ask him," Obermeyer said.

She turned back to McSwanson. "Are you?"

"I already did, this mornin'."

"What about our new contracts?"

"What new contracts?"

"The ones you promised over the phone. The deal you made with Obie. The reason we came back to work."

"I think ya must have misunderstood, lass." He paused theatrically. "Oh, perhaps I acknowledged something under duress, said something I shouldn't have. But then ya'd be talkin' blackmail, wouldn't ya?"

Obermeyer intervened. "No, we wouldn't. We'd be talking good old hard-nosed, get-the-deal-done business negotiation. We had a gentleman's agreement."

"Ya have proof of this? A written document? A secretly taped conversation?" A smirk crept across McSwanson's narrow countenance.

"No," Obermeyer said, "I forgot only one of us is a gentleman."

"Ah, well, then that's your failure, isn't it? Did ya think ya were dealin' with some ignorant Scottish shortbread vendor? A Highlander in his cups? A beggar from the streets of Edinburgh? Did ya think ya could beat me at my own game?"

The phone on Obermeyer's desk rang, a single ring indicating a call from within the building. He answered. A voice on the other end of the line informed him the guest he'd been expecting had arrived. "Please escort her down here," Obermeyer said. He turned back to McSwanson. "I can't beat you at your game, but I can beat you at mine."

"Too late," McSwanson said. "Game over. Ya did your job, very nicely I might add, a credit to the network and all that, but we can handle it from here. It was a team effort, ya see. No stars, no prima donnas, certainly no blackmailers. Your services are no longer required. Yours or the bawdy lass's. Now, do I call the police again, or do ya exit under your power?"

"And when the next major hurricane hits, what then? Who's your expert? How will the network meet the challenge?" Obermeyer asked.

"Like I said, Obie, this was a team effort. Everyone pullin' the load together. That's the way it'll be with the next big storm."

"You're a liar, Robbie McSwanson," Sherrie said, jabbing a finger at his nose. "You know it, I know it, Obie knows it."

McSwanson pushed her finger away. "Ah, yes, lass. That may be, but nobody else does."

"At the moment, no," Obermeyer interjected, "but by tomorrow morning, over two million people will." It was his turn to smile and he hoped he looked less like a crocodile than McSwanson had.

"Forget tryin' to threaten me, Obie. Out. Now. Both of ya."

"*Jawohl, mein Fuhrer.* But before we leave, there's someone I'd like you to meet."

McSwanson's gaze darted around the room, a small betrayal of sudden uneasiness, as though fearing something or someone that could do him harm might have slipped his notice. "Who?"

"My insurance agent."

McSwanson chuckled and brought his gaze back to bear on Obermeyer. It was then Obermeyer noted with satisfaction something in the Scotsman's eyes that hadn't been there before: uncertainty. The conveyance of a gnawing doubt, the festering apprehension that a carpet was about to be yanked out from underneath his feet.

A door to the operations area swung open and a plump little muffin of a woman followed by a corporate security guard entered. The odor of stale cigarette smoke, perhaps the residue of a clandestine drag in an exterior hallway, probably by someone other than the woman or her escort, trailed them into the sprawling facility.

The guard pointed in Obermeyer's direction. The lady nodded an acknowledgment, then waddled toward Obermeyer. Her clothes were so mismatched she looked as if she'd dressed in the dark in a Goodwill store. But her short hair was neatly clipped and groomed, and her face made up in a manner that offset the disarray of her wardrobe. A large tote bag was slung over her left shoulder. She smiled easily at Obermeyer as she extended her hand to him. "Mandy Offutt," she said, "I believe I've interviewed you before." Her visitor's badge read "Amanda Offutt, USA TODAY."

"Yes, several years ago after Rita," Obermeyer said, accepting the proffered hand. "Good to meet you again. I see your by-line often in *USA Today*." He turned to McSwanson. "I'd like you to meet my boss, Robert McSwanson, the executive vice president of production at the network."

McSwanson shook hands with Mandy, but glanced at her only briefly. Mostly his eyes bore into Obermeyer, and Obermeyer could see in them the look of an animal that knew it was about to step into a snare, but didn't know what it was, where it was, or how to avoid it.

Obermeyer returned McSwanson's glare, keeping, he hoped, his face expressionless, but feeling something entirely different. *Don't look now you son of a bitch, but a safe is about to fall on your head.* He turned away from McSwanson and gestured at Sherrie. "And this is Sherrie Willis who shared most of the on-camera duties with me today." *And almost shared my bed this morning.*

Sherrie and Mandy shook hands. Sherrie turned to Obermeyer. "Insurance agent?" she mouthed.

Obermeyer flashed her a one-second grin.

Offutt reached into her tote bag and withdrew a small tape recorder. "An unnamed source," she said, making little quotation marks in the air with her fingers, "by the name of Rick Keys at the National Hurricane Center called me this afternoon."

Obermeyer cocked his head at Offutt, a warning gesture.

"Don't worry," she said, "his name won't appear in anything I write. I understand the last thing a government agency wants to do is cast laurels around someone else's shoulder for doing its job better."

"The Hurricane Center did fine," Obermeyer said.

"But Rick, my unnamed source, told me you led the charge, got out in front of the cavalry, put your professional reputation on the line and probably saved a lot of lives. That's a great story. Front page stuff. John Wayne as a meteorologist." She chuckled softly, apparently warming to her own simile.

She turned toward McSwanson. "You gotta be proud of this guy. This was a real coup for the network. And you."

McSwanson opened his mouth, but no words came out.

Obermeyer stepped next to him and draped his arm across the back of McSwanson's shoulders, feeling him stiffen as he did so. "Robbie's the greatest boss in the world. Tell your readers that."

Offutt switched on her tape recorder.

Obermeyer continued talking. "Robbie saw the necessity for getting us on the air early, getting out in front of this thing. Luckily for us he's a guy with foresight, and we were able to jump on the situation." He patted McSwanson on the back.

McSwanson recoiled from the approbation and smiled wanly.

"I'll tell you something else about this man," Obermeyer went on, "he knows how to take care of his troops. I understand this won't be the focus of your story, but just as background, let me tell you that in the midst of the turmoil today, he rewarded our efforts, mine and Sherrie's, with new contracts. Quite generous tenders, I might add." He squeezed McSwanson's shoulder as if they were the best of buddies, then withdrew his arm.

"He's too kind," McSwanson said to the reporter. His words came out coated in invisible venom. If Offutt noticed the ire in the man's voice, she didn't let on.

"As a matter of fact," Obermeyer said, "Robbie was just on his way upstairs to retrieve the contracts for signing."

McSwanson stood his ground, glaring at Obermeyer.

"It's okay, Robbie," Sherrie said, picking up on Obermeyer's game. "Go ahead. We can fill Ms. Offutt in on the meteorological details of today while you get the documents. You can give her the production and corporate angles when you get back, and then maybe we can have a little celebratory signing." She stepped up to McSwanson and gave him a quick hug.

He didn't reciprocate. Instead, he took a step back and crooked his index finger at Obermeyer. Obermeyer followed him into an unpopulated corner of the ops area, out of sight of the reporter.

McSwanson's face had turned the color of a male cardinal. He stood standpipe straight, his fists clenched at his sides, and leaned into Obermeyer. "Ya mother fuckin' weasel, ya snivelin' wee cockroach, ya—"

Obermeyer laughed. "You look like a scarecrow with a broomstick up his ass, Robbie. For Christ's sake, relax. You got out-finagled in this round. Go type out a memorandum of agreement and we'll all make nice. Corporate headquarters can draft the contracts next week."

"You'll not intimidate me, ya supercilious son of a bitch. You'll not make a fool of me in front of the national media."

"The only way you'll be made a fool of, Robbie, is if you can the two meteorologists who were the canaries in the coal mine for the most powerful hurricane in history. Oh, yeah, and simultaneously landed the network on the front page of *USA Today*. Now go prepare an MOA and quit acting like I tossed a hand grenade into the bathroom while you were taking a dump."

McSwanson didn't move.

"Don't step on your poncho, Hotshot, not now. You think there's not a big enough bonus to buy a second home, and a corner office, waiting for you at corporate? Don't be a fool, Robbie. This is victory in defeat. I whipped your ass. But you climb the corporate ladder. Lose-win."

McSwanson expelled a long breath. "Don't ever let your guard down around me, Obie." He wheeled and stalked away.

"Don't worry, I won't," Obermeyer said to no one. He walked back to Sherrie and the reporter.

"Well?" Sherrie said.

"Sometimes love is the best revenge," he answered.

# Chapter Thirty-five

## ST. SIMONS ISLAND, GEORGIA
## LABOR DAY SUNDAY, 2000 HOURS

The water in the Hurricane Hunter at last receded, leaving the interior of the plane encrusted in a thin gravy of salt and mud. Janet had swirled inland. Karlyn poked her head out the crew door. The wind, she guessed, still blew at 30 to 40 mph, but compared to the fury of the eyewall, it was a summer zephyr.

The darkness was what struck her most. The sun had set, leaving the island, or whatever was left of it, in utter blackness. No street lights, no house lights, no headlights, no neon signs. Not even a firefly. A cave at midnight during a new moon.

She played her flashlight over the tarmac. It was layered in silt, sand and mud; strewn with tree limbs, shattered lumber, pieces of metal. The beam of her light caught a tattered shirt, an orphaned shoe, a twisted Atlanta Braves baseball hat. A mephitic vapor permeated the air, the stench of tidal flats at low tide. But there was something else, too. A vague odor of rot and maybe—she didn't want to dwell on it— death.

"Let's go," Major Best said from behind her. "Let's find our guys."

She turned toward him. "What are the odds?" she asked quietly, barely able to squeeze out the words. But she knew what the odds were. People caught in the open don't survive cat five hurricanes.

Best stared past her into the darkness. "Maybe you'd better stay in the plane, Karlyn, take care of our guests. It's not going to be pretty out there."

"I know that. But I can't . . . I don't want to stay behind."

Best laid his hands on her shoulders and looked her in the eye. "Chances are Bernie, Arly and that baby they found didn't make it," he said, his voice soft, compassionate.

She looked away from his gaze, knowing she was on the verge of tears. "I understand that. But me staying here won't change the outcome. One way or the other, now or later, I'll have to face whatever happened out there." She stepped through the crew door onto the steps. "Come on," she said.

Accompanied by Best and Sergeant McKenzie, she stepped down onto the soggy grass.

"Wait." A voice from the plane.

Best turned.

"I'm coming, too." Hemphill.

"I'm sorry, sir, but you'll have to remain in the aircraft with Lieutenant Smithers and the others," Best said.

Hemphill, his shoes squishing in the grass, walked toward Best. "I'm not in the aircraft now."

"But you're still my responsibility."

"You're relieved of duty, sir. Sorry, I appreciate the ride and everything, but I'm not in your chain of command and not on a military base. Free press and all that crap. Besides, I can help you search."

Best muttered something, then yelled to Lieutenant Smithers in the aircraft. "Give him your Maglite, Van."

Smithers tossed his flashlight to Hemphill.

"At least out here, Mr. Hemphill, how about following my orders?" Best said.

Hemphill nodded.

"We'll spread out, about twenty yards apart and walk north along the runway in the direction we last saw Bernie and Arly. Keep calling their names. Not only for their benefit, but ours, too. As long as we can hear each other, we'll know everything is okay."

They sloshed through the mud and grass around the nose of the Hurricane Hunter and headed up the runway. Karlyn swung her flashlight in the direction of Frederica Road. In a water-filled drainage ditch paralleling the road, her beam reflected off a pair of bright, egg-sized orbs. They seemed to float on the surface of the water, but as quickly as her light struck them, they disappeared in a soft splash.

Other than that and the rush of the wind, there was no sound. At least not the kind Karlyn had come to know on soft September nights: dogs barking, children calling, the burbles and peeps of night creatures, the blurt of an occasional automobile horn. Nothing. Silence as deep as the darkness.

The searchers called out as they pressed forward: "Bernie? Arly?"

The group moved slowly, spread apart, their flashlight beams playing back and forth across the muddy, debris-laced plain of the runway. Downed trees, large and small, jetsam of the storm, littered the airport grounds. They lay like the ragged skeletal remains of large animals, too slow-footed or dim-witted to have escaped the surge.

Karlyn's stomach knotted, rolled, then knotted again. The chances of finding anyone alive out here were virtually nil. She knew that, but refused to accept it. There were always tales of someone surviving for days, long after hope had been abandoned, buried in the rubble of an earthquake, trapped in the depths of a collapsed mine, surrounded by flood waters in an airless attic. Always.

But this. This was catastrophic. Hiroshima. Nagasaki. Dresden. The Twin Towers.

"Bernie?"

"Arly?"

No answer save for the distant, lonesome howl of a dog. But even that abruptly ceased, as though the pet suddenly realized the futility of his situation. Or . . . Karlyn swept the beam of her light more quickly over the ruined landscape, checking for something akin to the twin reflectors she'd spotted in the drainage ditch. But there was nothing, no sign of life, neither benign nor predator.

The flashlight beams of the others swung to and fro on either side of her, but their brightness illuminated only rubble and muck, nothing that hinted of their missing friends. Karlyn looked back at the Hurricane Hunter. A dim glow from the plane's interior, the craft's emergency lighting, filtered through the cockpit windows and crew door. The subdued brightness marked the only safe haven remaining on St. Simons Island.

Because of a baby they'd gone out, Arly and Bernie. Left the plane, racing the eyewall; losing. Because of a baby.

"You don't understand any of this, do you?" Karlyn whispered to the nascent life within her. *Neither do I.*

Ahead of her, the silhouette of a massive pine lying in state rose from the ground, like some prehistoric beast mired in a latter-day tar pit. Several shafts of light played over the dark tree, but illuminated only shattered limbs.

"Nothing here," McKenzie said.

"No, hold on," Best responded. "Listen."

A soft mewing sound floated through the darkness.

"A cat?" Hemphill said.

Karlyn darted toward the tree, slipping and almost losing her footing on the slime of mud and sand that coated the runway. "No," she said, "not a cat." She swept her flashlight back and forth, up and down, but still saw nothing, save for broken branches. Then she spotted a slight movement near a large limb. "Here, guys, here!"

A baby, fussing, but very still, turned its head to gaze into the beam of her light.

"Oh, Christ," she said, "it's wrapped in a flight suit."

"It's Arly's," Best said. He directed the glow of his light at the name tag on the suit.

"Hey, little fella," Karlyn said. "It's okay now." She pocketed her Maglite, then plucked the baby from its nylon cradle and kissed his scratched face.

"A boy," Sergeant McKenzie pointed out.

"Yeah, I see." Karlyn unzipped the top of her own flight suit, cuddled the baby inside of it, and nestled him against her breast. "I think the last time I did this for a man," she whispered, "was for the guy who saved you."

"What?" McKenzie asked.

"Nothing," she answered. "Just wondering where the guys are who rescued this little dude."

"Me, too."

"Search all around the tree," Best ordered. "They have to be nearby."

*Them, or their corpses?* Karlyn hugged the child tighter.

"Karlyn, you stay right here. Don't move. If we don't find Arly and Bernie nearby, I'll send Mr. Hemphill back to the plane with you and the baby."

"Sir—," Hemphill said.

"That wasn't a suggestion, Mr. Hemphill," Best snapped. "She needs someone to light the way. Besides, you've got your story: Moses, if not pulled from the bulrushes, at least from a slash pine."

Hemphill acquiesced.

"We'll be back in a few minutes, Karlyn. Hang tight," Best said. The group moved off, McKenzie and Hemphill to her left, Best to her right. Their flashlight beams cut through the black void, sweeping over the branches and ground in slow, methodical arcs.

Beneath Karlyn's flight suit, the baby whimpered and squirmed. He pushed his face against her breast. "Nothing there for you, junior. We'll find something when we get back to the plane. Just relax now." She patted his back.

"Do you believe the good die young?" she asked, lowering her head to speak to the baby. "I used to think that was just an old saw, but now I wonder. Kind of like 'no good deed goes unpunished.' The guys that saved you, Arly and Bernie? Good men. Young. Doing a good deed. Life isn't fair is it?" She sensed her eyes welling. "Don't mind me, I'm just a wuss."

The baby lifted his head off her breast. The dying wind swept a soft spatter of rain into her face.

"I think you would've liked Arly," she continued. "He's the guy who wrapped you in his flight suit, by the way. A true gentleman. No, really. There should be more like him. His wife's a real bitch, though. How does that happen? Do you think some people can be too nice, too tolerant, too forgiving? Well, I don't suppose you'll ever get a chance to meet him . . ." A sob leaked from her throat, surprising her. "Sorry about that. Like I said, you probably won't get to meet him, but I'll tell you about him someday when you're older. Deal?"

No answer. Nothing but a soft purr, a baby's barely audible snore.
*I miss you, Arly.*

She heard the men continuing to call Arly and Bernie's names; saw their lights dancing through the broken limbs; sensed the fruitlessness of their search.

"Gotta sit for awhile, kiddo," she said. "I feel like a rag doll." The fatigue of loss. She shuffled sideways, searching for a place she could lean back against the tree trunk. Her boots kicked through a pile of branches and cones and hit something semi-solid.

She bent to feel it, jerked her hand away. Saturated cloth. Clothes? Underwear? A body?

*Don't scream. Don't scream.*

She screamed.


**Too much pain.** *Can't be dead. Or in heaven.*

Walker opened his eyes. One of them, anyhow. The other wouldn't respond. His shoulder seemed to have been garroted. His head split with an iron wedge. His lungs seared by fire.

"Hurts," he said.

"Yeah, yeah. Take it easy. You're back in the plane," Major Best said.

"You're gonna be all right, Arly," Karlyn said. She stroked his forehead with her hand. Her eyes were puffy and red, but at the same time, soft and reassuring.

Wrapped in several blankets, Walker was lying on a bunk at the rear of the flight deck. He tried to sit up, but Best placed a restraining hand on his shoulder. "Not yet, Major. Mission complete. Time for some R and R."

"Bernie?" Walker asked.

No one answered.

"What happened to Bernie?" he repeated.

"I'm sorry," Best said. "We found him . . . his body . . . floating in pile of lumber and tree limbs. He had a nasty wound on the back of his head. I . . . I don't think he drowned. Something hit him . . . " His voice trailed off. Even in the dim light, Walker could see deep furrows etched in his navigator's face. On land, wind and rain require centuries to carve out canyons and valleys. On the human body, stress can do it in moments.

"He was holding Stormy when something hit him," Walker said. "Both of us. A door or window frame maybe. I don't know." He shook his head slowly. "When I came to, Bernie was gone and Stormy was underwater." His words were slurred in pain and fatigue. He squeezed his eyes shut, willing the tears not to come.

"Stormy?" Karlyn said after awhile.

Fighting to control his voice, Walker answered, "The baby. I named him Stormy. We had some long talks, him and me, sitting out there in the eyewall."

"I didn't find him to be much of a conversationalist," Karlyn said.

Walker attempted a smile, but an explosion of pain blew it up. "Shit," he choked out.

"Sorry," Karlyn said.

"But he's okay, Stormy's okay?"

"He's fine," Best said. "We found some juice for him and rigged a nipple. Now the kid's pissing like he swallowed a diuretic."

Again Walker tried to smile, or at least grin, but it ended in a grimace.

"I'd yell 'medic,'" Best said, "but we don't have one. Sergeant McKenzie's the closest thing. He's got some first aid training. You stay here with Nurse Karlyn, and I'll go round him up." Best scrambled down the ladder leading to the rear of the broken Hurricane Hunter.

"Nurse Karlyn?" Walker said.

"Female stereotype."

"Yeah. I never pictured you as a nurse."

"Me either."

Their conversation lagged momentarily, then Walker said, "After today, do you think you'll stay in the Reserve?"

Karlyn looked away, as though the question had touched a nerve he wasn't aware of.

"What?" he asked. He felt compelled to reach for her hand, but it seemed inappropriate.

"It's a loaded question," she said.

"How can it be loaded? It's sort of a yes or no thing."

She turned to look at him. He could read in her eyes there was something he had totally missed or didn't understand.

"It's not a simple yes or no thing," she said. "Starbucks when we get back, remember? I still have a friend, right?"

He nodded. Something inside his head was hammering to be let out.

She stepped back from the bunk. "Well, I'll go check on Stormy while Louie tends to you."

"A little bit of nurse in you after all."

"Maybe." She turned to go.

"Well, if nothing else about this day," he said, "you'll have a hell of a story to tell your kids when they get older."

"You're assuming," she answered, a bit sharply it seemed.

"Sorry, it was just something to—"

"You sure know how to rattle a person's cage," she blurted, and disappeared from view.

He waited for her to reappear, to deliver the punch line. She didn't. *What the hell did I miss?* Apparently about ten chapters, he decided. At least Donna he understood. Didn't like, but understood.

"Dr. Louie here, Major." Sergeant McKenzie came up the ladder. He walked to where Walker lay and bent over him, gently pushing at the dislocated shoulder.

Walker flinched. "You know what you're doing?"

"No, but I've got some little pills here that will take you to Happy Dreamland."

Walker shook his head. "I'll live without them."

"Please do, sir. Losing Bernie was enough." Walker could see McKenzie squeezing his lips together, suppressing emotion.

# Chapter Thirty-six

## ATLANTA, GEORGIA—THE NATURAL ENVIRONMENT TELEVISION NETWORK LABOR DAY SUNDAY, 2035 HOURS

After the interview with the *USA Today* reporter was wrapped up and Obermeyer had completed briefing his relief meteorologists, he stood to leave. "Hey, Obie," someone called from across the room, "pick up line four."

He did. It was Rick Keys from the Hurricane Center. "You're a hero, buddy," he said. "The Hurricane Hunter escaped the eye, then crash landed on St. Simons, but everyone survived. Well, except for the copilot. We heard he was killed after they landed, but we don't have any details yet. Oh, and the crew apparently took some people onboard who were unable to get off the island. So it worked out well for a lot of folks."

"Except the copilot," Obermeyer said.

"Yeah. But you know, the entire crew could have been lost."

Obermeyer considered his situation for awhile before responding, then said, "So, the repercussions of Rita are dead?"

Keys laughed. "Yeah, until the next hurricane. I'm sure you'll manage to yank a string around someone's balls again."

Later, Obermeyer and Sherrie stood together in the parking lot. The wind, warm and humid, gusted fitfully. Bats, in search of an evening meal, dipped and darted through cones of brightness shed by banks of overhead lights. The moon, barely visible through a gauzy overcast, sat atop a tree line to the east.

"We're in for it, too, aren't we?" Sherrie said.

"Should be blowing pretty hard by morning," Obermeyer answered.

"Lotta damage?"

"More than the city's ever seen."

"Not like the other tropical storms that have come a-calling, then?"

"Janet will still be a hurricane. First one ever for the city."

"Land-office business at Home Depot and Lowe's, I suppose. You know, for power saws and portable generators and stuff."

"Yeah, but after what happened to St. Simons . . ." His voice faltered.

"It won't be a big deal by comparison, will it?"

"No," he said simply. "Let's walk."

"Where to? Our cars are right here."

"Just walk."

Side by side, they strolled toward the perimeter of the fenced-in lot. A tiny whirlwind ran ahead of them, herding a ground blizzard of dust and sand.

"Do you think there's anything left?" she said.

"On St. Simons? No."

They sauntered on in silence.

"Janet will be your legacy," she said after awhile. "You did good today."

"Too many people still died."

"We don't know that. Not yet anyhow."

"There wasn't enough time to get everybody off the island."

"But maybe most of them, thanks to you."

"Look, don't canonize me. All I did was blow the bugle to sound the charge. There were a lot of others involved, including the guys at the Hurricane Center. They just needed a kick in the butt to get them energized."

"More like a stick of dynamite stuck up their asses. Don't be so damn modest."

The warmth of the evening closed in on Obermeyer; his dress shirt grew damp in perspiration. He stopped walking, removed his suit jacket and slung it over his shoulder.

Sherrie poked at the spot on his shirt where he'd spilled the Dr Pepper hours ago. "You should save this shirt," she said, "just as it is. A remembrance of the day."

He smiled. "There are others." He let his response hang between them.

A vigorous puff of wind coiled Sherrie's hair around her face. She brushed the tangled strands back and looked up at him. After the long day, she looked older, tiny etchings apparent at the corners of eyes and sides of her mouth. Now she seemed more his peer than underling. More his equal. More desirable.

*Don't.* He looked away.

She took his hand. "You don't know what to make of me, do you?"

"No."

"Sometimes I don't either."

The wail of a distant siren, an ambulance or fire truck, rode the wind, waxing and waning in the growing darkness. Then it faded completely and they were left in silence, save for the busy breeze.

He debated pulling her closer, wrapping his arms around her, kissing her. But lost in a conflicted limbo of desire and restraint, he didn't.

She spoke again. "You think you're too old for me, don't you? Maybe a little dumpy, a bit too nerdy?"

"Well?"

"Well, here's the deal. Not all women get dippy and swoony over firm butts, tight tummies and guys wearing Gucci and Armani. Sometimes we're just looking for a man who will take a stand, be honest, put the toilet seat down, and notice what we're wearing once in a while." Unexpectedly, she snickered. "Although I kind of obviated that last item this morning, didn't I."

"Meaning?"

"I think you noticed what I *wasn't* wearing."

"Oh, that. Well, you had ulterior motives."

"Did I?" Still holding his hand, she stepped closer to him.

Her perfume overwhelmed him, an invisible sweetness in the humid dusk pillaging his resistance. "There you go again."

"The enigmatic Miss Willis."

"Yes." Her face was inches from his. "Do you mind if I kiss you? Again?" he asked. *Idiot.*

"It'd be cooler if you just did it. As I recall, I took the lead this morning."

"I never claimed to be cool."

"With good reason." She dropped his hand and stepped away from him. "We need to work on that."

"That was a 'no' then?"

"No."

"What was it?" he asked.

"You figure it out."

"I'm no good with women."

"You handled Janet pretty well."

They resumed walking. "That was different," he said.

"Perhaps you'd like me better if I had one eye and could whirl like a dervish at 100 mph."

"I like you just as you are."

"But you do like me?"

"Yes."

"And you do see me as something more than a kid sister?" She kicked at an acorn bouncing across the pavement.

"Maybe."

"Try again."

"Yes."

"Good. We're making progress."

"So what's next?"

"You're a slow learner aren't you?"

"Not really," he said softly.

He dropped his suit jacket, grabbed her arm, spun her about and drew her into him. Their bodies met a little more forcefully than he intended, but she didn't resist or protest and already had her head tilted up as they came face to face. They kissed for a long time, separated, then kissed again.

"I'm glad we got over that hurdle," she said, finally breaking their embrace.

He was breathless, exhilarated, yet at the same time permeated by a strange hollowness. It was as if he'd attained a goal, but knew it was a fleeting victory, an illusory triumph. He attempted to deconstruct the feeling, to determine its roots and meaning, but came up empty.

Sherrie, seeming to sense the confusion raging within him, fixed her gaze on him.

He shrugged. "I don't understand what's going on."

She leaned toward him. "Yes, you do," she whispered.

He touched her hand, paused, then said quietly, "Let's go home."

"Okay," she said. "See you tomorrow?"

"That's not what I meant."

"I know what you meant. But I don't want you to think I'm easy."

He stared at her, not knowing whether to laugh or throw himself off the top of a building.

"Think you can leave the Black Jack on the shelf tonight?"

"Yeah."

"Think you can acknowledge you've won lady fair?"

"Have I?

She kicked him lightly in the shin. "I don't disrobe for just anybody."

"I still haven't figured you out."

"If you'd figured me out, you'd be a psychoanalyst, not a weatherman. Look, you're really good at what you do. And you're gonna have to do it again tomorrow." She nodded in the direction of distant lightning. "It's going to get nasty in Atlanta. Go home. Get some rest. I'm off tomorrow, but I'll come by the studio, get the keys to your house, pick up some steaks and cook dinner for us."

"I doubt it," he said.

"You don't believe me."

"No, I mean there probably won't be any power tomorrow, the grocery stores will have been plundered, and you shouldn't be out driving around anyhow."

"Well then, there's always anticipation, isn't there?" She leaned her body against his again, nestling into him until he could feel every hill and valley, every softness and firmness, every promise and lie in her topography.

The southern horizon trembled in electric flashes, tinting the skyline of the city blue and white. The wind had stiffened. No longer gentle, it sawed through the night with an urgency that warned of worse to come. Large raindrops, like stray gunfire, splattered onto the asphalt of the parking lot.

"Janet," Sherrie whispered in Obermeyer's ear.

"Yes, we'll always have Janet, won't we?"

"Funny, Bogie."

He took her hand and they walked toward their cars.

# Chapter Thirty-seven

## ST. SIMONS ISLAND, GEORGIA
## LABOR DAY SUNDAY, 2040 HOURS

After McKenzie completed his work, Walker drifted into a restless sleep. Disturbing visions swirled through a chaotic dream filled with green-gray water and the jet-engine roar of wind: an alligator festooned with Donna's head; a gleaming white stadium filled with cheering skeletons; a Hurricane Hunter plunging wingless and silent into the sea; Karlyn handing him a baby that stared at him with dead eyes—Bernie's eyes.

The alligator, this time complete with its own head, charged. Jaws agape and tail thrashing, it came at him. Stopped. Sat there, inches from his face, mouth open, ragged, serrated teeth gleaming in red light. A cell phone, covered in saliva and blood, rested at the back of the gator's throat. The phone rang. Walker, knowing he shouldn't, but somehow compelled, reached for it. The gator's jaws snapped shut. Walker jerked awake, yelling, "No, no, no." The phone continued to ring.

His flight bag. The cell phone in his flight bag was ringing. He looked around for help, but found himself alone, still in the bunk. Head spinning and exploding in pain, he sat up. Through blurred vision he spotted his bag on the floor next to the navigator's position. He stumbled to it, unzipped it, and pawed through a tangle of clothing, toiletries and paperback books until he found his phone.

"Hello?" he said.

It continued to ring. *Gotta push the button.* He did, and said again, "Hello?"

Silence.

"Any one there?"

"Yes, goddamn it, someone's here. Where the hell are you? Did you forget we had a cookout to attend tonight? You said you'd be back by seven at the latest. You'd think on your last friggin' flight for the Air Force you could make it home on time—"

"Donna?"

"Yeah. Who the hell else do you think? Like there are other ladies in your life? You aren't up to it, hotshot. Double entendre intended."

Walker let her jibe go, too tired to retaliate, too exhausted to care. "The flight turned out to be longer than we'd planned."

"Duh. But you don't give a flying fuck, do you?" Over the phone, Obermeyer heard music, people laughing, the splash of someone diving into a pool.

Donna went on. "You couldn't possibly care about showing up for a gathering at your boss's home, could you? Displaying a little executive interest in your coworkers and what goes on at the bank? Running up the colors and saying I'm committed to this? God, please tell me you're at least back at Keesler."

"We've been delayed." A white-hot lance of pain arced across his scalp.

"Delayed. Delayed where?"

The cockpit began to spin. Walker felt as if he were riding a precessing gyroscope tilted at an extreme angle. He staggered back to the bunk, sat and pulled a blanket over his legs. "On St. Simon's Island," he said.

"Fine and fucking dandy," Donna said. "How do you think that makes me look? Standing here alone, everyone else with a spouse, my husband stuck at some coastal resort? God, I'm glad this is over, that you're finally leaving the Reserve. That maybe we can at last make something of our lives."

Despite his weakness, Walker finally felt compelled to mount a counterattack. "*Our* lives? I think I have made something of my life, Donna."

"What? Captain Miracle putzing around in windstorms?"

He wasn't really hearing this was he? He took the phone away from his ear and set it on his lap. He closed his eyes; the pain abated. Donna continued to yammer into the blanket covering his thighs.

After a minute, he lifted the phone back to his cheek. "Donna?"

"Oh, I thought you'd hung up on me, you prick. Can't even show up on time for a—"

"Have you watched TV at all today?"

"No."

"No news? No weather reports?"

"I've been shopping. Played a little tennis."

"You haven't heard about the hurricane then?"

"The one you were flying into today? That wimpy thing going into South Carolina or someplace? Of course I heard about it. So what? You've always found excuses to put the Reserve first."

Excuses? He didn't respond immediately. When he did, he asked, "Whatever happened to us?"

"What?"

"Whatever happened to us, our relationship?"

"Us? You mean you?"

"Yes. Maybe that's what I meant." The words drained from him like water rushing down a sewer. His head began thumping again, the sensation almost audible. He opened his eyes and lay back on the bunk. He tugged the blanket over his chest as a shiver rippled through his body.

"What time do you think you'll get back to Keesler?" Donna said. "By eleven, maybe? This thing will still be going past midnight. So let's say you're here by then, okay? Tough day at the office, I'll tell our host. I'll cut you some slack this time. The final time."

"I'd appreciate that, honey." He didn't really. He just couldn't muster the energy to joust with her any longer.

"Look, just get here before I turn into a pumpkin. 'Roger that?' as you guys say." Her attempt at lightheartedness.

Karlyn poked her head over the top of the ladder leading to the flight deck. "You okay?" she mouthed to Walker, seeing he was on the phone.

"Yes," he said out loud, answering both her question and Donna's.

"Make sure," Donna said.

Karlyn started back down the ladder.

Walker, using his good arm, the one holding the phone, motioned for her to sit beside him.

She hesitated, looked back into the fuselage, then climbed onto the flight deck and sat near his feet. She fixed her gaze on his face, furrowed her eyebrows, and cocked her head—a tacit question.

"Donna," he said softly to her and placed his forefinger against his lips. He brought the phone back to his ear. Having Karlyn seated next to him seemed to spark something deep within him. A sudden realization—an epiphany?—that he'd taken enough of Donna's belittling and demeaning comments. Enough of her vulgarity. Enough of her self-absorbed, self-serving behavior. A surge of adrenaline, fueled by the nearness of Karlyn, rammed through his body. "Dear," he said, "forget the 'roger that' crap."

"What?"

"Look, stay at the party, drink yourself into oblivion, have a good time. I'll be home when I'm home."

"What?"

"I won't be back by midnight."

"You bastard!"

"It's about time, isn't it?"

"What the fuck are you talking about?" A harsh stage whisper. In the background, another splash, gales of laughter.

"I'm not tendering my resignation to the Reserve. I'm going to keep flying with or without your blessing. I really don't give a damn anymore."

Karlyn leaned closer to him, an affirming smile spreading slowly over her face.

Walker kept the phone pressed to his ear, but heard only music and muffled voices. "Donna?" he said. He brought the phone away from his ear and pressed the speaker button.

"You're such an asshole," Donna answered, her voice clipped and sharp. "What happened? You get laid by one of the squadron bimbos? Find a chippie with big tits at a Biloxi casino that brought your flopper back to life? God, you men are all alike. A little extracurricular nooky and you're king of the world. You think I can't play that game, too?"

"Maybe, if you found someone desperate enough."

"You—"

"See, here's the deal, Donna," he interrupted. "You can lure men with your physical assets. No one's ever complained about those. You're a looker, as the troops say. But I swear to God, once a man discovers the real you, realizes he's bedded a world-class harpy, he'd be out the door before you could pull your panties on."

Karlyn chuckled. Tried to stifle it. Too late.

"Who's that, who's there with you?" Donna shrieked.

"A good friend," Walker said.

"You goddamn prick, you fucking asshole." The words exploded from Donna, her anger reverberating through the phone.

Karlyn pointed at the phone, then at herself.

Walker understood what she wanted, but hesitated, unsure if he should involve her. But the dogs had been unleashed. He handed her the phone. She placed it between them on the bunk.

"Mrs. Walker," she said, "This is Captain Hill. I guess I qualify as one of your squadron bimbos." Her voice carried the even tenor of a flight attendant making an announcement over a PA system. "I was a bit of a failure with your husband, though. I never slept with him—tried, but was unsuccessful—don't have any further designs on him, won't steal him away, will never marry him, but he's going to help me give birth to a baby."

Walker did a double-take, like an animated cartoon character. He pointed at Karlyn, who shrugged.

"What kind of a sick fucking joke is this?" Donna shouted.

"It's not, Mrs. Walker," Karlyn snapped, losing her flight attendant coolness. "And in case you were too busy masturbating at the mouth to be worried about Arly, we crash landed on St. Simons with two engines out and category five hurricane breathing up our butts. We lost a good man, Colonel Harlow, but your husband's a hero." She paused, but Donna said nothing.

"You know," Karlyn continued, "I can't guess how your marriage will end up, but I'm rooting for Arly to drop you like a turd into a toilet, to put it in words you like to use. Well, enjoy the party, Donna. Nice chatting with you." She pushed the phone back to Walker.

He clicked it off. "Help you give birth?" he said.

"Well, that was the Starbucks part," Karlyn answered. "But I wasn't going to . . . do you know anything about The Bradley Method?"

"The what?"

"I can see you're going to be a big help." She stood. "I'll have Dr. McKenzie come take another look at you." She stepped to the ladder and clambered down, but stopped with only her face showing above the flight deck floor. "Janet, if she's a girl. Jan, if he's boy. And yes, a hell of a story to tell either one. You're gonna be a great godfather." She disappeared from view.

Walker closed his eyes and rested the cell phone against his stomach. In freeze-frame images, he played through the events of the day, more than once, and realized they somehow mirrored the events of his life.

Bernie, for instance. Bernie had been correct. He, Walker, did agonize over decisions when the right choices were neither ambiguous nor worthy of moral debate. *Bernie, damn you. Why couldn't I have told you that to your face.* Walker shifted in the bunk, trying to ease his discomfort, but knew the pain was more emotional than physical.

It seemed a lifetime ago, not two days, that the old soothsayer had held his hand and read his fate. Maybe the wizened chiromancer had sensed it before he did, but now it was clear to him: the eye of the storm in which he'd been trapped had not been exclusively Janet's. For too many years, long before Janet, it had been Donna. Donna, swirling around him on her own course, tracking her own agenda, careening toward her own goals; his be damned.

Well, no more. He'd been imprisoned within her self-absorbed eyewall for too many years, flying in cautious orbits, making no attempt to punch through the fortress. But if he could escape Janet's constraints . . .

His phone rang again, the sound muffled by the blanket. He let it continue to ring, allowing the vibrations from its signal to pulse across his abdomen like the gentle caress of a woman's hand.

"Your phone," a voice said.

He opened his eyes. Karlyn was standing over him, her chestnut hair veiling her face.

"Your phone," she repeated.

"I know," he said.

She reached out to touch him.

The ringing stopped.

# Epilogue

## ASTORIA, OREGON
## NINE MONTHS AFTER HURRICANE JANET

"This is a spectacular view," Walker said. He stood near a picture window in Karlyn's hillside apartment and gazed out at the broad mouth of the Columbia River where it slid into the Pacific Ocean at the end of a 1200-mile journey. A beat-up freighter plowed westward underneath the arcing steel spans of a long bridge. The scene was cast in shades of gray: the water tinted in gunmetal silver, the sky draped in slate-colored stratus.

"It's sunny in Mississippi now, isn't it?" Karlyn said. She held an infant against her shoulder.

"Not so dreary as here." Walker turned to face her.

"It's what we call the June Gloom," she said. "You should have planned your visit for later in the summer. It's absolutely gorgeous in late July and August."

"Hurricane season will be in full swing by then. Things can get kind of busy. But why am I telling you?" He hesitated, debating whether to say what he wanted to next. Yes, he decided, and continued. "I . . . well I thought you might be back in the South by then."

She shrugged. "Not much reason to return, now that I've resigned from the Reserve and quit my TV gig. Besides, I've got a good deal going here. I can afford my own place and my parents take care of the baby while I'm at work—oh, I didn't tell you. I got a job—you'll find this ironic—at a bank." The infant gurgled and Karlyn wiped away a tiny molasses-run of drool with a towel. "Here," she said, "you should hold your namesake." She handed the child to Walker.

He cradled the baby in his arms and looked down at him. The baby stared back with huge blue eyes. "It's kind of weird, having a kid named after me," Walker said.

"I thought it would be better to name him after you and Bernie, a couple of heroes, instead of that damn hurricane."

"Arlen Bernard Hill," Walker said softly, continuing to gaze at the child, "how are you? I welcomed you into the world a few months ago, but you were screaming and red-faced and seemed pretty pissed off about things so you probably didn't hear me." Walker looked up at Karlyn. "I don't feel like a hero. I was just doing my job. I wanted to survive as much as anyone in that airplane."

"But you and Bernie didn't *have* to leave the aircraft, didn't *have* to risk your lives, to rescue Stormy," she said.

"Yes, we did," Walker responded. "What if that had been Arly out there?" It sounded strange to say his own name when he was talking about someone else.

"Do you ever think about Stormy?"

"Every day."

"What happened to him?"

"His father has him. He was away on a business trip when Janet hit. I've met him. He's a good guy. He wants me to spend some time with Stormy—his real name is Sam—when he gets a little older and tell him what happened, how he was rescued, what happened to his mother." Walker hoisted Arly to his shoulder. Another trail of drool drained out of the infant's mouth and settled onto Walker's shirt.

"I'll get it," Karlyn said. She dabbed at the damp spot with a small cloth.

She smelled fresh, of talcum powder and scented laundry soap. Walker studied her. "You look good," he said. She did, but not so good as she had nine months ago. The crash, the birth, the job upheaval had taken their toll. There were dusky circles beneath her eyes; her skin was pale, albeit still flawless; and extra pounds adorned her hips and thighs. But Walker knew you didn't mention such things to a lady.

"You're a gentleman, always have been, but a shitty liar." She smiled brightly. "I look like hell. But not forever. When Arly gets a couple of months older and the sun comes out and I get my strength back I'll start working out and running again. I've been thinking about taking up sky diving, too."

"Well, good. Arly would certainly be unhappy if Mommy decided to do something *dangerous*."

"Maybe I'll take him with me." She chucked the baby under his chin and he blew a bubble when he tried to smile in response. "You could be the youngest sky diver ever, couldn't you?" she said in a sing-song tone, bringing her face close to the baby's. He squirmed in

Walker's arms.

"You always liked living on the edge, didn't you?" Walker tried to make the question sound non-adversarial.

Karlyn quit playing with Arly and looked at Walker. "Sky diving is an order of magnitude safer than riding a motorcycle," she said, her voice firm. "Here, let me have Arly and we'll sit for awhile."

Walker handed the baby to her and they sat on a leather sofa. The apartment, painted in pastel colors, was cozy but sparsely furnished: the sofa, a couple of cushy club chairs, a coffee table inlaid with tile, and a modest wide-screen television set.

"Rent-a-room," she said.

"It's you."

"You mean One-Night-Stand Karlyn?"

He colored. "I'm sorry. That's not what I meant. I . . . I—" *Way to fuck up.*

"I know what you meant," she interrupted, "I was just yanking your chain. You should realize by now I do that. You were suggesting, I think, that I tend to be, well . . . nomadic. That I can't be domesticated."

"More to the point."

"*Au contraire.*" She held Arly aloft. "Exhibit A for the defense."

Walker laughed. "You're saved? A changed woman?"

"Well, I don't think there was much to save or change. I never considered myself as living on the edge, as you put it. I liked pushing the edges out a bit, stretching the boundaries, but not deliberately hanging my toes over the brink. If and when I did that, it was an error in judgment and not inherent in my life style. Does that make sense?"

"Sort of." He stood and walked to a picture on the wall. It was a photo of the squadron, including Karlyn and Bernie, kneeling in front of a WC-130. He pointed to it. "These guys miss you," he said.

"Does the squadron commander?"

He smiled. "You heard, then?"

She nodded. "Congratulations, *Lieutenant Colonel* Walker."

"Yes, the squadron commander misses you."

"Personally or professionally?"

"Trick question. Let's start with this." He reached into his briefcase and pulled out a small rectangular box and handed it to her."

"Oh, my, you shouldn't have!" she exclaimed in mock surprise. She turned to the baby. "I think I'm being proposed to, honey." Arly Junior reached for her nose with a spastic little motion of his tiny hand.

Walker rolled his eyes. "It's your Air Medal, Captain Hill, since you couldn't be at the ceremony. Each of the crew was awarded one. Bernie received his second Distinguished Flying Cross. His widow accepted it for him."

"I'm sorry I missed that. I wish I could have hugged her."

"She got lots of hugs." He paused. "And we shared a lot of tears."

"And the other DFC recipient, was his wife there, too?"

"Donna couldn't make it."

"Oh."

Walker returned to the sofa beside Karlyn. "Well, there is some good news. The newspaper guy, Hemphill, is writing a book about his . . . our adventures. It's going to be called *Teal 37*, I think.

"And the family we brought on board, the Grants, they've moved to St. Simons, what's left of it, and Alan Grant's company is helping rebuild it. Also, from what he told me, it sounds like he kind of reconnected with his family because of the storm."

Arly snored softly on his mother's shoulder. Karlyn shifted his head so his nose wasn't buried in her blouse. "Have you seen St. Simons recently?" she asked.

"It took several months to clean up. New construction is just now getting under way, so not too many folks have moved back yet. Quite frankly, it looks pretty ugly at the moment. About the only trees that survived were the live oaks. The pines will come back fast, though, and I understand they're going to truck in hundreds of hardwoods. They'll get the resorts up and running again and the island will eventually come back stronger and better than before."

"Did you ever meet the TV guy, the one who guided us out of Janet's eye?"

"I did. I bought dinner for him and his lady friend, Sherrie, in Atlanta a few months ago. He told me a hell of a story. Turns out *USA Today* didn't have the inside scoop on what really went down at The Natural Environment network the day of the storm." Walker retold the saga of the behind-the-scenes Obermeyer-McSwanson battles and Karlyn couldn't stop laughing.

"Obermeyer actually finagled McSwanson into hiring him and Sherrie back at twice their salaries after he'd fired them?" she asked between whoops.

"Not only that, but the network mounted a huge ad campaign featuring Obermeyer and Sherrie, and then they quit."

"So where are they now?" Karlyn wiped tears of laughter from her eyes.

"Obermeyer went to CNN, Sherrie got a job at a local station and McSwanson is in charge of operations at corporate headquarters for Asian-Pacific."

"So, a happy ending for all."

"Maybe not for McSwanson. When I told Obermeyer about the book Hemphill was writing, his eyes lit up. 'You got his phone number?' he asked."

"The guy knows how to leverage a victory, doesn't he?"

"When you've got your opponent down, kick him."

"Tell me about Obermeyer's lady friend. Their relationship sounds kind of May-Decemberish."

"I don't know. She's very attractive, very bright, but it's hard to tell how old she is. As they say, 'a woman of a certain age,' but clearly younger than Obermeyer. I just couldn't tell by how much. I guess it doesn't make any difference. They seemed to enjoy each other's company."

A ray of brightness poked through a thin spot in the overcast outside and illuminated the room. "Maybe it'll be sunny after all," Karlyn said.

"Yes." He found himself staring at Karlyn, not looking outside.

"Arly?"

"What?"

"Why did you come here?"

"To see how you and the baby were doing and bring you your Air Medal."

"Oh, bullshit. You could have emailed me and asked how I was doing. The Air Force would have sent me my Air Medal."

He let her rejoinder go unanswered for several moments, then said, "Maybe I'm like Obermeyer, kind of smitten by younger ladies."

"I didn't realize Donna was that much younger than you."

"Stop it, Karlyn. You know I'm not talking about her."

"But we have to."

He moved closer to her and took her free hand. "Donna and I are divorcing," he said. "God knows, we tried to make it work. At least I did. We went to counseling, she underwent anger management therapy and got some medications that seemed to help her. But she wouldn't take them consistently and she wouldn't lay off the booze." He looked away from Karlyn, out at the brightening sky. He shook his head. "I don't know, it's . . . it's almost like she's happier being miserable. Anger and frustration seem to be her daily bread, what keeps her going, what gives her life meaning, if you can call it that. Maybe she gets an adrenalin rush from it or something, like a narcotic fix. I don't understand it. I do know I can't live with it anymore." He turned to face Karlyn.

She leaned forward and kissed his cheek. The sensation was electric.

"But you didn't answer my question," she said. "Why are you here?"

"I loved Donna once, very much. But I don't know where that woman went. It's as if she disappeared from the face of the earth. There's no love left, no feeling, nothing but a hollow existence. I don't want to live that way. And I see in you everything Donna wasn't, at least the way she ended up. You're accepting, compassionate, funny and—"

"A fallen woman."

"Yes, a fallen woman with courage and integrity who once told me, 'I wish I'd met you before Donna did.' I remembered those words. I'm calling your bluff. I want you to come back to Mississippi."

Tears welled in Karlyn's eyes. She looked away from him and didn't speak for a long time. Walker sensed he'd overstepped some undefined boundary. "Maybe I'd better get back to my motel," he said. He rose, retrieved his briefcase and walked toward the door. "We can talk later."

"Wait," she said. "Here's the deal. Promise me one thing, only one. If this works—if I come back to Mississippi, if you like being a daddy, if you aren't terrified of walking down the aisle again—promise me you'll take me back to St. Croix. To The Buccaneer Hotel and the Terrace Bar and mai tais with crappy little paper umbrellas. And that we'll drink too many and then make love all night with the windows in our room open and the curtains flapping in the wind. St. Croix, promise me, because that's where I fell in love with you, and that's where I realized I could never have you."

He went back to the couch and sat beside her. "I promise," he said.

She wiped her eyes. "Well, we'll see. Here's your first test." She handed Arly, suddenly awake, to him. "Let's see how you are at changing diapers."

"Oh, no. Colonels delegate those sorts of things."

"Forget about it. I'm a civilian now. You can't pull rank on me. Arly's room is down the hall, to the right."

Out on the Columbia, an oil tanker riding low in the water sounded its horn, long and loud, as it plowed beneath the bridge and churned upstream toward Portland. The clouds had parted and the sun reflected in a kaleidoscope of glittering diamonds off the broad sweep of the river.

# Author's Note

The idea for *Eyewall* was born of a real event. In 1989, a NOAA Hurricane Hunter was trapped briefly in the eye of Hurricane Hugo. The WP-3D Orion lost an engine during a low-level penetration of the storm's eyewall, but was able to fly to safety after only a brief imprisonment.

I chose, however, to use the Air Force Hurricane Hunters as the focus for my novel for several reasons. One was purely partisan: I'm a retired Air Force officer and once flew a mission with the 53rd Weather Reconnaissance Squadron, the Hurricane Hunters.

Another was the fact that while I was on active duty I spent a good deal of time riding around in C-130s, the aircraft now used by the Air Force to stalk hurricanes. I'm familiar with all the whining, grinding and shimmying that goes on in the venerable old airplane.

I also had access to a former C-130 pilot (and retired Delta Air Line captain), Mike Klindt, two houses down the street from me. I peppered him—a patient man, fortunately—with numerous questions about flying.

But there were other reasons. At The Weather Channel, I worked with an Air Force Reservist, Nicole Mitchell, who's an airborne meteorologist with the Hurricane Hunters. I think I wore her out with questions about flying through hurricanes. Still, she was kind enough to arrange a chance for me to prowl around inside the new J-model WC-130 and introduce me to Lt. Kevin Olson, a Hurricane Hunter pilot.

Warren Madden is also a Reservist who flies with the Hurricane Hunters. He's a part-timer with The Weather Channel and he, too, pitched in to answer my endless questions.

Dr. Steve Lyons is a former Weather Channel veteran who aided my efforts. Steve is one of the foremost tropical weather experts in the world and knows more about the mechanics of hurricanes and storm surges than anyone I know. He helped immensely with *Eyewall's* meteorological details, even to the extent of calculating a storm surge for the novel's mythical Hurricane Janet.

Both Nicole and Steve served as inspirations for characters in the book. Having a female weather officer as part of the Hurricane Hunter's crew opened up a lot of possibilities to me as an author, but Nicole was concerned people would think the character was her. No, no and no. If anything, Nicole is a responsible, mature antithesis to the female officer portrayed in *Eyewall*.

Steve's astounding knowledge of hurricanes was an absolute must for the book. So I packed his wisdom into a character that otherwise bears no resemblance to Steve.

Janet, by the way, is a hurricane name that was "retired" by the World Meteorological Organization after the 1955 season. Janet, a category 5 Caribbean storm, swallowed a Navy hurricane aircraft, claiming the lives of 11 crew members and two newspaper reporters. The storm later hit Mexico's Yucatan Peninsula where winds were clocked at 175 mph before the anemometer blew apart.

The plot for *Eyewall* rolled around in my mind for many months—and through at least one false start—before it came to fruition. I finally ended up with characters not only in conflict with a catastrophic hurricane but, in many cases, with each other.

Writing a novel is a craft. A number of successful writers generously shared their knowledge of the trade with me and helped me become a more accomplished writer: Brian Jay Corrigan, whom I consider my mentor; Steve Berry; David Fulmer; Vicky Hinze; Elizabeth Sinclair; and Cheryl Norman. You can read more about these people on my Website www.buzzbernard.com. My critique group at the Alpharetta (Georgia) Barnes & Noble also did its share in making *Eyewall* a better novel, especially Terry Segal who read most of the first draft. Thank you, one and all.

There were a couple of "non-writers" who helped move the project forward, too. Gary Schwartz, a long-time friend; and Christina, my wife of many decades. Gary is an avid reader who had no reluctance in expressing his criticism of the early drafts of *Eyewall*. He helped me make numerous improvements. Chris, for the most part, accepted the realities of being married to a writer. "Sometimes when you're here," she said, "you aren't really here." She's right. I often was lost in my *Eyewall* world. Thanks for your patience, honey.

Finally, *Eyewall* would never have come to life without an agent and editor who believed in it. Thus, I will be forever grateful to my agent, Jeanie Pantelakis of Sullivan Maxx, and Deborah Smith, vice president and editor at BelleBooks, Inc.

# ABOUT THE AUTHOR

 H.W. "Buzz" Bernard is a writer and retired meteorologist who worked more than a dozen years at The Weather Channel. He lives in Georgia and is a frequent visitor to St. Simons Island. Visit him here at www.buzzbernard.com.

CPSIA information can be obtained at www.ICGtesting.com
Printed in the USA
LVOW081527010512

279888LV00005B/85/P